*continued . . .*

"*Daisies for Innocence* is masterfully composed, and Cattrell enchantingly infuses the novel with lessons on the language of flowers and the lore of perfumery."

—*Mystery Scene*

Praise for Bailey Cattrell writing as Bailey Cates
and the *New York Times* bestselling
Magical Bakery Mysteries

"Katie is a charming amateur sleuth, baking her way through murder and magic set against the enchanting backdrop of Savannah, Georgia."

—*New York Times* bestselling author Jenn McKinlay

"A smooth, accomplished writer who combines a compelling plot with a cast of interesting characters that are diverse and engaging . . . while the story's magical elements bring a fun, intriguing dimension to the genre."

—*Kirkus Reviews*

"[A] promising series."

—*Library Journal*

# FOR
# MALICE

## AN ENCHANTED
## GARDEN MYSTERY

# BAILEY CATTRELL

BERKLEY PRIME CRIME
New York

BERKLEY PRIME CRIME
Published by Berkley
An imprint of Penguin Random House LLC
375 Hudson Street, New York, New York 10014

ISBN: 9780451476906

First Edition: September 2018

Printed in the United States of America
1 3 5 7 9 10 8 6 4 2

Cover art by Adrienne Langer
Cover design by Emily Osborne
Book design by Laura K. Corless

*For Stacey*

# ACKNOWLEDGMENTS

So many people helped this book come into being. The amazing team at Berkley Prime Crime includes Jessica Wade, Miranda Hill, Tara O'Connor, Elisha Katz, Emma Reh, and Angelina Krahn. A big thank-you also goes out to Kim Lionetti and the team at BookEnds, LLC. I'm incredibly grateful for the valuable feedback from Mark Figlozzi, Laura Pritchett, Laura Resau, and Bob Trott throughout the process of writing this story. A big shout-out to Stacey Kollman, who first sparked my interest in aromatherapy and who has a real superpower when it comes to horses. And, as always, thank you to Kevin—for everything.

# CHAPTER 1

WALLFLOWERS get a bad rap.

For some reason, the shy girl who stands all by herself at the party, talking to no one and radiating awkward social anxiety, is called a wallflower. However, the actual plants are transfixing—rangy, branching stalks that end with clubs of delicate, four-petal blossoms in dusky shades of orange, yellow, purple, and red. *Erysimum cheiri* are some of the first flowers to erupt into bloom each spring, reaching into the cool air with a verve and cheerfulness not at all associated with the human version of a wallflower.

Oh, and the scent! That was what made me pause in front of Heritage House, my hand frozen on the wrought iron gate that opened into the small square yard. The Poppyville town council had funded the restoration of the Old West log cabin and moved it from its original location to the wide lawn behind the library with the intention that it would house a museum dedicated to the California gold rush. Now the spicy, sweet, verdant fragrance of the wallflowers Thea Nelson had planted around the foundation was so thick in the air that I was surprised it wasn't somehow visible.

Yet a woman ushered her two small children past my corgi, Dash, and me without even a glance at the blooms of Chelsea Jacket and tiny, double-leaved Harpur Crewe. Shaking my head, I inhaled again, nearly swooning at the intensity of the aroma. It sparked the memory of my grandmother, her calm voice echoing through time from my childhood.

*See the white violets, Ellie? Breathe of them deeply. Can you smell how they're different than the modest purple blossoms? The white ones embrace challenge, want to take chances. And here—the wallflowers. So strong, though they seem so delicate. They need to be strong, though, for they represent fidelity in adversity. They only appear fragile.*

My corgi brushed against my leg as he turned to look behind us. Moments later, a familiar voice reached through the scented haze of my past, and Gamma's voice faded from my mind.

"Hey, Ellie! Sorry I'm a little late. You didn't need to wait out here for me, though."

I looked over my shoulder to see my best friend Astrid Moneypenny striding toward us from the side entrance of the Poppyville Library. Almost a foot taller than my four feet ten, she'd tamed her wild, coppery tresses into a complicated updo held together with wooden combs. Her willow green eyes flashed affection, and the freckles on her nose stood out against the paleness of her early spring complexion. When we hugged, I smelled cloves and vanilla with just a soupçon of wet dog. My guess was that she'd been baking cookies or washing one of her pet-sitting clients. Probably both.

"Couldn't help myself," I said. "Every time I come to the museum I have to stop and—"

"Smell the flowers," she finished, and stooped to rub Dash's velvety ears. Panting, he gave her his best doggy grin.

Standing again, she said, "I would expect nothing less, Ellie. They're delightful. But I don't think my humble nose can appreciate them quite the way yours can."

I rolled my eyes. I knew what she meant, though. It was true that I had a rather, er, *well-honed* sense of smell. Which was a nice way of saying it was almost freakish. But it had saved me when I'd divorced my husband after finding him in flagrante delicto with Wanda Simmons in the walk-in freezer of our restaurant, the Roux Grill. I'd always wanted to try my hand at perfumery, so, newly single, I'd sold him my half of the Roux, purchased a storefront at the end of Corona Street, and started my own business.

Scents & Nonsense was where I indulged my love of aromatherapy and created custom perfume blends for a growing list of clients. Throughout the shop, every product featured lovely, lovely, natural smells. As a bonus, the more I worked with scent, the more I was able to understand exactly what kind of fragrance combination would help any particular customer.

Of course, that didn't account for the bits of weirdness since I'd opened Scents & Nonsense, planted the elaborate garden behind the store, and moved into my tiny house at the back of the lot. There had been a mysterious plant that provided memory-enhancing essential oil, strange whispers in the garden, and a few experiences that bordered on the otherworldly.

Okay, sometimes they crossed the border.

However, I wasn't the only one of our friends with what Astrid had dubbed "superpowers." Gessie King, who owned the stables on the edge of town, had a gift with the horses that went beyond "whispering." Thea Nelson of Terra Green Nursery had a thumb so green I sometimes wondered if chlorophyll ran through her veins, and Maria Canto had a knack for knowing what you needed when you walked into the library before you knew you needed it. As for my best friend in the whole world, Astrid could diagnose most of the pets that came into the animal clinic where she worked as a veterinary technician with little more than a glance. That was part of why her personal business as a self-proclaimed petrepreneur was so successful. There wasn't anyone in Poppyville who wouldn't trust their pet's welfare to Astrid.

Opening the gate to Heritage House, I pointed at the half-open door and said, "We'd better get to work. The others have been hard at it since noon. I think Felicity and Gessie are gathering the last of the boxes from the basement of the Hotel California, and Thea and Maria are unpacking what we brought over yesterday."

"Are they finding anything suitable for display?" Astrid asked as we entered the old cabin. "Seemed like there was an awful lot of stuff that was old and falling apart."

"You've got that right," a voice said from the dimness inside.

We blinked. A few seconds later, my eyes had adjusted to the lower light, and I recognized Eureka Sanford crouched over a pile of hodgepodge metal implements. The knees of her khakis were dusty, as was the wrinkled white dress shirt tucked into them. She'd bundled up her gray-streaked hair under her signature red newsboy cap, and her dark eyes gleamed at us from beneath the short brim. I caught a whiff of fountain pen ink and mountain mahogany flowers.

Dash ran over to her, and she patted him on the head a few times, then stood. Satisfied, he continued over to the corner and flopped down for a nap. Eureka turned toward us and held out a dented disc classically used to pan for gold. It had a gaping, rusted hole in the bottom.

"We've unpacked so many of these things we could build a sculpture. Call it *Pan Man* or something." She shook her head, then pointed to our left. "Pretty good stuff over there, though, once we weeded out all the crap from the last century. Seems like the *collection*, as Felicity keeps calling it, was just a bunch of things people didn't want to throw away over the years and didn't know what else to do with." Her eyes narrowed. "But old doesn't mean valuable, you know. Or even interesting."

"Well, we sure appreciate your expertise, Eureka," Maria Canto said as she stepped from the shadows. Almost as height-challenged as me, the town's librarian wore jeans and an electric yellow sweater with a matching headband to hold back her thick black hair. She smelled slightly of orange blossoms.

"Not to mention your backing with the town council," I said.

A retired history professor from UC Berkeley, Eureka had moved to Poppyville the year before to work on her book about everyday life during the California gold rush. She'd been instrumental in getting the rural cabin fixed up and transported to Library Park. It had provided the perfect spot for the museum our women's business group, the Greenstockings, had been trying to jump-start for a few years. The previous option had been a paltry display in the basement of the Hotel California, but Eureka had felt this location would be more of a draw for the tourists that were the lifeblood of our little town's economy, and she'd convinced the council to pay for it.

She beamed. "Glad to do it! Can't let myself go to seed just because I'm not bossing around graduate students anymore."

"Where's Thea?" Astrid asked, fingering a length of somewhat yellowed lace on a table next to an embroidered crazy quilt.

"Right here," our friend said from the doorway. The scents of fresh soil and green seedlings drifted into the museum. She wore a Terra Green Nursery T-shirt and baseball cap, and her long tan legs emerged from cargo shorts. Tall and lanky, Thea generally moved with a deliberateness I found calming. Today, however, she stomped into the cabin with a frown.

"What's wrong?" I asked.

"How hard is it to get good help in this town?" Thea

grumbled. "I mean, jeez. That new guy I hired doesn't want to do anything except read comic books behind the register, and now he's messed up an order so badly I'm not going to make a cent on it. You have no idea how lucky you are to have Maggie working for you."

"Yeah," I agreed quietly.

Thea started to go on, then stopped. Turning pink, she said, "Oh, gosh, Ellie. I didn't mean . . . Josie was . . . oh, darn it."

I smiled. "I know what you meant. And believe me, I also know how lucky I am that Maggie can work for me at Scents and Nonsense as well as for Harris at the Roux."

Harris was my ex, and he sometimes snarked about his star bartender also tending my shop part-time. Thea's discomfort had nothing to do with Maggie, though. Josie Overland, my employee before Maggie came to work for me, had been murdered the previous June.

"Relax," I went on. "We all know it's harder to find good workers during the off-season."

Astrid and Maria nodded.

Thea's shoulders dropped. "At least that brother of mine will be coming back from Alaska in three weeks. In between his wooing you, Ellie, maybe I can get some real work out of Ritter."

Now it was my turn to blush. "I'm sure he'll have plenty of time to help out at the nursery." I tried to ignore the swoopy feeling in my stomach at the thought that I'd finally be able to see the handsome mountain man I'd only been in contact with via phone and the Internet for the last five months. See, hear . . . touch . . .

I cleared my throat.

She winked. "And plenty of time to spend with his little Ellie-boo."

My eyes widened. "No. Tell me Ritter does *not* call me that behind my back."

Astrid laughed.

"*Ever*," I said.

Thea let a few beats pass, then relented. "Of course not. You think I'd put up with a brother who talked baby talk about his girlfriend? Sheesh." At least she seemed to be in a better mood than when she'd come in.

Shaking my head, I said, "Try putting a bouquet of goldenrod or black-eyed Susans on the counter by the register. Maybe it'll help give your employee a little motivation and strength of character."

She quirked an eyebrow. "Really? Well, okay. You haven't steered me wrong with your flower lore yet."

As Thea turned away to unpack another box, Astrid murmured low enough that the others couldn't hear, "I bet Tanner Spence isn't going to be too excited when Ritter comes back to his Ellie-boo."

I shot her a look. "I've been pretty darn clear that I'm not dating Spence."

"Maybe not. But you two sure spend a lot of time together."

"He's my friend!"

She quirked an eyebrow, but before she could continue, we were interrupted by footsteps and voices outside announcing that Gessie and Felicity had arrived. They came in, each holding a big box that they carried to the back of the cabin and put on the floor next to all the others we were supposed to be unpacking, instead of yakking about my love life—or current lack thereof.

Gessie wore a plaid flannel shirt and Wrangler jeans imbued with the rich, musky scent of the horses she tended, but for once her iron gray curls were uncovered. Felicity, formerly the editor of the *Poppyville Picayune* and now the manager of the Hotel California, had on a pair of coveralls over a black T-shirt, and her long dark hair was gathered into a single braid that snaked down her back. Dirt smudged her heart-shaped face, and I detected a hint of bergamot from the Earl Grey tea she liked so much.

"Need some help unloading?" Astrid asked.

Gessie nodded. "We finally cleared out the storeroom over at the hotel, but my truck is packed chock-full of the last of it."

"Let's start putting things outside that can go to the dump," Eureka said. "Then when we have enough to fill Gessie's truck, a couple of us can make a run."

"Need to empty the truck first," Thea said, and strode toward the door.

Astrid and I nodded to each other and followed her outside.

L ATE in the afternoon we'd sorted through nearly everything and filled the back of Gessie's pickup, and she and Thea had made the trip to the landfill.

Inside Heritage House, items that would be displayed together were gathered in rough groups. There were several samples of the equipment used for gold mining, including picks, axes, short-handled shovels, placer cradles, hip boots, and a few of the sluicing pans Eureka had complained about. An example of the convoluted-looking assaying machines sold to gullible—and hopeful—miners by entrepreneurial inventors who likely knew nothing about gold or mining sat in one corner. There were also examples of clothing and footwear. Nearby was a display of home goods and women's clothing ranging from calico bonnets and long skirts to a skimpy red dancehall dress that would have raised some eyebrows even now.

Near the door, we planned a reception desk and educational displays. Visitors could browse through old newspapers, letters, and other ephemera, though the items Eureka had deemed most important would be displayed under glass.

"Oh, no!" Gessie exclaimed from the corner.

We all turned to look at her.

She stooped and lifted what looked like a tall jug out of a box in the shadows. "I thought we were done. What the heck is this thing?"

Eureka hurried over. "It's a butter churn! Here, put it on this table."

As we crowded around to see this new treasure, she quickly ran her hands over the yellow ceramic vessel. It was chipped here and there but looked to be in good shape. Stylized flowers and birds decorated the sides of the churn, all painted in blue.

"I thought butter churns had dashers," I said, trying my best to ignore the strange sensations that had erupted in my solar plexus. There was something about this simple vessel that gave me the inside shivers: part trepidation, part anticipation, and part something that felt almost like . . . need?

Dash must have sensed something, too, because he abandoned the corner to trot over and lean against my leg.

Maria frowned from the other side of the table. "Look at the lid. It's been sealed with wax. Even the hole where the butter dasher would fit." She reached toward the churn. "What's this?" She untwisted a thick cord and loosened a flat square of thick paper about three inches by four inches.

"There's writing," Felicity said.

Maria angled it toward the natural light coming in the window. "The writing is so faded. It looks like 'For' and then something I can't make out, and then 'Poppyville, 1850.'" She squinted again, then looked up. "You guys! You know what I think this is? A time capsule!"

# CHAPTER 2

❧

SURPRISED, we looked around at one other.

Felicity suddenly broke the silence with a laugh. "Oh, wouldn't that be amazing? Eureka, you're the expert. Do you think it really could be a time capsule?"

Eureka nodded. "I do indeed. It's a miracle the seal is intact at all. And that tag! I'm surprised it's not completely illegible."

"Let's open it." I had to make an effort to keep my tone light.

The erstwhile professor grinned at me, and I saw she was as curious about the contents as I was. She reached for a screwdriver on the table behind her.

"Now, hang on!" Felicity held up her hand. "We can't just go willy-nilly opening up a time capsule that's almost a hundred and seventy years old!" She looked around at us. "We have to do this right."

"Yeah." Astrid said. "This might be a big deal."

"It's *publicity*, ladies. For Poppyville, and therefore for our businesses." A satisfied smile played on the lips of the de facto leader of the Greenstockings.

Impatience swelled beneath my sternum, but I kept quiet.

"We'll have a ceremony," Thea said thoughtfully.

Gessie nodded. "Invite the press. Get the mayor involved."

"Put Poppyville on the map—or at least hit a news cycle or two," Felicity said, sounding determined. "It's a great opportunity to bring some people into town during the off-season."

Astrid turned to me.

"Yes," I managed to croak out around the unexplainable desire I felt to immediately see what was inside that butter churn. "That's exactly what we need to do. Have the mayor speechify and reveal the contents with a flourish."

Astrid's eyes narrowed. "You okay?"

I nodded and pasted on a bright smile, not trusting myself to say more.

"Okay, then," Eureka said. "First thing we need to do is get the thing under lock and key."

A few faces showed surprise.

"Who knows what's in here? There could be gold dust!" Eureka said.

"It is kind of heavy, but not full-of-gold heavy," Thea said, her tone dry. "But you're right. Where do we take it?"

"The bank?" Astrid suggested.

"The police station," I said.

Felicity snapped her fingers. "That's it! And it's right

by city hall, so we can drop by the mayor's office afterward."

I kept my face neutral and shrugged, trying to quell the subtle vibrations I felt coming from the churn. Besides the scent of old honey in the beeswax seal, there was something else teasing my nose. Something I couldn't identify.

The last time there had been a mysterious scent I couldn't pin down, things hadn't ended so well for my shop assistant.

"I'll come with you, Felicity." Eureka shrugged on her jacket.

"I'll stay here and lock up," I said.

Eyeing me, Astrid said, "I'll stay and help Ellie."

Oblivious, Thea and Gessie wrapped the time capsule in an extra quilt and took it out to Felicity's SUV before going back to their workaday lives.

Astrid watched them go, then turned back to me and crossed her arms. "What's going on?"

"Nothing."

"Bull pucky."

I hesitated, then made a face. "I don't know how to explain it. There's something in that churn that . . . well, it feels like it's calling me or something. Like an itch I can't scratch." I rolled my eyes. "Good Lord. I sound like a crazy person. Don't mind me."

Her expression remained concerned. "Ellie . . ."

I looked at my watch. "Have to get back to the shop so Maggie can get to her shift at the Roux on time."

"Really? You sure you're okay? I know that empathy thing you do can hit you hard."

"*Pfft*. Empathy for a butter churn? I'm fine." I took

my key to Heritage House out of my pocket. "Come on, Dash. Let's get going."

Dash wiggled his tailless behind and ran out the door as soon as I opened it. I locked up behind us, and we began walking toward the street.

Out in front of the library, Astrid said, "You know, I'm pretty curious about what's inside that thing, too."

"We'll find out soon!" I infused cheer into my tone, even though "soon" seemed a long time away.

The itchy feeling continued to twitch in the back of my mind as I walked down Corona Street to Scents & Nonsense.

T HE Greenstockings worked like crazy women, though, and it was only a week later that we were ready for the big time capsule reveal. The displays inside Heritage House were arranged with care, press releases had gone out, and the history and anthropology departments of California universities had been alerted to our find.

It was a Wednesday, and I woke even earlier than usual. Ever since we'd found the time capsule, random speculations of what might be inside had littered conversations around town and in Scents & Nonsense. None were enticing enough to account for my fixation, though.

*Probably just a bunch of moldy, rotten, unimportant memorabilia . . .*

Didn't matter. I still wanted to know what was inside the butter churn.

"Come on, Dash!"

He jumped off the bed and headed toward the spiral staircase that led down to the first floor of my tiny house. I donned a warm fleece robe and followed at a more leisurely pace, trailing my fingers along the railing as I descended. The staircase was perhaps my favorite feature of my small-scale home. The contractor I'd hired to transform the rambling potting shed at the back of the Scents & Nonsense property into a place where I could live was a creative genius when it came to saving space. There were built-in shelves, drop-down furniture like the dining table that could be tucked out of the way when not needed, and super-efficient pieces like the ottoman that also served as a coffee table and storage. But I'd fallen in love with the bookshelves he'd fashioned between each of the circling steps that led up to my skylit bedroom. They were the ideal place to house my collection of aromatherapy, gardening, and perfumery books. Having room for a library even that size was usually unheard of in tiny house construction, and every evening I had the pleasure of climbing a bookcase to bed.

At the bottom, I paused to push my palm against the battered garden journal my deceased grandmother had left to me. I'd rediscovered it when clearing out the basement in my old house after the divorce, and over the course of many consultations among the pages, I'd learned it was a strange volume indeed. Changeable, and bizarrely informative in obscure situations. It had helped me find scentual solutions to enough of my clients' problems that it had become a habit to touch it each morning. The warmer it felt, the more information was waiting inside for me to find.

This morning it was cool. I moved into the abbreviated kitchen to brew strong coffee and rummage in the nearly empty cupboard for a quick breakfast. Peanut butter and saltines it was. I washed down five with the first swallows of searing caffeine and then went to take a shower in the deep, Japanese-style tub in the bathroom.

Feeling refreshed, I dressed in brown jeans, a white silk mock neck, and a navy blue peacoat. I slipped on comfortable loafers and led Dash out to the Enchanted Garden. I usually indulged in my second cup of coffee while letting my crazy dark curls—longer now than they'd been in years—dry in the sunshine that streamed obliquely from the east.

The air was crisp but pleasant as we wended our way past beds spilling over with pansies and yellow trillium. Tulips were in full riot, bordered by short rows of grape hyacinth and faded crocus. A few irises had burst forth, their stems heavy with more silky buds in wait. Chartreuse ice plant and dusky mother-of-thyme spilled from the rock garden, punctuated by pink rock rose and purple phlox waterfalling over the edge. The delicate white petals of oak-leaf hydrangea sparked subtly in the shade of the fence between my property and Flyrite Kites next door, and hellebore, bleeding heart, and snowdrop anemone brightened the spaces among a myriad of perennials and herbs greening up for later bloom.

I paused, smiling at the gnome door set into the base of the apple tree. Another one—smaller—cheerily beckoned from a rock near a stand of cress and the wee pansies Gamma had always called Johnny-jump-ups. Near it, a miniature picnic table and benches invited the fairies to come sit, and a tire swing the circumference of my forefinger and thumb touching swung from the branch of a bonsai pine.

Similar tableaus were tucked in surprising niches and cozy crannies throughout the gardens. I'd created my first fairy garden by the birdbath near the shop—a tiny gazebo surrounded by pint-size Adirondack chairs and landscaped with baby tears and delicate ferns—and had been adding new ones ever since. Most were hidden, or at least not obvious, and the Enchanted Garden—declared by those very words etched into a large rough boulder in the center—had become a regular attraction for children and adults alike. They would come to explore the fairy scenes, enjoy the flowers, sip a hot beverage or lemonade, and browse in the shop. I loved providing a place for people to relax, away from the rest of the world, and the additional business was more than welcome, too.

Dash bounded ahead to the patio at the back of the shop. Nabokov, the Russian blue shop cat, waited there for him. Nabby languidly stretched his back before deigning to touch noses with the corgi. Together they ambled out of view, no doubt heading for the mosaic retaining wall where they liked to hang out.

My phone vibrated in my pocket, and I drew it out. The messaging app Ritter and I used since there was no cell service where he was in the wilds of Alaska showed an incoming message. I opened it with a smile.

Good morning, Elliana! Just wanted to check in and say hi. I'll be out in the field for the next twenty-four

hours, so won't be able to chat. Didn't want you to
worry when I don't respond. MISS YOU.

My smile broadened, just as it did every morning that
he was able to contact me. Between messaging, online
chats, and the occasional video call, we'd managed to
stay close despite the physical distance between us. It
would have been easier if all his contact with the outside
world hadn't been through his research project's expensive satellite connection, but we took what we could get.

Standing in the middle of the Enchanted Garden, I
messaged him back.

Good morning right back atcha! Be safe out in the
tundra. Miss you, too. Can't wait to see you. Only two
more weeks! <3 <3 <3.

I'd settled into one of the mismatched rocking chairs,
when the smell of coconut reached my nose. A moment
later, the latch rattled, and Astrid pushed open the gate
that led from the covered boardwalk out front. She wore
leggings with boots and a tie-dyed tunic that flared at the
bottom. In one hand, she held a lidded container and in
the other the leash of a gray Nubian goat wearing a red
harness.

I stood. "What do we have here?"

She grinned. "Coconut squares." My friend hated to
cook but was crazy about baking cookies. Said it was the
perfect way to start the day. Of course, she wasn't about to
eat a batch of cookies every day, so Scents & Nonsense

and yours truly were the happy recipients of her labors. Her delicious concoctions had gained enough of a reputation that sometimes customers came in just to see what the treat of the day was.

"Yum!" I said. "Though actually I was wondering about . . ." I pointed to the goat.

Awkwardly juggling the leash, Astrid opened the plastic lid and handed me a gooey lump of goodness. "Oh, this is Hector. He belongs to Charlene Gibbon."

"Chief Gibbon's wife?" I mumbled around a mouthful that was far superior to the saltines and peanut butter I'd scrounged for breakfast.

She nodded. "The most recent addition to her backyard menagerie. Says with Hector around there's no need for a mower anymore. Keeps the ducks company, too."

I swallowed and side-eyed the creature. His mouth parted enough to reveal two perfect rows of teeth designed to tear plants to shreds, and he blinked long lashes over unsettling horizontal pupils.

"Looks like he's flirting," I said.

"Oh, he is." Astrid ruffled his soft ears. Dash made a noise of disgust and trotted over from the retaining wall to inspect the newcomer.

"Well, at least someone is." I regretted the words the second they left my mouth.

Astrid rolled her eyes. "Poor you. When Ritter gets back, you're going to have more flirting than you can stand between him and Spence."

Ignoring her, I pointed to Hector. "Do *not* let him off that leash. The last thing I need in this garden is a rogue goat."

Astrid thrust the container of cookies at me. "Oh,

please. You know I'd never. I was just giving him a walk and thought I'd drop these off early. Is Maggie covering for you this afternoon during the ceremony at Heritage House?"

I shook my head. "I don't want her to miss out, so we're closing the shop for a couple of hours."

My friend let out a whistle. "Wow. You never close the shop."

"I don't think I'll lose too many sales with everyone in town gathered at Library Park."

Astrid made a sound of agreement, then led Hector back to the gate. "See you later, Ellie-gator."

Raising my hand in farewell, I said, "Thanks for the treats!" and proceeded to eat another one on my way into Scents & Nonsense.

Inside, I emptied the rest of the coconut squares onto a plate and set it on the table by the back door. I started brewing dark roast coffee, flipped on the overhead lights, and turned back to scan the interior of the shop.

My breathing deepened, and contentment settled into my bones as I surveyed the business I'd built from dreams and determination. Sunlight streamed through the back window, sparkling through the brightly colored glass bottles that lined the sill, ready for use. The air smelled of dozens of scented products, the natural floral and herbal fragrances melding into a heady miasma of welcome. My work area was clear except for a basket of fresh evergreen fronds and a half dozen jars of dried herbs and petals from the garden, soon to be blended into potpourri. The kids' corner was scattered with scratch 'n' sniff books and offered shelves of child-friendly products like

scented play clay, nap pillows, and diffusers. The front
windows boasted more colorful bottles, while on the
boardwalk out front, hardy pansies and ornamental kale
spilled from planters on each side of the door.

With a happy sigh, I wended my way through display
tables, turned the hand-lettered wooden sign from CLOSED
to OPEN, and went back to get ready for the morning's
business.


THAT afternoon a little before two o'clock, a growing crowd of people milled around the edges of
Library Park, chatting in pairs and groups or helping
themselves to the catered refreshments from the Kneadful Things Bakery on the long table at the back. Clouds
scudded across the sky overhead, and the air grew chilly
each time the sun tucked behind a white puff. Rain was
unlikely, but there were light jackets and sweaters all
around.

Some of the Greenstockings had arrived early to help
arrange the rows of folding chairs on the grass, a few of
which were already occupied. Eureka was bustling
around, making sure everything was just so, accompanied by Maria, whose typical calm offered balance to the
professor's high energy.

I spied a lot of people I knew, but there were also a
few unfamiliar faces in the crowd. There was a reporter
whose press pass said she was from the *Sacramento Bee*,
as well as a guy I recognized from our own *Poppyville
Picayune*. Three or four historians from academic insti-
tutions had come, interested in seeing what might be

found in the time capsule since there hadn't been many discovered in the West. There was even an anthropologist in attendance. However, it looked like Felicity's hope of national news coverage was not to be fulfilled.

Perhaps I should have felt upset about that, as a good Greenstocking interested in boosting tourist trade to Poppyville, but instead I found myself almost glad. Upon reflection, I realized I felt quite proprietary toward the quaint butter churn and its mysterious contents.

To one side, Chief Gibbon chatted with my friend Detective Lupe Garcia and a uniformed officer who was there to provide nominal security. Off duty, Lupe wore dark jeans and a black T-shirt, and her dark hair brushed the shoulders of her leather jacket as she laughed at something her boss said. The chief was pushing fifty-five, though his black hair, combed straight back from his brow, showed not a single gray. He was medium height and wiry, with bushy eyebrows that arched over dark crow eyes. I wondered what he thought of his wife's newest caprine addition to their property.

Larken Meadows, my half brother Colby's girlfriend, waved to me from the other side of the seating area. Colby was on an extended camping trip in his Westfalia van, while Larken worked to develop their new property outside of town into a self-sustaining mini-farm. Theirs was a relationship of compromises, but they were happy, and that was all I cared about.

I waved back as a movement to my left caught my eye. I turned to see "Bongo" Pete Grimly, the homeless man who camped down by the river by Gessie's stables, hanging at the edge of the crowd. He was an odd duck, shy and poetic and not entirely in touch with reality, but along with a few other homeless souls, the people of Poppyville took care of him as best we could. As I watched, Gessie filled a plate from the food table and handed it to him.

A tall figure with sandy blond hair and a scowl came up beside her, frowned briefly at Pete, then kept going. It was the other detective on the force, Max Lang, who strode through the park as if he owned the place. Trotting behind him was his best friend, Harris Madigan.

Whom I'd once been married to.

Astrid walked up then, and I happily turned away from them. "Where have you been?" I asked.

She'd exchanged Hector for a canine companion—this time a timid-eyed greyhound that leaned against her leg as if she were a lifeline. "Checking on Ruthie here. I'm watching her today while her owner is out of town, and she didn't want to be left alone. She gets nervous."

"Ah." I looked down to where my corgi was sit-staying like a trouper. "Dash, this is Ruthie. Ruthie, Dash."

He grinned and glanced at me. At my nod, he got up and went over to the greyhound, his behind waggling gently as they touched noses.

Felicity caught my eye, held up her wrist, and pointed to her watch. I nodded and passed on the same gesture to Gessie and Thea.

The ceremony was about to begin.

"Who's *that*?" Astrid asked in a low voice.

Her tone made me look toward where she'd subtly pointed with her chin. A man who appeared to be in his late thirties stood by himself about forty feet away, hands clasped behind his back and a bemused expression on his face as he surveyed the crowd. He was tall and slender, with long lashes and a Eurasian cast to his features. His good looks were exactly the kind that my friend was attracted to—handsome with a delicate edge.

"No idea," I said, about to make a teasing comment, when something made me stop. What was it about the guy that set off my internal alarm? Not the big, clanging alarm that said *run!* or *fight!* but the smaller, subtler one that I'd nonetheless learned it was wise to heed.

"Keep your hands off him," she said with a grin. "He's mine."

"You might want to tell him that."

"Oh, I'm planning to, believe me." She sounded sure of herself.

Felicity made her way over to the mayor and shook his hand, then went behind the podium and began adjusting the microphone.

"Excuse me, ladies and gentlemen." Her voice echoed from the microphone, and she turned it down a bit before continuing. "Could we all find our seats? We're about to begin."

# CHAPTER 3

A STRID and I led our dogs over to the first row, where the members of the Greenstockings would sit. Dash plopped down on the grass in front of me, and Ruthie sat right by my friend's leg, still leaning against her.

Eureka slid onto the seat next to me. "Whew! I'm so glad we got everything arranged inside so folks can check out the museum after we find out what's in that dang butter churn. I'm thinking of this as a kind of grand opening for Heritage House, you know?"

I smiled. "You've worked your tail off. We'd never have been able to do it without you."

"Oh, *pshaw*." She blushed a little, and I knew she was pleased.

A man walking between us and the podium paused by her chair. "Eureka," he said to her. "There you are." His voice was silky smooth. His eyes were gray, a dark reflection of his mane of white hair that fell a few inches below his ears.

"Odell!" She smiled. "I'm so glad you were able to come see what's in our little time capsule."

I watched them, frankly curious. Sitting like we were, I could hardly be accused of eavesdropping.

"That and to see you, my dear. How's your book coming along?" the man asked.

She beamed. "I want to talk to you about it! Will you be in town long?"

"A few days. Perhaps you'll allow me to take you out to dinner? We can reminisce about the old days."

"Not that old. And yes, dinner sounds delightful," she murmured, holding the man's gaze.

He broke eye contact after a few seconds and turned to Astrid and me. Holding out his hand, he said, "Hello. I'm Odell Radcliffe, an old colleague of Eureka's from Berkeley."

We shook his hand and introduced ourselves.

Fingers tugged at Odell's sleeve. He stepped aside to reveal a young woman who looked to be in her midtwenties. She had wispy hair the color of seasoned oak, and behind the thick lenses of her frameless glasses, her hazel eyes looked too big for her face. She hugged herself as if chilly in her cotton shirtwaist dress.

"My daughter, Haley," he said.

"Hi." Her voice was as wispy as her hair.

"Hello," I said with a smile.

She bit her lip and offered Astrid and me a tentative smile of her own, then looked at Eureka. "Nice to see you."

"How have you been, dear?" Eureka asked, but Felicity tapped the microphone before the young woman could reply. The Radcliffes nodded to us and went to find seats as the murmurs of conversation faded to silence.

"Welcome to the opening of Poppyville's historic Heritage House," Felicity said with a broad smile. "First off, I want to extend sincere thanks to everyone who made this possible." She went on to list everyone who had been involved. When she was finished, she waited for the applause to fade.

*Enough already. Let's see what's in that butter churn.*

"Now, you all may have heard a little something about an extra-special element to this first day that Heritage House is open. In the process of sifting through the items that eventually went on display inside, we ran across what appears to be a time capsule."

She leaned forward conspiratorially. "At least that's what we think it is, because we haven't looked inside yet. But that's about to change! Mayor Ward?" She stepped back and handed him the microphone.

"Thank you." The mayor scanned the crowd with smiling brown eyes that matched his movie-star hair. "I think Ms. Donovan covered everything, so I'll save the speeches for my campaign next year. What do you say we get down to the business of seeing what the enterprising folks of Poppyville left us back in the day?" He grinned. "Let's just hope this goes better than when Geraldo Rivera opened Al Capone's vault."

The uniformed policeman who had been talking to Chief Gibbon earlier stepped to the podium with a small hammer and chisel in his hands. He bent to carefully loosen the wax around the top of the churn. After a few taps, he straightened with a puzzled expression. Leaning over, he said something to the mayor, then went to join Felicity.

The mayor flashed the onlookers a smile and said, "Officer Danielson made short work of the wax seal on our butter churn here. Shall we have a look?"

With a flourish, he pulled off the wooden lid. Murmurs ran through the crowd, and my own heart stuttered. Very slowly, he reached in and extracted the first item. I craned my neck to see. He held a piece of thick paper between his thumb and forefinger.

After a quick glance, Mayor Ward held it over his head like a boxing champion. "Everyone, this is a menu from our very own Hotel California! There was no Empire Room in the hotel back then, just the busy hotel dining room. Ms. Donovan here is the current manager of the hotel, so I'll give her the first look." He held out the menu.

With a nod, Felicity stepped forward, glanced at it, then placed it on the table next to the podium.

I took a deep breath as the mayor reached into the time capsule again and pulled out a smaller piece of paper. He frowned as he scanned it, then turned it over. Then his face cleared, and he looked up.

"Ladies and gentlemen, this appears to be a page from some kind of diary."

I heard Eureka's intake of breath beside me. No doubt a diary would be helpful to her book project.

"It relates the writer's activities on a Sunday morning." He laughed as he placed it on the table beside the podium. "Apparently, Sunday was laundry day. It must have been included to show some of the mundane aspects of mining life."

I looked around to see the reporters scribbling in their notebooks. One of the history professors was typing on an electronic notepad. The cute guy Astrid had been drawn to stood to one side with his arms crossed, avidly watching the proceedings. Professor Radcliffe looked on serenely, his hands folded in his lap as his daughter typed on her phone with her thumbs, lower lip clamped between her teeth. She was probably bored to death and texting with her friends.

"And here we have a claims map." The mayor held up another piece of paper with a wink. "That should come in handy for modern gold hunters, don't you think? Who knows how many of those old claims weren't completely played out?" He tipped his head to the side and peered at the map. "Looks like a couple are up there by Clary Springs."

The reporters scribbled again at that, and I mentally congratulated Mayor Ward for giving them fodder that might attract tourists not only to try their hand at mining gold, but also to visit the local hot springs.

He added it to the other items on the nearby table and reached into the churn again. "And here we have a photograph of Corona Street." He held that up, too.

From the front row, I could make out the classic Old West covered boardwalks on either side of the main street. They looked just like the ones that Poppyville still boasted, only some of the buildings now had been mere tents then, and the street itself was a muddy mess. Horses stood at the hitching posts, and piles of wooden barrels crowded the road.

My heartbeat had quieted, but that strange pull still emanated from the churn. Was there something inside that caused that slight vibration in the air? Or was it something about the churn itself? I sniffed the air but only smelled someone's aftershave and more faintly the marigolds from a nearby garden.

The mayor pulled out an envelope. He slid out the contents, and grew very still. Licked his lips. Everyone watched, mirroring his sudden quiet. I found myself holding my breath.

Then Mayor Ward looked straight into my eyes and turned the photograph in his hand toward me. I blinked, then squinted. From where I sat fifteen feet away, I could see it was a portrait of a woman, black and white like the one of Main Street. She had long dark curls and a small face, and was wearing a modest, high-necked dress with a lace collar.

The scent of marigolds increased, filling the air and making me a little dizzy.

*There aren't any marigolds around here,* a voice whispered in the back of my mind. *They aren't in bloom yet.*

"Well, I'll be," the mayor said in a wondering tone. "This is a photograph of a woman who could be Elliana Allbright herself." He pointed right at me. "Ellie, you'll have to take a good look at this when we're done. But for now, there are still a few more goodies in our time capsule!"

Astrid elbowed me. "How weird is that?"

I flashed her a questioning look, feeling the eyes of the crowd on the back of my head. I resisted the urge to turn around and somehow managed to keep my expression placid.

Was *that* what I'd been waiting for? Why would someone in an old picture look like me? If she really did. It was entirely possible the mayor, who was not known for his attention to detail, had simply conflated the similarities between two women with dark hair who had lived more than a century apart.

Then I saw the envelope it came in as he placed it on the table. It was slightly open to reveal ancient dried petals that I somehow knew had been from an orange marigold. The scent intensified again, which was impossible because there couldn't be the slightest smidge of volatile essential oil left in that husk of a bloom.

To say the least, I was distracted when the mayor drew the next item from the churn and held it up.

It was a book—really a sheaf of paper, roughly stitched together and covered with writing and drawings. The hair on my arms flew to attention, and the colors in my peripheral vision brightened to neon. Everything around the strange volume suddenly seemed a little out of focus. My breath quickened, and I realized I was quietly panting.

Beside my foot, Dash perked his ears, and he looked up at me.

"Huh," the mayor said, apparently baffled. "Can't say that I know what this is. Heck, I don't even know what language this is." He looked over at Eureka. "Professor? Maybe you can help."

She stood and hurried to the podium. Taking the proffered pages, she tenderly turned each one with a fingertip while her gaze flitted over the contents. After several seconds, she looked up with a perplexed expression.

"I just don't know what this is. I've never seen anything like it." She started to go on, but then stopped and shook her head. "I can't understand why such a thing would be in a Poppyville time capsule from the gold rush. This vellum is quite old, much older than the other items." Puzzlement deepened across her brow, and she shook her head again. "How very odd." Gingerly, she placed the sheaf on the table next to the other items.

The mayor looked skeptical. "All right, then. Tell you what, Professor. We'll just leave it to you to figure out what this is."

Eureka gave a sharp nod. "Happy to try, Mayor." She returned to her seat and nibbled on her thumbnail.

I sensed confusion and frustration as well as excitement, and a part of my brain absently concocted a perfume blend of ylang-ylang and lavender oils, with bergamot as the heart note.

Aching with a combination of curiosity and an unexplainable feeling of protectiveness toward the newly discovered book, I spoke in an undertone. "What's wrong?"

Her response was barely audible. "That manuscript needs to be archived under glass. It shouldn't be touched with bare hands."

Astrid leaned over. "Why not?"

"The oil from human skin can harm old parchment like that," Eureka murmured.

"You're right. It does look a lot older than the other items," I whispered. "Is it valuable?"

"Perhaps, to the right person. She shook her head, then stopped. "That language, though . . ."

"What is it?" I asked.

"I've no idea," Eureka said, her voice still hushed. "It appears to be a combination of Greek and Cyrillic alphabets, but there are a few Latin letters as well. I made out an 'X,' and what I think are a 'V' and an 'R.'"

Someone behind us made a hushing sound, and I looked up to see the mayor glaring at us like an irritated schoolteacher.

I gave him a weak smile.

He reached into the butter churn again. His gaze suddenly brightened, and he looked down at his own hand as he drew out the next find. Oohs and aahs erupted from the crowd when he held it up.

It was a misshapen gold nugget the size of an orange. I remembered Thea scoffing at the idea that the butter churn contained gold.

"Holy crow," Astrid breathed from beside me. "That's got to be worth a boatload of money."

The sun broke through the sketchy clouds, and in its light the metal shone a dazzling yellow even though parts of it were still smeared with dirt.

They could have at least cleaned it off.

"Hoo boy! This thing is a lot heavier than it looks!" He hefted it a few times, looking at it in wonder before transferring his gaze to us. "Well, everyone, that was the last item in the time capsule, and what a find! I'll put it with the rest of the bonanza over here, so you all can take a look." He nodded to the policeman who had wielded the hammer and chisel. "No touching, though. Officer Danielson will be right there to keep everyone honest. And there are some other members of our illustrious police force here to help him." He winked at Chief Gibbon and Lupe and stepped down from the podium.

They exchanged glances and then moved wordlessly toward the display table.

"Well, good Lord," Eureka said. "That chunk of gold needs to go straight to the bank, not sit on a table waiting for some ambitious looky-loo to grab it and run."

"No kidding." I stood.

"Don't you think it's a little strange that the citizens of Poppyville would go to all the trouble of making a time capsule, but not include some kind of note to the folks who would open it in the future?" Astrid asked as she unfolded from her chair.

"Come to think of it, you're right," I said, already walking away.

People crowded forward to see the chunk of gold, but I elbowed my way to the other end of the table, where Mayor Ward had placed the marigold-scented picture of the woman and the manuscript.

The woman in the picture looked up at me. She had a bow mouth and wide eyes. Even though the photo wasn't in color, I knew they were cornflower blue.

Because my eyes were cornflower blue, and the mayor had been right. The woman in the photograph looked *exactly* like me. Furthermore, I caught something besides the scent of marigolds wafting from the photo: a faint whiff of melancholy drifting from the past to the present.

However, next to the photo sat the manuscript, and my

reaction to it was more intense. I could hear it singing to
me, a song without words or sound, but one that reached
a sense I didn't even know I had—beckoning, inviting,
beseeching. I estimated there were about ten pages. The
rough book had fallen open to reveal two interior pages
filled with a language that was strange indeed and drawings that felt eerily familiar. Then I realized why. My
gamma's garden journal looked very similar—a free-
form compilation of lore and botanical sketches, verse
and decoration, information and artwork.

An unmistakable drawing of a marigold was centered
on the left page, with words that swirled out from it in a
spiral like that of a conch shell.

Cruelty. Grief. Jealousy. Malice.

Words that weren't in any language I recognized, yet
I *knew* what they said. And on the right page, some kind
of symbol. A tree with roots that perfectly mirrored the
shape of the branches above. The whole thing was en-
circled within a series of linked spirals. Next to it were
more words in script. I made out the letters "X," "V," and
"R" that Eureka had mentioned, and my mind filled in
the rest:

Xavier.

The author? The subject?

The police had their hands full preventing the enthusi-
astic gawkers from touching the gold nugget. No one saw
me reaching toward the pages. When the pad of my fingertip touched the rough paper, a hot jolt shot into my hand for
a split second before fading to a subtle vibration that made
my blood thrum beneath my skin. Light-headed, I swayed
and had to take a step backward.

Hands reached out to steady me on either side.

"You okay there?" the slender man who'd snagged Astrid's attention earlier asked from my left elbow at the same time Odell Radcliffe said, "Whoa!" on my right. I hadn't realized they were standing so close.

"Ellie!" Astrid bustled in before I could say a word, flashing a flirtatious smile at the man on my left. "Come on, honey. Let's sit down."

"No, I—"

"You didn't touch it, did you?" Eureka demanded from behind us.

I clasped my hands, my fingertip still tingling, and turned. "Sorry."

"Dang it, Ellie!" She sounded truly angry. "I told you, the oils from your fingers . . ." She clamped her mouth shut and glared at me.

"Come on," Astrid insisted, and pulled me away.

Right into Detective Max Lang.

"Doesn't sound like Professor Sanford cared for you getting so grabby there, Ellie," he said with an unpleasant smile. "Might want to keep your hands to yourself."

Tugging my arm out of Astrid's grasp, I said, "Thanks for the advice, Max." No longer light-headed, I was irritated that I hadn't been able to examine the manuscript further.

And it didn't look like I would anytime soon. At least two dozen people were gathered around the table by now, and a glance at my watch reminded me I had to get back to open Scents & Nonsense.

"Listen," I said to Astrid. "Are you sure it's okay to leave you ladies with the cleanup?"

She waved her hand. "No worries. But I'm a bit concerned about you."

"Oh, I'm fine. Really. Come on, Dash." He and Ruthie had remained by our front row seats, and now he trotted over to me.

"But—"

I pointed over her shoulder to where the man who had caught my left elbow was approaching. "Better go introduce yourself to Mr. Right."

Or at least Mr. Right Now.

I wasn't proud of distracting her like that, but it worked. I glanced one more time toward the manuscript that had bewitched me, but my view was blocked.

*Tomorrow. I'll look at it tomorrow. That'll be soon enough.*

As I was leaving, I saw Astrid approaching her quarry. He was on his cell phone, a hundred feet away and partly facing away from her. I paused to watch. His expression was almost angry as he scanned the milling crowd in the park. When he finally saw Astrid marching in his direction, he said a few last words into the phone and abruptly hung up. As he turned, the intense look on his face morphed into a relaxed, welcoming smile.

*He's hiding something.*

Dash and I walked back to my shop, and I stopped worrying about Astrid's soon-to-be conquest and instead scrambled to make sense of the contents of the time capsule. First my doppelgänger and the dried marigold. Then the marigold and the tree symbol on the manuscript pages. But what was the most troubling was that even though I didn't know the language in which the words around the marigold were written, I'd nevertheless *understood* them. How was that possible?

Cruelty. Grief. Jealousy. Malice.

Furthermore, I'd understood part of what had been written near the symbolized tree in a circle.

*After violence*
*Keep the balance.*

That was all I'd gleaned from what I was already thinking of as the Xavier manuscript, but I recalled something very similar my grandmother had said to my mother when I was too young to reasonably be able to remember such things.

*We all help keep the balance, whatever our gifts. This daughter of yours will bring solace, but also right wrongs . . . and that will be triggered by violence.*

I shivered. There had been plenty of violence in the last year. I liked to think I brought solace to my customers, and in my own bumbling way I'd righted a few wrongs, too. But why this reminder, and why now? And why did it feel like a threat?

# CHAPTER 4

A FTER I closed the shop at five o'clock, I cooked some linguini and tossed it with leftover bacon, lemon zest, the last two farm fresh eggs, and Parmesan. I took my carbonara out to my back porch, which looked out on the expanse of a meadow and Kestrel Peak beyond. It was chilly, and I sat on the porch swing with an afghan draped across my lap as I ate. Dash sat at my feet, watching a rabbit play near the copse of evergreens on the left side of the meadow.

When I was finished, I washed the dishes, tidied up, and turned off the kitchen light. In the postage-stamp living room, I paused by the bookcase. After a moment's hesitation, I grabbed Gamma's journal off the shelf, ready for it to be hot to the touch after the events of the afternoon.

It was warm, but not overly so. I sat down and flipped through the pages. A kaleidoscope of blue butterflies like the ones that tended to follow Nabokov around the garden in the summer months filled one page. Another page showed meticulously rendered cross-sections of *Datura stramonium*, which demonstrated my grandmother's scientific knowledge as well as her artistry. I had one of the purple variety overwintering in the small greenhouse I'd added to the back of the property the previous fall, along with potted jasmine and gardenias and dozens of herb starts for the Enchanted Garden.

I turned the page. There: a drawing of a marigold, the ink outlines filled in with orange colored pencil. Gamma's voice echoed from the past.

*They look so sweet, don't they? But do not be fooled. If someone sent a floral message that contained marigolds in Victorian times, it was a sign of danger and ill will toward the receiver, for those sweet orange blooms represent cruelty and malice.*

Danger, cruelty, and malice.

Great.

I felt antsy as I put the journal back on the shelf. I knew I'd never get to sleep feeling so anxious, so I dug out a book of Gladys Taber essays that never failed to relax me and read for an hour or so. Reveling in her descriptions of cocker spaniels and life in an old Connecticut farmhouse, I went back into the kitchen and made a cup of strong passionflower and chamomile tea. It steeped while I took a hot shower and dressed in my softest pajamas.

* * *

I DRANK the tea and turned off the light a bit after eleven thirty. I stared up at the stars that shone beyond the skylight. Cassiopeia sat upon her celestial throne, perpetually circling the North Star, which was beyond view from the angle of my pillowed head. I closed my eyes and waited.

And waited.

My eyes popped open, and I felt Dash come to his feet beside me on the down comforter. Watching me.

"Hey, guy. Sorry. You can relax. I'm sure I'll be able to sleep soon."

He lay back down, still watching.

Two minutes later, I sat up. "Okay, okay. You're right. I'm not going to be able to sleep until I get a closer look at that manuscript."

*Woof.*

It came from deep in his chest, soft and low and replete with understanding.

"Let's go," I said, and swung my feet to the floor.

T HE smell of evening primroses greeted us on the front step. Above, the budding branches of the ancient oak tree rubbed against one another in dusty whispers. A mockingbird called from the meadow, echoed by its mate farther away. The bright moon streamed through the panes of the greenhouse, outlining silhouettes of leaves reaching up from terra-cotta pots inside. The path to the shop stretched in front of us like a blue-gray ribbon through the shadowy garden beds. Humidity filled the night air, promising ample dew by morning.

Dash and I went down the path and out to the boardwalk, and I closed the gate to the Enchanted Garden behind us. We crossed the street. Headlights swept the empty asphalt as a car turned onto Corona from Gilpin Avenue, then quickly faded as it continued toward the state highway north of town. The streetlights added a paltry yellow glow to the silver cast of the moon, giving an eerie aspect to the deserted downtown.

In front of the library, I hesitated, suddenly doubting my midnight mission. What was wrong with me? Still, if I went back home without further examining that manuscript, I'd end up staring out the skylight until dawn. The smell of the wallflowers wafting from the direction of Heritage House urged me forward.

We followed the sidewalk around to the side door of the library and then started across the lawn to the museum. Another scent joined the floral one—something with a metallic tang, like rust, but with an electric undercurrent that made the hair on the back of my neck rise like a dog's.

Without warning, Dash stopped right in front of me. I stumbled and nearly fell over him.

"What—" I began.

A quiet growl rumbled in the back of his throat. I froze, my heart beating double time.

Listening.

"What is it, boy?" I breathed, so low I could hardly hear myself. My gaze flicked from shadow to shadow, and my nose twitched as I sniffed the air. I knew that smell. What was it?

My dog looked up at me, brown eyes flashing, then back toward Heritage House. Another warning issued from deep in his chest, this time a little louder.

I took a deep breath and called in a loud voice, "Who's there?"

A rustle sounded near the cabin as a thick cloud scudded in front of the moon, and the entire scene was plunged into inky darkness. Cursing myself for relying on the moon instead of bringing a flashlight, I turned to go back home.

*Wait. There's a flashlight on my phone.* I took it out of my pocket, turned it on, and flashed the tiny beam around me. The shadows at the edge of Library Park were too far away to illuminate, but there was nothing in my vicinity except manicured lawn and a concerned corgi.

Still, light or no light, the damage was done. I felt jumpy. The next morning would be soon enough to look at the manuscript, right? I could get up super early and come over before opening the shop . . .

Dash *woof*ed and took off for Heritage House at a run.

I whirled and ran a couple of steps after him. Paused. "Dash!" I hissed in a loud whisper-call.

A tall streak of vertical yellow light split the squat building. Confused, I took a few more steps. Then I realized it was simply the door, open nearly a foot now. My corgi stood in the gap, peering into the cabin.

Slowly, I advanced. The wrought iron gate was ajar. Why? Why was the light on inside? And why was the door unlatched? It must have been if Dash was able to push it open. Fear crawled down my spine like a spider.

*Call the police.*

I fumbled with my phone. Dash looked over his shoulder at me, and I got the distinct idea he was urging me to join him. Then he looked back and went inside.

*Great.*

Glancing around, I quickly entered 911. Thumb hovering over the CALL button, I sidled toward the door. Standing with my back to the cabin wall on one side like some cop on television, I pushed it the rest of the way open with the flat of my palm.

The lamp on the information desk was on. Dash stood beside the desk. The fur on his back was smooth, and his head was cocked to one side, small details that calmed my alarm. Swinging around, I stepped onto the threshold and scanned the interior of the museum.

A yellow legal pad sat on the desk beneath the lamp. It was at an odd angle, as if it had been knocked askew. A ballpoint pen lay on the floor near my feet.

Another rustle hissed behind me, and I looked over my shoulder. The cloud had moved along, revealing the bright moon again. In its light, I saw nothing amiss. A strong breeze pushed at the azaleas at the edge of the yard, and they made a rasping sound against the metal fence. Was that what I'd been hearing?

I took a deep breath.

*One of the Greenstockings is probably here. God knows Thea and Felicity are both night owls. And we all have keys to the museum. No big deal.*

My shoulders relaxed a bit more. I turned back, scanning the shadows. "Hello? Thea? Felicity?"

There was no response. Turning the light on my cell off, I flipped on the overhead. The cabin appeared empty.

Dash moved behind the desk, sniffing at something behind it. I realized the metallic smell was a lot stronger inside the cabin. And I knew what it was, too.

Blood.

My stomach clenched in denial. Phone still in hand, I made myself walk over to where my dog stood and look down.

The chair was lying on its side. Next to it, Eureka Sanford was sprawled on her back between the desk and the wall. A short-handled mining shovel, streaked with rust, rested on the floor beside her. Her eyes were closed as if she were sleeping, and her red newsboy cap lay a foot away. Her hair was dark and matted on the left side of her head.

Closer examination revealed the red on the shovel wasn't all rust.

I set my phone on the desk, dropped to my knees, and started to reach for her wrist. Then I saw she was wearing white cotton gloves that came halfway up her forearms, so instead I gently probed her neck with my fingertips to feel for a pulse. As I did so, my mind flashed back to the last time I'd had to do the same thing, less than a year before.

Eureka was just as dead now as Josie Overland had been then.

My hand fell away, and my eyes closed against the sight in front of me.

After several deep breaths, I opened my eyes and hoisted myself to a standing position. I felt like I'd aged twenty years. My gaze slid away from Eureka's body and settled on the shovel. She was the one who'd suggested hanging it on the wall behind the reception desk.

And tonight, someone had killed her with it.

Instinctively, I reached for my phone on the desk, but then stopped with my hand hovering over it. The specter of Detective Max Lang rose on my mental movie screen, in full scowl and with his eyes narrowed in disbelief. He'd tried to pin one murder on me, and another on my brother's girlfriend. I'd proved him wrong both times. That he was Harris' best friend meant the dislike we held for each other was even more personal.

Well, I couldn't help it if I kept finding bodies. It wasn't as if I went looking for them, for heaven's sake. I was just . . .

My head jerked up. The vibrational *zing!* I'd felt when I was near the Xavier manuscript was absent. Panicked, I left the phone where it was and moved to the glass case where Eureka had planned to display the items in the time capsule.

It was open. And completely empty except for a color picture of the dirt-streaked gold nugget. Next to the photo was an information card about the piece of gold, including the weight—nearly twelve pounds!—the current estimated value of around $250,000, and a note that it had been taken to the bank for safekeeping. Everything else was gone, including the reason I'd trekked to the museum in the first place. Only a single dried marigold petal remained, an orange speck against the black velvet lining.

Grief for Eureka arrowed through my solar plexus,

followed closely by sadness and anger. I had to admit some of those feelings were also because the Xavier manuscript was gone.

It made no sense. I knew that. I couldn't explain why I'd come to Heritage House, either. Not that it mattered. Max Lang wouldn't give a shake anyway. He'd remember that I'd been interested in the manuscript, and that Eureka had been angry at me for touching it. Now she was dead, and I'd found her body in the middle of the night in a museum neither one of us was supposed to be in. I could almost see the smirk on his face when he realized he might have another chance to put me in prison.

My hand was shaking as I reached for the phone again. Dash gave me a quizzical look as I slowly slipped it into my jacket pocket.

No one knew I was here. I could just leave. Shut the door behind me and go back home through the empty streets of slumbering Poppyville. Latch the gate, lock my door, crawl into bed, and wait for someone else to find Eureka's body.

I took a step toward the door. Looked over my shoulder at the dead woman I had only begun to become friends with.

I couldn't do it. I couldn't leave her lying there all alone. Besides, now that I really thought about it, Maria would be the one most likely to find her. I knew how awful it was to find a dead body. This was my second one, and no way could I do that to the cheerful, gentle librarian. Other than her work for the museum, Eureka had largely kept to herself, but Maria probably knew her better than anyone else in town.

The phone felt heavy as I pulled it back out and regarded the 911 on the screen. I'd been ready to call for help, but this wasn't what I'd had in mind.

The screen went blank. I'd been staring at it too long.

An impulse struck. From my contacts, I selected Lupe Garcia's number. She might be the other detective on the force, but at least she knew I wasn't a killer.

# CHAPTER 5

You found who? Where? Jeez, Ellie, give me a minute." I heard a rustling, and seconds later, Lupe was back on the line. "Now let me get this straight. It's after freakin' midnight, and you're in Heritage House, and Eureka Sanford is dead."

"I'm sorry," I said again. The first time had been when she'd picked up the phone with a groggy hello. "But yeah, that's it. Looks like someone hit her over the head with a shovel."

"What?" she said, her incredulous voice fading on the word. Then the swishing sound of fabric got louder as she put me on speaker. She was getting dressed while we spoke. Her next words were strong. "Could her attacker still be there? Did you look in the restroom?"

Fear shot through me, and for a moment I didn't breathe.

I looked over at the closed door at the back of the cabin. Then I saw Dash gazing placidly up at me from where he seemed to be guarding the body. I let out my breath, realizing on a subconscious level I'd already known we were alone by my dog's behavior. "Dash is with me, and he would have let me know if there was anyone else here."

"Yeah, I guess," she grumbled over the sound of a zipper.

"But I'm going to check now," I said. "While you're on the phone with me."

"You should just go outside—"

"Hang on." I walked over to the closed restroom door, opened it, and flipped on the light. "No one here."

"God, Ellie." She sighed. "All right. You get a hold of Nan?" She was referring to the police dispatcher. Emergency calls were forwarded to her home at night during the middle of the week in the off-season.

"Um . . ."

A pause, then, "'Um'? What does that mean? Ellie, you called nine-one-one, didn't you?"

"Um . . . no. I called you."

"What?" she spluttered, then fell silent. Finally she said, "Is there something you're leaving out?"

"Of course not!" Not like she meant, at least.

"Then what on earth . . ." She sighed again. "You're afraid of Max. Okay, I get it. But listen, you *have* to call nine-one-one. If I call it in, then they'll know you called me first, and that'll raise suspicion you don't need."

"Oh. Right. God, I've made it worse," I said in a shaky voice.

"Just call them. I'll get there as soon as I can."

"Okay." I hung up and, gritting my teeth, made the call I should have made in the first place.

The whole time, I was staring at the yellow legal pad on the desk. It wasn't until I'd hung up that I realized what I had been looking at.

Eureka had been taking notes. Not many, just a few words.

*Try GPS overlay with claims map?*

*Check Bible.*

And below that, a doodle of a tree with arching branches above and sweeping roots that echoed them below. Sure enough, it was surrounded by a circle made up of a series of spirals.

It was the same symbol I'd seen on the manuscript page earlier. She must have copied it before someone killed her.

I turned on the camera on my phone and took a picture of the page. I pocketed it, called Dash, and went outside to wait. Then I remembered the rustle I'd heard in the bushes and rethought that decision. Azaleas or not, nighttime noises took on a whole new character after discovering a dead body.

The scents of blood and ink lingered in the air behind me, though, and I didn't want to stay inside. In the end, I hovered on the threshold, nervously peering into the darkness. After a few minutes, I slipped down to a half-squatting, half-sitting position, resting on my heels with my back against the doorframe. The air had grown quite cold, and I shivered. Dash pushed against my flexed thigh for comfort—his as much as mine.

Since I'd called her first, I expected Lupe to show up first.

She didn't. Chief Gibbon did.

I saw the beam of his flashlight before he rounded the corner of the library and strode toward me. He played the light over the ground, probing the bushes, and ended by shining it in my face. I'd scrambled to my feet by then, and stood blinking at him like a myopic deer in the proverbial headlights.

He lowered the light and regarded me with a gaze as bright as a bird's. My guess was that he hadn't been asleep when his phone rang with the news of another murder in his town.

"Ellie Allbright." He swore loud enough that I flinched. "Dispatch told me you made the call. This is the third time you're in the middle of a suspicious death, Allbright."

"Hey, it's not my fault," I said, and immediately regretted the high pitch of my voice, not to mention the playground protest.

Grimacing, he pushed past me. "It's that professor?"

"Eureka Sanford." I followed him into the reception area and pointed behind the desk. "She was at the ceremony this afternoon." I glanced at my watch. "Er, yesterday afternoon."

"Leave the dog outside." His tone was blunt as he squatted and touched Eureka's neck as I had.

Dash stood in the doorway. I pointed to the ground and murmured. "Sit. Stay." He obeyed instantly.

The chief stood and turned to regard me. "So? What's the story?"

Before I could answer, he looked over my shoulder.

"Detective Garcia, I'm glad you're here. Ellie was just about to tell me the tale of how she happened to come across a dead body in our brand-new museum in the middle of the damn night."

Lupe pressed her lips together, sidestepped my dog, who was partially blocking the entrance, and came inside. She wore her plainclothes uniform of blazer, slacks, and button-down shirt, but her cheek still reflected a crease from the pillow I'd roused her from.

"Chief. You made good time." Unasked was the question of why he was there in the first place, but I could tell she wondered. He was a politics and paperwork guy, and he'd always left the fieldwork to his officers—and murder investigations to his detectives.

"I was still up watching *The Late Show*, and I live closer than you do," he said.

Which was true. However, she'd known before he had. She didn't mention that. I owed her one.

"Now, back to Ms. Allbright." He raised his eyebrows and waited.

If I hadn't just discovered a murder victim in the middle of the night, I might have had the good sense to come up with a reasonable story. After all, telling them that I wanted to see what was in the Xavier manuscript when there was no way I should have been able to decipher any of it, or that I'd felt its buzzing energy when I'd touched it earlier that day . . . no, they'd never buy it.

"I, uh, I couldn't sleep, and so I came over to make sure the time capsule display was, you know . . . nice," I finished lamely.

The chief's expression was skeptical. So was Lupe's.

"I don't understand," she said. "You knew the other Greenstockings would take care of that."

I tried again. "Sure. I just wanted to see it, you know. Since I couldn't sleep. And Dash wanted a walk."

They exchanged a look.

A deep voice came from outside. "She wanted to get her hands on the papers that were in that urn, Garcia. I caught her trying to grab them after the ceremony, and—" Detective Max Lang stopped short upon entering the room and seeing Chief Gibbon.

"What're you doing here, boss?" he blurted out.

"I heard there was a murder," Gibbon said mildly. "Seems to be a lot of those in the last year." At this he shot a look at me.

Max noticed and smirked. The smirk faded when the chief continued.

"And my detectives don't like each other, which has made it difficult for them to work together." He looked between them. "So, I decided I needed to be personally involved before another murder has to be solved by a civilian."

I looked down at the ground.

Lupe said, "Sounds good to me." She'd been the one who requested not to work with Max after he'd bungled the investigation into my assistant's death.

Max looked like he always did: complexion ruddy, blond brush cut standing to military attention despite his never having served, and an expression on his face that hinted that he'd just eaten a sour grape. However, tonight he smelled of beer. Maybe that accounted for why he stood and gaped at his superior's announcement that he'd be detecting along with his detectives.

"I do hope that meets with your approval, Lang?" Gibbon prompted with a subtle layer of sarcasm threading his tone.

"Well, yeah. Yeah, of course, boss. You'll do great."

"Why, thank you for the vote of confidence." This time the sarcasm positively dripped from the words.

Max blinked.

Lupe's lips twitched, and she looked away.

A swirl of lights painted the night outside, announcing the arrival of emergency personnel. It had taken them nearly twelve minutes, but that was pretty good time in the middle of the night in Poppyville.

"Outside." Chief Gibbon waved us out the door. "Detective Lang, I want you to coordinate with the scene techs. Garcia, you're with me."

Max reddened but turned obediently toward the two jumpsuit-clad figures coming across the lawn.

I motioned to Dash to come with us as Gibbon led us to the portico over the side entrance to the library. He took something flat and narrow out of his pocket and held it up. It took me a few seconds to realize it was a digital recorder. The green light indicated it was on.

"Your name is Elliana Allbright?"

"Yes."

He stated the date and time, then said, "Tell us what happened this evening."

I told them as much as I could. I left out the unexplainable twitchy feeling I had about the Xavier manuscript, but emphasized that I'd nearly turned around when I'd thought I'd heard someone in the park.

"But Dash was kind of, you know—" I glanced at the

recorder. "Insistent about going into Heritage House. So, I kind of had to follow."

The chief looked down at my corgi, who sat obediently at my feet. "He seems pretty well trained."

"He is."

"But he didn't respond to your commands?"

I shook my head. "He's a good dog. Really. It's just—"

"It's just that he sensed something was wrong inside the museum," he said thoughtfully, still watching Dash.

"Yeah," I said in a tired voice.

"Smart," he said, and I dared to hope Chief Gibbon was one of the good ones.

His attention returned to me. "Is what Detective Lang said true? Were you looking to take the items that were found in the butter churn?"

"No, sir." I raised my chin. "It's true that I tried to look at the manuscript from the time capsule this afternoon, but then Dr. Sanford informed me that if it was indeed as old as she suspected, then it would be harmful to touch it with bare hands."

"And now it's gone, along with the other items in that case." Gibbon glanced back toward Heritage House as it was suddenly illuminated with xenon lights. "Or did I miss something?"

I shook my head. "No, all the items are gone." I felt sure I'd be able to sense the Xavier manuscript if it were on the premises. "Eureka was going to put the contents of the time capsule in the locked glass case. The one that's open by the reception desk. I think she was examining the manuscript, and whoever killed her took it and all the rest."

"Tell me why you think that," he said.

"Well, for one thing, she's wearing gloves. And I could tell she was excited about it this afternoon, even if she downplayed it to the crowd."

"Hmm," he said.

I looked at my watch. It was after one a.m.

"The case was open, not broken," Lupe said. "Professor Sanford would have the key. What Ellie says makes sense."

"Hmm," he repeated. What about that big ol' gold nugget? Maybe someone thought it would be in the case, too."

"Nope," Max interrupted, striding over to join the discussion. "Thea Nelson asked me to go with her when she took it to the bank. Bank manager said it's worth something like a quarter of a million dollars."

Lupe blinked, then looked at me. I nodded.

Max waved toward Heritage House, where the two technicians had moved inside to do their crime scene magic. The paramedics lingered near the doorway, waiting to escort Eureka to the morgue in Silver Wells. "He put it in their vault. Those women obviously hadn't thought much about security until that gold nugget showed up," he said.

I glared at him but kept my mouth shut.

"Yes, I'm aware of where the gold nugget actually is, Detective Lang. I was the one who suggested that Ms. Nelson take it to the bank, and to ask Officer Danielson to serve as her escort. He was obviously otherwise occupied, so she asked you."

Max reddened enough for it to be noticeable in the dim light of the portico.

The chief didn't seem to notice. "My question was whether anyone might *think* the nugget was in the museum." He looked thoughtful. "I bet there were at least some people who didn't know it went to the bank." His gaze cleared, and he nodded to himself. "It would only take one gold digger—literally. That nugget would sure be a better motive to kill someone than some old manuscript. And I can't imagine the other stuff that was in that butter churn would be worth taking."

"But all those items are gone," I said slowly. "And the nugget was never there."

"True," he said. "Dr. Sanford must have seen the thief's face and became expendable as a result." He nodded to himself again. "Her attacker might have taken the other contents of the time capsule once he—or she—realized the nugget had been stored elsewhere."

"She wrote a something on that notepad on the desk," I said. "Something about—" I stopped when I saw anger flash in his eyes.

His lips thinned. "Exactly how much snooping did you do before calling us, Ellie?"

"It was right there on the desk. That's hardly snooping." I couldn't keep the defensiveness out of my voice.

With a skeptical expression, he turned off the recorder. He was sliding it into his pocket when light suddenly spilled from the doorway behind us. The chief whirled to reveal Maria standing in the opening. She wore pink flannel pajama bottoms under a long coat and had a black watch cap jammed over her dark hair. Her face was devoid of makeup, which gave her a vulnerable air that was only exacerbated by the quaver in her voice when she asked, "Did I hear you right? Someone is dead?"

I grimaced. "It's Eureka, hon."

She gaped for a moment, then covered her face with her hands. "No," she whispered.

Of all the people who had joined Dash and me after our grisly discovery, Maria was the one who triggered my empathic response. I had to take a step to catch myself under the onslaught of her natural compassion for others, now ramped up to two hundred percent.

Neroli. Sandalwood for the heart note. And something else. I ached to give her the solace of those aromas.

"I'm afraid so, Maria." Lupe's voice was kind.

Chief Gibbon's face remained neutral as he asked the librarian, "How is it you happen to be here tonight?"

She dropped her hands. "Well, for Pete's sake, Chief. You have this place lit up like a ballpark. We live right around the corner, and all the lights woke up my little girl. When I looked out and saw they were coming from the library, well, you can bet your sweet patootie I hustled myself right over to see what was the matter."

I suppressed a smile.

Then the verve faded from her voice as she said, "And now you say Eureka is dead. She said she wasn't going to be here long. What happened?"

I opened my mouth, but Gibbon held up his hand.

"You knew she was here?" he asked.

Maria nodded and hugged her coat closer, as if to ward off more than the chill in the air. "She said she wanted to look at some of the stuff that was in the time capsule. Just a quick look, she said. It was kind of late, but she'd worked a lot of evenings getting Heritage House ready, so I didn't really think anything of it."

"What time was this?" Gibbon asked.

"She was parking out on the street as I was leaving for home," Maria said. "The library closes at eight this time of year, but I had some ordering to do. I stayed late to finish. It must have been almost nine thirty."

Chief Gibbon nodded and turned to me. "And you arrived here after midnight?"

I said, "Just after, I think."

"So, are you going to tell me what happened to Eureka?" Maria sounded perturbed.

"She was—" I began.

"Ellie," Lupe said.

"What? Everyone is going to know tomorrow. Is it a big secret?"

"Ms. Canto," Gibbon broke in. "I'm afraid it looks like Dr. Sanford was attacked on the premises of Heritage House."

Her eyes widened. "Attacked?"

"Yes. I'm afraid she died from her injuries. Did you happen to see anyone else around when you left work this evening? Anyone acting suspicious?"

She shook her head, eyes round. "Mrs. Paulson was walking Precious across the street, is all."

"Precious is her dog, then?" He ducked his head to make a note.

"Pig," I corrected.

He looked up.

"Precious is a fifty-pound pot-bellied pig," I said. "I'm surprised your wife hasn't gotten one yet."

He rubbed his eyes. "God forbid." The hand dropped, and he returned his attention to Maria. "Okay. You saw Mrs. Paulson and her, er, pig. No one else?"

She shook her head. "Did you catch who attacked Eureka?"

"Well, now—" Max started.

"No," I said.

She looked around the library grounds, so bright by the floodlights that it could have been high noon but surrounded by deep dark night. "I have to go."

"All right, that's fine," Gibbon said. "If you could—"

"No, I have to go now. My little girl will be frightened, and I think I might have left the front door unlocked. My husband is fast asleep."

"Chief," I said. "Maybe someone could go with her."

I thought he'd call over one of the patrolmen, but he nodded at Lupe. "Garcia."

"Sure, boss," she said easily, and followed Maria back into the library to lock up before escorting her home.

"Chief?" a voice called from Heritage House. "Do you want us to wait for the state patrol to get here before we move the body?"

I shuddered.

"Ellie, I'll catch up with you if I have more questions," he said. "You need an escort home, too?"

Glancing at Max, I said, "No thanks. I have Dash."

Gibbon looked down at my dog, nodded, then motioned to Max. Together, they moved back toward the museum.

I followed as far as the wrought iron fence that surrounded the yard around Heritage House, as if I could somehow still help. But I couldn't. I stuttered to a stop, watching, something in me unwilling to leave poor Eureka alone.

She was hardly alone.

No, there were a half dozen people there with her. It was Eureka who was gone.

I glanced down at that thought, whether in a moment of reverence or prayer, I couldn't have said. That was when I saw the corner of paper poking out from under one of the azaleas inside the fence. Without thinking, I kneeled to pick it up. Dash had been right on my heels and nosed my hand for a scratch. Absently, I fondled his ears and reached for the half-hidden item with my other hand.

The second I touched it, a strange sadness shot through me, familiar in an unsettling way. Usually when I felt someone else's pain, I could tell it was theirs. This felt like my own, but it was coming from an outside object.

I tugged it out and saw it was the envelope that had been missing from the glass case. The one with my look-alike's picture inside. And the dried marigold. Without opening it, I knew it still contained both. Why was it out in the bushes? Had the killer dropped it?

*Take it to Chief Gibbon,* said the smart voice in the back of my head.

*Who was this woman? Why does her photo make me feel this way?* asked the other, not-so-smart one.

I sighed and took the advice of the smart voice for once. I backtracked inside the fence, and Max nearly ran over me as he bustled out the door of the museum.

He glared at me. "Can't help snooping a little more, eh, Allbright?"

"No, I found—"

"Time for you to go home and let the real police investigate this." His tone was heavy with condescension.

"But—"

"Go on, now. We don't need your help."

"Max! I—"

He looked over his shoulder, then back at me. "I'm serious. Get out of my way," he gritted.

Anger flared through my weariness and sadness, and at the same time the need to know more about the picture of my doppelgänger flared even stronger.

"Fine." I turned away, slid the envelope into the sleeve of my jacket, and walked toward Corona Street.

# CHAPTER 6

✗

I N front of the library, I paused by the collection of emergency vehicles. Rapid footsteps behind me made me whirl around.

"Astrid?"

She was hurrying toward me, the cute guy from the time capsule ceremony trying to keep up. A long silk skirt swirled around her ankles, and her hair was plaited in a single braid over one shoulder.

"Ellie! What the heck?" She nearly knocked me off my feet with a bear hug. "What are you doing out here so late? What are all those lights? Are you okay?" Her face was flushed.

"I'm fine. But Eureka . . ." I trailed off, suddenly so tired I wasn't sure I had the energy to walk the two blocks home.

Her date stepped up to stand beside her.

"This is Dylan Wong," Astrid said. "And, Dylan, this is Ellie Allbright."

"Hi, Ellie." His voice was deep and pleasant.

I nodded to him.

"Something happened to Eureka?" She scanned the police cruisers and ambulance, the skin around her eyes pinched with worry.

"Um, could I call you later?" My eyes cut to her companion.

"No!" she said. "Tell me now. What happened?"

I sighed. "I'm afraid she's dead." I wished I could have said it better.

My best friend's mouth dropped open. "But . . . what?" she finally said.

"Did she have a heart attack or something?" Dylan asked, not unkindly.

Locking eyes with Astrid, I shook my head. In that instant, understanding passed between us, and all the blood drained from her face.

"No," she whispered.

I cleared my throat. "What are you doing out and about?"

"We were taking a stroll after the Horseshoe Bar closed at midnight." She flashed a distracted smile at Dylan.

He slid his arm around her. "We saw the lights, and Astrid had to come see what was going on." He smiled at her. "Like a little moth to the flame."

*Yuck.*

Astrid's eyebrow twitched as she turned toward her date and stepped away. "Tell you what, Dylan. You go on back to the hotel, and I'll give Ellie here a ride home in my car."

"Well, why don't—" he began.

"And I'll see you tomorrow, okay? Give me a call when you get a chance."

"Um . . ."

"Come on, Ellie," she said, and marched across the street to where she was parked.

Dylan looked surprised but followed obediently after, as did I. Standing by her ancient Peugeot, Astrid allowed him to give her an awkward kiss on the cheek. Then she waved good-bye as he continued down the block to the Hotel California, where he was evidently staying. Dash and I slid into the passenger side as she got behind the wheel.

"I didn't mean to break up your date," I said as she started the engine. "It's only a couple of blocks . . ."

"Nonsense. You're my bestie, and you need me. Plus, Dylan seemed to want to continue our date in his hotel room, which I had no intention of doing."

"On a first date?"

"Yup. Besides, I want to know what the heck happened to Eureka."

"Ah," I said, and filled her in on everything.

"Hit with a shovel?" she asked with horror when I was done. By now her car had been parked in front of Scents & Nonsense for quite a while.

I nodded. "It was pretty awful."

"I bet." She grimaced, and then her expression turned thoughtful. "And that manuscript was why you were acting so funny yesterday afternoon. Huh. You say it felt like it was calling you?"

I nodded, glad Astrid knew me well enough to take my "feelings" seriously. The one thing I'd left out of my narrative was taking the photo of my twin.

I'd take it to Chief Gibbon tomorrow.

Slumping in my seat, I said, "Yep. And now the Xavier manuscript is gone."

"Are you going to try to find it?"

I blinked. "I hadn't thought about it."

"Well, maybe the police will find it." She sounded doubtful.

"Maybe." But what if they didn't?

Suddenly, Astrid let out a huge yawn.

"Ohmagod," I said, looking at my watch. "It's almost three. Are you working tomorrow? Er, today."

She rolled her eyes. "I work every day. But yes, I have to be at Dr. Ericcson's at nine sharp."

"I'll let you go, then," I said. "No cookies tomorrow."

"And disappoint your customers? Are you kidding? I have a bunch of chocolate crinkles in the freezer. I'll drop them by on my way to work."

I adored her chocolate crinkle cookies. "You don't have to do that." I opened the passenger door, and Dash jumped to the ground.

"Pshaw," she said with a wave. "I'll wait until I see you flash your porch light."

"Thanks," I said, and shut the door.

As I hurried through the gate and down the path, I sensed nothing awry. If anything, it was eerily quiet. Every leaf and bloom was still, and not a trace of a breeze moved the cool night air. It was as if everything in the Enchanted Garden was holding its breath.

Dash seemed most intent on getting inside for a late-night snack, which I gave him after flashing the porch light three times for Astrid's benefit. I felt so weary I barely managed to climb my bookshelf staircase to the bedroom. Once there, I tumbled onto the bed, pulled the quilt over myself, and plummeted into unconsciousness.

M y alarm buzzed insistently at seven o'clock, jerking me out of a sound sleep. Usually, I woke up long before it went off, but not this time. Groggy, I slid my feet to the floor and realized I was still wearing the long-sleeved T-shirt and yoga pants I'd put on to walk to Heritage House the night before.

*Heritage House. Eureka. The mysterious manuscript.* I sighed.

At least I'd taken my shoes off. Dash watched with interest as I grumbled my way to the built-in cupboards at the end of the bed where my fleece robe was stashed. I donned it, then stumbled to the staircase and made my way down. Without thinking, I grazed Gamma's garden journal with my fingertips like I always did in the morning.

It was so warm I jerked my hand away in surprise.

Blinking blearily, I considered the well-thumbed and dirt-stained volume. There was something in there I was supposed to read—the sooner the better.

*Coffee first. Whatever it is, I definitely need coffee first.*

While the caffeine dripped into the carafe at an agonizingly slow speed, I splashed water on my face at the kitchen sink and dried it with a paper towel. Gazing out the window toward the meadow out back, images from the night before played on my mental movie screen.

Eureka lying on her back. Blood on the shovel. The open display case. Legal pad on the reception desk, glowing yellow in the lamplight.

Shaking my head, I filled my largest mug with fresh brew, retrieved the garden journal on my way through the living room, and stepped out back. The afghan was still draped across the porch swing, so I snuggled under it while Dash went to the edge of the meadow to take care of his morning business.

A few bracing swallows of caffeine later, I set the mug down on a table. Gamma's book still felt warm as a puppy, even in the brisk morning air. Taking a deep breath, I allowed it to fall open.

And blinked. The page showed the colored pencil drawing of the marigold that I'd seen the night before, but now there were a few additions. Next to the flower were three lines of writing I could have sworn weren't there before, and on the opposite page a new drawing had appeared.

The words were neatly penned in Gamma's handwriting. How did she do that? I looked around as if I could see her spirit but saw only wind-bent grasses and a hawk drifting on a thermal above the meadow.

Frowning, I turned my attention back to the journal and read.

*Violent death times three*
*Will summon thee*
*Daughter of Kell*

I felt my brow knit as I reread the lines. Okay, "violent death times three" made sense, since Eureka's murder was the third one in the last year. But who the heck was Kell, and who was her—or his—daughter?

Sighing with frustration, I took a sip of rapidly cooling coffee and examined the drawing on the opposite page. The picture wasn't typical of Gamma's usual crisp renderings. It looked as if it had been crafted with only a few smudged strokes of black charcoal. A woman in a high-necked dress and with long, dark curls.

It could have been the same woman in the photo from the time capsule. There wasn't enough detail to be able to tell whether the drawing looked that much like me. However, there was one thing that stood out clearly among the otherwise dusky lines.

The brooch nestled at her throat showed the same tree symbol I'd seen in the Xavier manuscript. The one Eureka had drawn right before her death. In fact, it was the most clearly drawn thing in the picture.

A chill ran down my spine, and it had nothing to do with the slight breeze coming off Kestrel Peak.

Leaving Dash to nose at the dew-covered grass, I went back inside and retrieved the pilfered photo of my doppelgänger from where, in my exhaustion, I'd left it by my jacket on the love seat. Returning to the porch where the light was better, I carefully extracted the picture by the edges so as not to smudge any possible fingerprints on the surface.

It was as if I were looking into a mirror through time.

Holding it next to the vague drawing in Gamma's journal, I compared the two. The necklines of the dresses in each were high and lacy, and the buttoned yokes were similar. The photo showed the pattern of the dress to be a flowered calico, but the drawing showed no pattern. The face in the drawing hinted at a narrow chin and wide eyes.

Putting the journal aside, I stepped off the porch and into the direct sunlight.

*There. Can it be?*

It was. My photo twin was wearing a brooch at her throat where one might expect a cameo pin. But this was no cameo.

It was the tree symbol all over again, just like in the drawing.

"What the heck?" I muttered out loud. Dash came trotting over.

Gingerly, I turned the photo over and held it at an angle, hoping to see if there was the name of a photographer or photographic studio on the back. There wasn't, but I did see the faint outline of a name penciled in one corner.

*Alma.*

"Okay, Alma. Who were you? And what's up with that tree?"

Dash cocked his head as I slipped her likeness back into its envelope.

I smiled down at him. "Don't worry. I'll figure it out." Somehow.

The hawk's hunting cry echoed from the blue-green

foothills. A breeze kicked up, bending the dry, dead grasses with a susurrant whisper. Movement in my peripheral vision caught my attention. A pure white doe stepped from the copse of trees at the edge of the meadow, moving from the shadows on delicate, strong hooves. The morning sunlight struck her glowing coat with supernatural brilliance. She stopped and blinked at me, and I saw that she wasn't a true albino at all. Her eyes were deep brown and luminous beneath long lashes.

"Well. Hello there," I breathed. "It's been a while since I've seen you."

Her head dipped, and she tugged at a spray of emerging spring grass with her teeth. I watched, transfixed, as she roamed from one green delicacy to the next. Dash settled next to my foot, also watching, but somehow knowing not to disturb her.

Then she suddenly stood tall and looked around as if something had startled her. She met my eye, tipped her head to one side in an oddly human gesture, then spun and bounded back into the trees.

I let out a long breath. It seemed like the last twenty-four hours had been fraught with signs, most of which didn't make any sense, and the doe's appearance felt like another one. However, I'd seen her before—when I'd needed to be reminded of my own delicate strength.

And I'd been investigating a murder that time, too.

# CHAPTER 7

THE coffee helped. A shower helped. Two of the chocolate crinkle cookies Astrid dropped by on her way to work, still slightly frozen and dunked in more coffee, helped, too. Add in a big sniff of my energy essential oil blend—peppermint and rosemary mixed with eucalyptus and tea tree oil—and I felt as bright and awake as if I'd slept a full eight hours.

Well, sort of.

Inside Scents & Nonsense, I fed Nabby and fluffed his bed. I set out the rest of Astrid's cookies by the coffee urn and arranged the mismatched rocking chairs in front of the plate glass window that looked out on the Enchanted Garden. I dusted the displays of scented bath products, replenished the stacks of soap, and put a batch of newly labeled cinnamon lip balms out with the other flavors. The kids' section needed a quick tidying, and then I turned on the cool LED lights in the glass-fronted case where I displayed my custom perfume blends in the tiny, elaborately scrolled bottles I collected from wherever I could find them.

The soft light shining through the colored glass made me smile as I turned my attention to concocting a scentual remedy for Maria. When I felt like I had the right blend—a bit of calming rose oil added to the neroli and sandalwood I'd been thinking of the night before—I set the bottle aside and texted her.

> I have something for you but can't leave the shop until Maggie comes in this afternoon. If you're out and about, drop by.

At ten o'clock, I unlocked the front door and flipped the sign in the window to OPEN. As soon as I did, the door to the Kneadful Things Bakery on the other side of Corona opened, and Tanner Spence exited with a paper bag in his hand. He waved to me and jogged across the street.

Despite being nowhere near a beach, Spence looked like a California surfer dude through and through. His streaky blond hair was blunt cut and just long enough for him to pull straight back into a stubby ponytail, and he wore board shorts and flip-flops most days unless the temperature dipped below forty degrees. His green eyes flashed as I opened the door for him.

"Hey, Ellie. Want a bagel?"

I half smiled. "Because you just happen to have an extra, right?"

A grin spread across his face. "Well, sort of. I've been waiting for you to open the shop." He thrust out the bag. "Cinnamon with extra cream cheese. Just the way you like."

The thick paper of the bag crinkled as I opened it and stuck my nose in for a heavenly sniff of spicy goodness. "Mm." I carried it over by the register, where Nabby was snoozing the morning away in his red velvet bed.

"And to what do I owe this treat?" I asked, not mentioning that I'd already eaten two cookies.

"Just you being you," he said.

I rolled my eyes. "Be serious."

He leaned his elbows on the glass top of the display counter and gave Nabby a scritch under the chin. "I heard you might be feeling kind of wiped out this morning."

I paused with a bite of cream-cheese-lathered bagel halfway to my mouth. "What's that supposed to mean?"

"What happened to Eureka," he said. "It's all over town."

"Yeah. I guess it would be." I popped the bite into my mouth and chewed, considering what Chief Gibbon would want me to tell him.

"Jeez, Ellie. I leave for a three-day photo shoot at El Capitán and come back to this." He shook his head.

"What did you hear?" I was curious about how well Poppyville's grapevine was working.

"That she was killed at Heritage House with an axe." He grimaced.

"It was a mining shovel, actually."

He pointed at me. "Which you know because you found her."

I made a face.

"At two o'clock in the morning? Jeez."

"A bit earlier than that, but yeah. I found her."

His mouth turned down. "Well, okay, but it was still the middle of the night, right? Kind of a weird time to be at the museum. Why were you there? And all alone?" He shook his head again.

"Dash was with me."

"You know what I mean. You put yourself in danger. I hate that." He took his elbows off the counter and straightened, waiting for me to explain myself.

Spence had accompanied a journalist to Poppyville a few months back, as his photographer. The journalist had been going to interview me about my tiny house for a conservation magazine, but was killed before he'd had the chance. My half brother had just come back to town with Larken, who had immediately become the prime suspect in the murder—thanks to Detective Max Lang—so I'd had to step in to try to clear her name. For a while I'd even wondered if Spence had had a motive to kill the guy. *Enough* motive, I should say. It seemed like everyone had disliked the guy, including me.

Spence and I ended up being pretty good friends. He'd asked me out at first, but I'd made it clear I was involved with Ritter—long-distance relationship notwithstanding. Astrid had hinted that my friendship with Spence was more than that. That he'd moved from Sacramento to Poppyville didn't help dispel her delusion, but he'd told me he really liked small towns and that, as a photojournalist, he could pretty much make his home base anywhere he wanted. I utterly adored Poppyville and would never want to live anywhere else, so how could I blame anyone else for wanting to live here?

However, now I faced a quandary I seemed to encounter more and more: how to explain the curious feelings that sometimes came over me, or the things that I alone seemed to sense? How someone was feeling when they entered my shop, or the wordless messages that plants sometimes broadcast in the Enchanted Garden—not only messages Gamma had taught me from the Victorian language of flowers, but also what I could only describe as a kind of botanical telepathy.

*We need more acid in the soil over here.* Or: *Cutworms on the move—help!*

That kind of thing.

Spence was a good guy, but like a lot of my friends, if I tried to explain those things—or, in this case, the *zing!* I felt from an old manuscript that I understood despite not knowing the language it was written in—well, he'd think I was nuts. So I ended up answering his question the same way I'd answered Chief Gibbon's—that I hadn't been able to sleep, Dash wanted a walk, and I was curious to see how the time capsule display in the museum had turned out.

The look that Spence gave me was pretty much like Gibbon's, too.

"You can't go wandering around at night like that, Ellie." He reached out and took one of my hands in both of his. "Promise me you won't do that anymore."

"Spence—"

The bell over the door jingled as it opened, and I looked up to see a handsome mountain man standing in the doorway. His hair was a deeper chestnut than the last time I'd seen him, and the short beard was new, but he was the same gorgeous guy I'd fallen for back when he was just Thea's older brother in high school, and then fallen for all over again after Harris and I had divorced.

Our eyes met, and the electric attraction I felt every time I saw him arced across the room. Then his gaze fell to where Spence was still holding my hand. I yanked it out of his grasp as if it were on fire, but not fast enough to stave off the surprised hurt that flickered across my boyfriend's face.

Spence frowned and turned to see who had interrupted us.

"Ritter!" I rushed out from behind the counter and threw my arms around him. He smelled of leather and green moss.

After a second's hesitation, he returned my embrace. When I let go and looked up at him, though, I saw he was watching Spence instead of looking at me.

"You're home early!" I said, a little too brightly. *This shouldn't feel so awkward.*

"Surprise," he said, finally directing his gaze at me. When he spoke again, his voice was lower. "It's good to see you, Elliana. You look fantastic."

*Elliana.* Ritter always called me by my full name. However, considering that I hadn't done more to my hair than jam it into a high ponytail and hadn't bothered to cover the dark circles under my eyes with concealer that morning, I highly doubted I looked anything near fantastic. Still, his smile was so genuinely appreciative I felt myself blush.

Clearing my throat, I said, "That last text of yours . . ."

"A little lie so you wouldn't worry if you couldn't get a hold of me while I was traveling. I hope you'll forgive me." The corners of his eyes crinkled.

Spence stepped forward. "You must be Ritter Nelson. Ellie told me all about you."

Ritter regarded him. "Has she now. I don't think she told me anything at all about you."

"Sure, I did. This is . . . was . . . Blake Sontag's photographer," I said.

"Who lives in Poppyville now. Right. Spence something?"

"Tanner Spence. My friends call me Spence." The way he said it implied that the jury was still out regarding whether Ritter qualified.

They shook hands. On the surface it looked civil enough, but I could feel the enmity rolling off Ritter. Off Spence, too, for that matter.

Men and their testosterone.

So why did *I* feel so uncomfortable? And guilty? I hadn't done anything wrong. But I needed to explain to Ritter why Spence had been holding my hand when he walked in.

Yeah. No problem.

"I can't believe you didn't tell me you were coming home," I said, again too brightly.

He half smiled. "Maybe I should have."

"Ritter . . ." I trailed off.

"I missed you," he said with a sudden, brilliant smile that left my knees feeling a little wobbly. "So I left the research project a couple of weeks early. They'll just have to finish it up without me."

Warmth swelled from my chest all the way down to the tips of my toes. "That's . . . wow."

"Drove in from the airport this morning. Not telling you was Thea's idea. She was going to invite you to dinner at the Sapphire Supper Club tonight," he said. "Only I'd be there instead of her." He looked pointedly at Spence. "That was where Ellie and I had our first date."

"Nice place," Spence said.

"It is," Ritter said, then returned his attention to me. "But this morning I heard about the professor being killed, and that you were the one who found her. I couldn't wait until tonight to see you. It must have been terrible for you, finding her like that."

"See?" Spence said. "I'm not the only one who's worried about you."

Ritter looked past me again. "Well, I'm back now."

The smile Spence gave him didn't quite reach his eyes. "And I'm still here." He nodded to me. "I'll let you two catch up. Give me a call later. I brought you something from El Capitán."

"Um . . ." I was flustered by the tension in the atmosphere, none of which Spence was helping one little bit. "Good-bye," I said firmly.

"See you," he said, walking toward the door. He made it sound almost intimate.

Baffled, I wanted to clear the air right then and there but sensed it would only make things worse. So I ignored his exit altogether and pulled Ritter over to the counter to give him a proper hello kiss.

What should have been a romantic interlude after a five-month absence turned out to be awkward and fumbling. Our noses bumped not once, but twice. I stepped on his toe only one time, though. At least we were able to laugh at ourselves—sort of. Still, I felt a thread of disappointment at our very un-movie-like reunion.

After we'd made a start at reconnecting, I poured us both coffee and, between customers, told Ritter all about the night before. Even if we hadn't seen each other for months, we'd communicated regularly via satellite telephone and e-mail, and by now I felt confident that he understood what Astrid called my superpower, but what he simply termed intuition. So I didn't hold back on the baffling effect the Xavier manuscript had on me.

"Huh. That's pretty strange," was all he said when I was finished. We were sitting in a pair of rockers looking out at the Enchanted Garden from inside the shop.

I waited for more, but he didn't elaborate.

"You're mad at me." I sighed. "Listen, I can explain about Spence. We weren't holding hands when you walked in. He was just trying to comfort me after what happened to Eureka."

Ritter's eyebrows arched.

"Not like *that*," I protested. "He's just a friend."

"If you say so. I get the feeling he sees things a little differently."

Shaking my head, I said, "I don't know why he was acting so weird. And believe me, I made it clear I was waiting for you." Putting it like that made me sound like a wartime bride or something, and I grimaced.

He nodded slowly and reached over and took my hand in his. "I see. I'm just tired after the long trip. You know, Ellie, we've been apart a long time. Maybe we need to back up a little. Are you still up for that dinner tonight? Thea made reservations."

I felt the tension in my shoulders dissipate and smiled. "Yes, Mr. Nelson. I'd love to have dinner with you."

I SHOULDN'T have been in such a good mood after the events of the night before, but having the guy you've been dreaming about suddenly show up at your door can do that to a person. I caught myself humming as I stirred vanilla granules into powdered goat's milk and colloidal oatmeal. Then I added baking soda and citric acid, so the mixture would fizz when mixed with bathwater. When I had the formula right, I began funneling the milk bath into old-fashioned milk bottles.

When I was nearly finished, I looked up and saw a sour-faced woman standing on the boardwalk in front of Scents & Nonsense with her hands on her hips. Next to her, a little girl who looked about five years old tapped on the window. Nabby was sitting inside on the window-sill, and when she did it again, he stretched and put his paw on the glass.

"Lookit, Mama," I heard her say as her mother opened the door. "The pretty kitty wants to play."

"Be careful. He might scratch."

I hurried up to them. "Nabokov is a gentle cat. He's

never scratched anyone, so you go right ahead and pet him, honey." I smiled at the woman. "Welcome to Scents and Nonsense."

"My daughter wants to see the fairy gardens."

"They're right out back," I began.

She interrupted me. "We know."

They made a beeline for the Enchanted Garden, and I let them go. After filling the last bottles of milk bath, I moved to the rear window and looked out. The little girl was making the rounds of the fairy tableaus, while her mother followed at a slower pace. At first, she seemed impatient, but by the time she'd made a complete circuit of all the flower beds, the expression on the woman's face was much more relaxed.

Dash whined at the door, and I let him out to join them. He ran to the little girl and flopped over on his back, begging for tummy scritchin's. Her laughter sparkled through the air, and soon her mother joined in.

I smiled at the sound, too, and breathed out a murmur of gratitude to the universe for this place, my life, and the people—and animals—in it.

# CHAPTER 8

A BIT before noon, Maria walked in. "Hey, Ellie." Her voice was flat, and her eyes were bloodshot. I immediately felt a twang of her reflected grief deep in my solar plexus.

I moved out from behind my worktable, where I'd been decorating jars of fir-scented bath salts with sprigs of evergreen branches, and walked over to give her a hug.

"How're you doing this morning?" I asked, my hands still on her shoulders.

She shrugged. "Okay, I guess."

Nodding, I went back to the area behind the register and removed a small brown bottle from a shelf where I kept custom aromatherapy blends until clients came to pick them up.

"Here. I made this for you. It should help you feel a little better." I handed it to her across the counter.

Gratitude flooded her face as she took it. "Thank you, Ellie. Your blends always soothe." She unscrewed the cap and took a deep whiff. "Mm. What's in it?"

"Neroli and sandalwood, with a faint note of rose."

"Oh, Ellie. It's lovely."

I felt my own shoulders ease and knew it was the right blend to help her feel less anxious and sad.

"I can't believe she's really dead," Maria said, passing her hand over her face. "Last night seems like a bad dream." She took another whiff of the sandalwood blend.

My chest loosened a little more in response.

She hitched herself onto the bar stool at the end of the counter. "Have you found out anything new?"

I shook my head. "I haven't talked to the police today."

"That's not what I meant. Aren't you going to look into Eureka's death, Ellie?"

"It's not exactly my place. Chief Gibbon will take care of it." I went around to stand on the other side of the counter.

She waved that away like a foul odor. "Don't even try that on me. It wasn't your place when the last two people were murdered in Poppyville, either. But if it weren't for you digging harder than the police and figuring things out—"

I interrupted her. "Then I might have gone to jail, or Larken might have. I really had no choice."

"Eureka was my friend," Maria shot back, making me blink. "She was a friend to the rest of you, too. She deserves justice."

"Of course she does, Maria," I said quietly.

"Do you think Chief Gibbon can solve this?"

"I honestly don't know. But Lupe—"

"Is a terrific detective. Really good at her job. But last night when she walked me home, she told me the chief appears to be spearheading this investigation." One side of her mouth pulled back. "She wouldn't come right out and say it, but she hinted that he might be too busy being chief to be a detective, too."

"Chief Gibbon does have a full plate," I agreed.

"He thinks someone broke into the museum to steal that gold nugget, right?"

I sighed. "He did mention something about that. It's certainly plausible."

"So, Eureka was just in the wrong place at the wrong time?" Maria looked away, obviously unsatisfied.

Silence settled over us for a few moments, broken only by the rumble of Nabokov's purring as he strolled down the counter toward Maria. I watched as he sat down next to her elbow and lowered his head. She knew the drill and lowered her own, so he could butt her forehead with his own velvety one. Soon she was rubbing the space behind his ears, and his eyes were closed with happiness. The gentle smile on her face reminded me that Nabby had his own kind of comfort to offer during rough times.

I leaned forward and put my elbows on the counter. "Okay, say the chief is wrong about the gold nugget being the motive for Eureka's murder."

Her head came up.

"I'm not saying he *is* wrong," I clarified. "The guy has a lot of experience and knows his business. But hypothetically, if we were to entertain other motives, do you think someone might want that old manuscript badly enough to kill for it?"

She shrugged. "Nah. I mean, maybe."

"It's missing," I pointed out, slightly disappointed. It wasn't that I wanted Eureka to have been killed because of that mysterious old sheaf of papers. I just wanted to know why it had been stolen. More importantly, I wanted it back.

"Yeah." Maria sounded doubtful. "But no one seemed that interested in it besides you two."

Maybe. Maybe not. Astrid's new love interest and Odell Radcliffe were both standing close enough to reach out and steady me when I stumbled after touching the manuscript. They must have been looking at it, too, but I was so intent on getting close to it that I hadn't noticed.

My head tipped to one side as I regarded Maria. "Okay, if the killer wasn't there to steal the gold nugget or the manuscript, then what do you think happened?"

She hesitated, then shook her head. "I don't know. Everyone seems to think Eureka was killed because she was in the wrong place at the wrong time. What if she was killed precisely because someone knew she'd be there, alone and vulnerable?"

I frowned. "Like who? Did she have any enemies?" My eyes widened. "Maria, what do you know?"

A hesitant, pensive expression crossed her face. "I don't *know* anything."

Still puzzled, I asked, "If someone wanted to get Eureka alone, why do it at Heritage House? Why not go to her house? She lived by herself, didn't she?"

"She did, but she had a security system."

"In Poppyville? Gosh, that puts this whole thing in a different light, Maria. She must have been afraid of someone."

"Well . . ." Maria drew the word out. "It was her sister who put the security system in, actually."

"She has a sister in town?" I heard the surprise in my voice, and realized I really knew very little about Eureka Sanford.

"Not anymore. See, her sister died a couple of years ago and left her house to Eureka. When Eureka retired from Berkeley, she decided to move here and live in it."

My shoulders slumped. "Which already had a security system. I guess that would make it harder for her to be attacked in her home." I looked up. "I wonder why her sister installed it. Did you know her?"

"Not really. Her name was Victoria Perez, and she worked in the county clerk's office for years. However, from some things Eureka told me, I could make a guess about why her sister installed that security system."

I propped my chin on my hand. "Do tell."

"Her son's wife had threatened her."

"Victoria's son." I spoke slowly, trying to get it straight in my mind.

"Right. Eureka's nephew, Warren Perez. He and his wife live here in Poppyville. His new wife, I should say. Apparently, he divorced the old one and picked up a trophy model." She rolled her eyes. "*Trixie*. Ugh. His mother didn't approve, and there were, um, issues between her and her new daughter-in-law."

"Issues that necessitated a security system?" I asked.

"Maybe. I'm only guessing here, Ellie. But here's the thing—Victoria hated Trixie so much that she left her house to her sister instead of her son. And *that* did not make Warren or his new honey happy *at all*."

"Oh ho . . ."

She went on. "They were furious at Victoria, and at Eureka as well. Trixie suggested rather strongly that Eureka do the right thing and give the house to them anyway. Eureka refused, saying she couldn't go against her sister's wishes like that, but that she would *leave it to them when she died*." Her hand banged down on the counter in emphasis, eliciting a baleful look from Nabby.

I whistled. "Did you tell Lupe this when she walked you home last night?"

"Not really. I was too stunned and worried to talk much, but I did mention that the police should look into Eureka's nephew as a suspect. I mean, I could be wrong, but—"

"No, it's good that you told Lupe that," I interrupted. And then, because I couldn't help myself, I said, "Tell me more about Warren Perez."

She gave Nabby another scratch behind the ears. "He's in his forties. Trixie's closer to thirty. He sells farm equipment around the valley. Has that dealership on the Silver Wells Highway?"

I nodded. "I've driven by it. It's big. Looks profitable."

Maria lifted one shoulder and let it drop. "Hard to tell with some businesses. I've heard rumors."

"Is the house she inherited from Victoria worth a lot?"

She looked at her watch and slid off the bar stool. "It's nice enough. Older but well cared for. But it's on Swallow Avenue, and that location alone would increase the price significantly."

"No kidding."

Swallow Avenue had been the ritziest street in Poppy-ville during the height of the gold rush, and still was a coveted address, at least in the older part of town. It was lined with houses built by the most successful merchants who supplied the prospectors—and a few homes built by profits garnered from less reputable means. Pauline "Poppy" Thierry, local madam, city founder, and eventually the namesake of the town, had died in her mansion on Swallow Avenue when she was eighty-eight.

"Do you know the address?" I asked.

Maria gave me a knowing smile. "Five twenty-five." She turned toward the front door but held my gaze. "Thanks, Ellie."

"I can't guarantee anything."

"I'm not asking you to. Just do what you can. For Eureka."

M AGGIE Clement came in at noon on Thursdays so I could run midweek errands in the afternoon. I had the deposit ready for the bank and a grocery list to restock my larder. I'd added a few things to have on hand for entertainment purposes now that Ritter was back in town. I smiled to myself as I imagined sipping wine and nibbling on cheese in the garden before regaling him with my coq au vin.

I'd also made a copy of the old photograph of "Alma"

before replacing it in the envelope and sealing them both in a plastic bag. I'd handled it very carefully once I realized what I was dealing with, but not when I'd first picked it up the night before. As I recalled, Mayor Ward hadn't been all that careful with it, either. So, my fingerprints and his—and who knew how many others'—might be on the photo. I could only hope some of them might lead the police to Eureka's killer. Dropping it by the police station was first on my list of errands.

Precisely on the hour, Maggie strode through the door. A sixty-something grandmotherly sort, her blond hair came from a bottle, her jewelry from Rexall Drugs, and her big heart from a lifetime of practicing psychology from behind a bar. She made the best dirty martini I'd ever had the pleasure to drink, babysat her grandkids every chance she got, and worked harder than any one person I knew.

"Elliana Allbright, what have you gotten yourself into now?" was her greeting as she breezed past me to stow her purse in the office. "Harris is fit to be tied."

I felt my brow wrinkle. "Why? What does he care?"

"Thinks you going around and finding dead bodies somehow reflects badly on him."

"Good. At least something worthwhile came out of this tragedy," I muttered.

She came out of the office, tying on one of the chefs' aprons I kept on hand. "I know you don't mean that because you are too nice a person."

"Not when it comes to Harris."

Maggie grinned. "I can relate, honey. That man is only my boss, but sometimes I want to take him over my knee and teach him what his mother should have. I can only imagine what it was like to be married to him. Now." She put her hands on her hips and surveyed the shop. "What do you have for me to do today?"

I set her to work printing and cutting out tags for the milk bath I'd made earlier, called to Dash, and went across the street where my old Wrangler was parked. As I climbed inside, I considered how to order my errands.

"Police station first. Then the bank and Doggone Gourmet," I said to Dash, who was sitting in the passenger seat. He grinned at the mention of the purveyor of his favorite peanut butter treats. "And we're out of beeswax for lotion bars, so let's go by the Bee's Knees for more. We can stock up on clover honey while we're there." I started my vehicle and continued my list in my head.

My metal watering can was leaking, so I needed a new one at the hardware store. As long as I was there, I could pick up kitty litter for Nabby and more heavy plastic to line the planting benches in my greenhouse. Then the wine store for a bottle or two of something nice for Ritter and me to share, and the grocery store last. If I hurried, I might be able to detour by Eureka's house for a quick look-see.

I was so distracted by my thoughts that I almost didn't notice Detective Max Lang coming down the steps of the Hotel California. He had a manila file folder in his hand and strode purposefully toward the parking lot at the side of the building. I slowed and watched as he got into a dark SUV. As he pulled onto Corona, I veered into a parking spot across from the courthouse half a block down and grabbed my cell. He drove by the Wrangler without a glance.

"Hello, Felicity?"

"Hey, Ellie."

"You at work?"

"I am."

"I just saw Detective Lang coming out of the hotel."

She snorted. "You're at it again, aren't you?"

"At what?" But of course I knew what she meant.

"The girl sleuth thing," she said. I began to protest, but then stopped.

*For Eureka.*

"I guess I am," I admitted.

"Good," she said. "Max wanted the names of people who stayed here during the last three days."

"And you just told him?"

"Sure. He had a warrant. Gave him a full printout with all the names. Max actually didn't seem very happy about it." I could hear the smile in her voice. "Said Chief Gibbon wanted him to track down every single person and find out where they were when Eureka was killed."

I let out a sigh of relief. "That makes me feel better."

She laughed. "To know Max is stuck with a bunch of grunt work?"

"Ha. Well, I don't mind that a bit. He seems to have avoided the tedious part of crime investigation in the past. But really, I'm happy to know the chief is making sure the t's are crossed and the i's dotted in Eureka's murder case." I didn't mention that I not only wanted justice for our friend, but also hoped that finding her killer would mean finding the manuscript.

"Are they all gone?" I asked. "The people on the list, I mean."

"Not all of them. And not all were here for the time capsule ceremony. There's a wedding this weekend, and some of the people on Max's list are here for that. But the reporters are gone, and most of the professors. Dr. Radcliffe is the only one left. He had a reservation for four nights."

"I wonder why," I mused.

"No idea. Try asking him yourself. He's walking out to sit on the veranda right now."

I opened my door and stood on the running board to see down the block. Sure enough, Odell Radcliffe was settling into a wicker chair on the deep porch of the hotel.

"Has Max already talked to him?"

"Nope. Just took the printout I gave him and left."

I thanked Felicity, and we hung up. I looked at my watch. *So many errands.* I really didn't have time to talk with Dr. Radcliffe.

But it sounded like he'd known Eureka a long time, and Max hadn't even bothered to check in with him. What had the relationship between Radcliffe and Eureka been? Were they more than colleagues, by any chance? But his daughter—Hallie? No, Haley—was with him. Would he bring his daughter to a romantic assignation? Doubtful. Still, I thought I'd sensed a subtle flirtation between Odell and Eureka before the ceremony the previous afternoon.

Perhaps he could shed some light on who might want to harm his former colleague. It was also possible he could shed some light on why the Xavier manuscript had been included in a time capsule full of gold rush memorabilia.

I made a decision. First, I'd take the photograph to Chief Gibbon, and if Odell was still sitting on the veranda of the Hotel California when I was finished, I'd drop by for a chat.

"Stay here, Dash." I took a deep breath and opened my door.

How angry would the chief be about my keeping evidence in a murder investigation overnight?

THE police station was in an annex added to the back of the courthouse in the 1970s. The courthouse was still stately and regal, built in the mid-1880s and then updated several times on the inside. The exterior brickwork was original and beautifully maintained over the decades. The annex, however, was ugly, boxy, and luckily tucked out of sight from the street.

The tiny waiting room boasted dirty linoleum, four cheap plastic chairs, and a half-empty bulletin board. Nan looked up from behind the glassed-in reception desk, nodded at me with a grin, and buzzed the door open.

I pushed through the door and found myself separated from her by a narrow counter. Three desks lined the walls of the small room, and a hallway with an EXIT sign over it led to the back door.

"What can we do for you, Ellie?" Nan had big bones, big hair, and a big voice.

Slipping off my daypack, I asked, "Is the chief in?"

She glanced over her shoulder and nodded. "I think so. Hey, Chief!" she called. "You in?"

His voice drifted from an open door down the hallway. "Can it wait?"

She looked at me and raised her eyebrows.

"Not really," I said.

"Nope," she called. "It's Ellie Allbright."

Chief Gibbon appeared in the door of his office, frowned, and then beckoned for me to come back. I wended my way past the desks, sidestepped an overflowing trash can, and stopped in his doorway.

The chief wore a dark suit with a crisp blue shirt and a red tie. He was standing behind his desk, flipping through several papers in his hand. His sharp crow eyes glanced up at me, then back at the papers. "Is this about Eureka Sanford?"

"Yes."

He found what he was looking for and put it in the open briefcase on his desk. Then he snapped the case shut and perched on the edge of the desk to give me his full attention.

"I'm already late for a meeting," he said.

I unzipped my pack and took out the plastic bag with Alma's picture in it. "I found this on the ground in Library Park. Eureka's killer must have taken it with the other items from the time capsule and then dropped it." I handed it to him. "My fingerprints might be on it, but I put it in the plastic just in case the killer's are, too."

One eyebrow slowly rose as he took it. "In Library Park? When exactly did you find this?"

I hesitated. However, where—and when—I found it might be important to his investigation. I sighed and told the truth.

His eyes narrowed, and his lips thinned as he listened. When I was finished, he regarded me for a long moment. "You know you shouldn't have taken this."

I looked at the floor. "Yeah."

"You say Lang wouldn't listen when you tried to tell him?"

My head came back up. "Yes! He's—"

Gibbon held up his hand. "I know very well what Detective Lang is. And I also know you could have insisted on seeing me or shown him what you found even if he dismissed you at first."

"I guess so," I mumbled.

"I'll admit this into evidence and get it to the lab." His gaze flicked to the big round clock on the wall. "And hopefully the budgeting committee will understand why I'm later than usual to our meeting. I need you to fill out a written statement about finding this evidence. Include all the details." He paused. "*All* of them."

"Absolutely," I said.

He stood and reached for his briefcase.

"Um, have you found out anything so far?" I was blocking his way. "About the murder, I mean?"

"Just go fill out your statement, Ms. Allbright," he said. "Nan will get the paperwork for you. Give it to her when you're done."

My lips pressed together, but I said, "Okay," and turned to go.

"Ms. Allbright?"

I turned back.

"Thank you for bringing this to my attention." His harsh eyes softened. "We're going to find Dr. Sanford's killer."

Slowly, I nodded my head. "Good."

I wanted to believe him. I did. But between Max's bumbling and Gibbon having to go to a meeting rather than tracking down clues, I didn't know if I should.

But at least he hadn't yelled at me.

# CHAPTER 9

I FILLED out the paperwork Nan gave me as quickly as I could and left the police station. Back at my vehicle, I checked on Dash, then eyed the Hotel California. Sure enough, Odell Radcliffe was still reclining in a chair out front, his feet propped on a stool. His face was partially obstructed by the copy of the *Poppyville Picayune* he was reading. Leaving Dash in the Wrangler again, I took a deep breath and hurried down the block.

"Hello, Dr. Radcliffe," I said from the top step of the wide veranda.

He'd watched me walk up the sidewalk, and now stood. "Hello, dear. I know we met at the museum opening, but I'm afraid I don't recall your name." His jacket lacked the patches on the sleeves, but his half-glasses, Beethoven hair, and the rich smell of pipe tobacco all screamed "academic."

"Ellie Allbright." I closed the distance between us and took his outstretched hand. "I saw you sitting here and wanted to extend my sympathies. I got the impression you and Dr. Sanford were old friends."

He blinked.

For a moment I had the horrible thought that no one had told him Eureka was dead. Then he passed his hand over his eyes and took a deep breath before gesturing to the settee across from his chair. We both sat down.

"Poor Eureka," he said.

"She was very well liked here in Poppyville. I wish I could have gotten to know her better," I said.

He nodded, looking into a distance I suspected had more to do with his own memories than the view across the street.

"There you are, Daddy."

I looked up to see his daughter had joined us. She wore a midcalf skirt and turtleneck, and clutched a misshapen cardigan around her, though the afternoon was pleasantly warm. Her hair was pulled back with a headband, and the sun flashed off the thick lenses of her glasses. I caught the scents of baby powder and maple syrup.

She was in her twenties, and I was no fashion maven, but I itched to give her a makeover for no other reason than to boost her confidence.

"Haley, my dear. Please join us. This is Ellie Allbright. She was a friend of Eureka's."

"Hello," she said with a tentative smile, and sat on the other end of the settee. "I remember you from the museum yesterday."

"Hi," I said with an answering smile. "I remember you, too."

She looked momentarily surprised, as if people didn't often remember her.

"I was just telling your father how sorry I am about what happened to Eureka Sanford."

Haley nodded. "Dreadful. Just dreadful."

"Did you know her well?" I asked her.

"I should say so," Odell answered for her. "Eureka and I were, well, old flames, I guess you might say. For a time there, Haley and I both saw a lot of her."

Haley had been watching her father and nodded before turning to me. "Yes, Daddy and Dr. Sanford were quite the item when I was eleven and twelve. Mama had been gone for what? Five years by then, Daddy? Even as young as I was, I remembered thinking that it was good for you to have a girlfriend."

Odell flushed and cleared his throat. "Girlfriend, indeed."

"I liked Eureka. It's too bad it didn't last," she said regretfully. "But that's how these things go, I suppose."

Looking wistful, he said, "We continued to be quite good friends."

"In the subsequent years," Haley said with a nod.

"After all, our offices in the history department were right—"

"Across the hall from each other," she finished. "I often chatted with her when I stopped by to see Daddy." She leaned forward. "I'm in another building on campus. Psychology department."

"And you must have stayed in touch after Eureka re-tired," I said to Odell.

"Oh, yes," Haley answered.

They were like an old married couple, one answering for the other and finishing each other's sentences.

It sounded as though her mother must have died when Haley was just six or seven years old. My own mother had died when I was four, but my grandmother had stepped in as a mother figure until she passed when I was eleven. By then my father had married my vivacious yet very maternal stepmother.

"Eureka invited me to come to Poppyville to see the opening of the time capsule," Odell said. "She did love this little town. I can see why. Haley decided we could both use a little vacation and tagged along." He smiled at her over his half-glasses.

I heard a buzzing sound, and she took her phone out of her pocket. "Excuse me," she said, and began typing with her thumbs.

Irritated, I reminded myself that such behavior was becoming the norm, and turned back to her father. "So you must have known Eureka for a long time, Dr. Rad-cliffe."

"Odell, please. For nearly twenty-five years, I'd say. She was an amazing woman."

Something about the way he said it made me wonder if he'd still carried a torch for his "old flame."

"Do you have any idea if she had any enemies?" I asked.

"Eureka? Good heavens, no. I mean, she could rub a person the wrong way, that's for sure. A bit prickly at times, you know. Didn't suffer fools gladly. Disliked authority. Could be a bit caustic. Irritated the powers that be because she couldn't have cared less about the politics of the university. But enemies? I don't think she made anyone angry enough to be considered an enemy."

Haley gave a tiny snort, and I looked over at her.

"Oh, Daddy. You just described someone who has lots of enemies." She tipped her head toward me in a conspiratorial gesture. "My father is not a connoisseur of social relationships."

Odell shrugged and nodded at his daughter. "It's true. Human interactions can be quite baffling, don't you think?"

I suppressed a smile. No wonder it didn't work out between him and Eureka.

"Um, I suppose so," I said. Resisting the urge to check the time, I pushed on. "Do you remember the manuscript from the time capsule? The one the mayor called Eureka up to look at when he was taking things out of the butter churn?"

"Indeed, I do," he assured me. "Fascinating thing isn't it? I saw how it interested you yesterday afternoon."

"It's missing," I said bluntly. "Along with all the other items from the time capsule except the gold nugget, which is at the bank."

"Ah, of course. They couldn't keep it at the museum, now could they?" His eyes flashed, and he leaned forward. "But the manuscript is missing?"

"Yes. And, apparently, Eureka was examining the manuscript when she was killed." Hopefully, I hadn't just revealed something I wasn't supposed to. On the other hand, no one had told me to keep any of the details about Eureka's murder under wraps.

"Is that so?" he said. "And you say all the other items from the time capsule are missing as well?"

"Well, all but one."

He gripped his knees with both hands. "Thank God there's at least something left. What is it?"

I frowned, not wanting to go into detail about the photo I'd found. "The police have taken it as evidence," I hedged. "But back to the strange manuscript. Do you have any ideas about what it might be, or why it was in the butter churn?"

He shook his head. "Such things aren't exactly my bailiwick. I'm a Civil War guy myself."

"And I believe Eureka's focus was on Western US history," I said.

"Exactly!"

"Nonetheless, she was interested in the Xavier . . . I mean, in that old manuscript," I pointed out.

He nodded. "Eureka had a lot of interests. Always looking for ideas for her next big book project."

Haley tore her attention away from her phone. "Oh, Daddy. Her book was on the gold rush, wasn't it?"

"I know, dear." He absently patted her arm. "But Eureka told me she had some new ideas—"

"About how to incorporate the time capsule into her research," Haley finished. "I remember what she said, too, Daddy."

I hazarded a look at my watch, and when I saw the time I bolted to my feet. "It's been lovely chatting with you, Odell. You, too, Haley."

Her smile widened. "I'm afraid I was a bit distracted. I'm trying to set up an interview with someone for my thesis. So sorry if I was rude."

Suddenly I felt like a heel. "No worries. Master's thesis?"

"PhD."

"What's the subject?" I asked.

"Reality-testing interventions for hindsight bias."

"Hindsight bias?" I asked.

"Basically, it's when something happens, and you think you knew it would happen all along, when in reality you didn't, because you couldn't."

I stared at her.

"It's a trick our memories play on us all the time. Someone wins a sports match or an election, and all of a sudden people start saying they knew it would turn out that way."

"Oh! Like twenty-twenty hindsight," I said. "Monday morning quarterbacking."

She sighed. "Well, yes."

"Sounds fascinating," I said.

"Doesn't it?" Odell said with an indulgent look at his daughter.

Glancing at my watch again. I said good-bye as gracefully as I could manage and returned to the Wrangler.

I SPED around town for the next forty-five minutes, frantically loading up supplies in the back of the Jeep. In the parking lot of the Grape Escape, I checked my watch and saw there was barely enough time to swing by 525 Swallow Avenue on my way to the grocery store.

The avenue was wide, with a mix of deciduous and evergreen trees shading the sidewalks and lovely homes. I thought of them as mansions because that was what they had been considered to be by the people who lived in them in the 1800s, but they weren't that large in terms of square footage compared to what would be considered a mansion now. They were tall and formal looking, though, with lots of red brick and dormer windows. A few smaller homes were scattered among the larger ones, most set farther back from the street. These had once been carriage houses or servants' quarters, renovated to meet modern standards of comfort and style.

Eureka's house fit someplace in the middle, size-wise, and had probably been built by a lesser baron than some of the others on her block. It had two stories, a sprawling wraparound porch, a tile roof, and wide windows. A cedar picket fence surrounded the yard, the lawn had been edged recently, and a sprightly mix of spring bulbs brightened the symmetrical garden beds on either side of the porch steps.

A black pickup was parked in the drive that led to an unattached garage in back. As I drove by, I saw the John Deere and Kubota stickers in the back window. Warren Perez sold farm equipment and was sure to have plenty of machinery from those two companies on his lot. Besides, Eureka had driven a maroon Camry, which had probably been towed from where she'd parked it on Corona Street before walking back to Heritage House.

Curious, I pulled to the curb, told Dash to stay, and

got out. As I walked up the front sidewalk, a man and a woman suddenly stepped out of the house. He smelled of stale cigar smoke and had unnaturally dark hair, heavy eyebrows, and impressive jowls that jiggled as he turned his head to look up and down the street. She was pretty and delicate, with long highlighted waves, distressed jeans that fit like a glove, and the fake watermelon scent of designer hairspray.

They stopped cold when they saw me.

"You're not the police," he said.

"Of course, she's not, Warren," she said with a deprecating smile. "For heaven's sake. You just called them."

*Warren. And that must be Trixie. They sure didn't waste any time.*

"You're expecting the police?" I asked. "Is everything okay?"

"No, everything is *not* okay," Warren said. "My aunt has been robbed."

His wife sniffed. "'Burgled,' I believe, is the more correct term."

My eyes widened. "You're saying someone broke into Eureka's house?"

She stepped forward and held out her hand. "I'm Trixie Perez. Eureka was my aunt. Are you one of her friends?"

"Ellie Allbright." I shook her hand. Her grip was like a vise. "I worked with her on the museum at Heritage House."

"Of course." She waved dismissively toward her companion. "This is my husband, Warren."

A city patrol car pulled to the curb behind my vehicle,

and then the unmarked Ford Taurus that Lupe usually drove parked behind that. Both drivers exited their cars at the same time and hurried over to us. Lupe's eyes widened when she saw me, but she spoke directly to the couple.

"I'm Detective Garcia," Lupe said. "And this is Officer Danielson." I recognized the same policeman who had been guarding the gold nugget at the time capsule ceremony.

The couple introduced themselves.

"We got a call there was a break-in," the patrolman said.

"You're darn right there was a break-in," Warren growled. "The lock was gouged right out of the wood, and the door was hanging open when we got here."

"What about the security system?" I asked.

Lupe raised her eyebrows.

"Maria told me," I explained.

"Well, I don't know anything about that," Eureka's nephew grumbled.

"We would have been notified by the alarm company if it had gone off," Officer Danielson said. "It must not have been activated."

"Ellie," Lupe said. "Could you come over here for a sec?" Her tone was mild, but the look she gave me was not.

*Uh-oh.*

"Sure," I said as lightly as I could, and followed her to the edge of the yard.

# CHAPTER 10

W HAT are you doing here?" she hissed when we were out of earshot.

"I was driving by and saw the truck in the driveway with the John Deere decal," I said. "I knew it wasn't Eureka's, and Maria told me she'd had problems with her nephew, who happens to deal in farm equipment. It seemed a little suspicious, so I stopped. Then those two"—I gestured with my chin—"came running out of the front door. You know the rest."

Lupe frowned. "They were inside the house?"

"Yup."

She turned around and marched over to where Warren, Trixie, and Officer Danielson were still standing in the yard. Out of the corner of my eye I saw a woman come out on her porch across the street to watch the proceedings. Her arms were folded disapprovingly.

"Mr. and Mrs. Perez," Lupe said. "Would you mind showing me your key to this house?"

Warren looked down at the ground, but Trixie straightened her shoulders and answered. "We don't have a key."

Surprise, surprise.

"Then why are you here?" Lupe sounded genuinely curious.

They exchanged a look, then Trixie took a deep breath and let it out with a huff. "We thought someone might be here. A friend, or . . . well, even you guys. The police. Because of the murder, you know."

That actually made sense. My eyes cut to Lupe. Had the police already come and gone? If they had, they would have already known about the break-in. Unless, of course, it had happened after they'd left.

Like right before I'd driven up.

"We were hoping you'd let us in," Trixie said.

"I see." Lupe waited for more. "And why would you need to go inside Professor Sanford's house?"

Trixie licked her lips, then seemed to make a decision. "We wanted to look for a copy of Eureka's will. She told us she was going to leave us this house, and we wanted to see if she kept her word."

Officer Danielson turned from where he'd gone to inspect the damaged door lock and stared at them. I didn't blame him.

Lupe had her poker face firmly in place. Her words belied it, though. "Well, you sure didn't waste any time."

Trixie grimaced. "You're right. We should have waited."

"I imagine it's hard to think straight in the middle of your grief and all," Lupe said.

The barbed remark appeared to be lost on the other woman, who shook her head. "Hardly. There was no love lost between Eureka and us."

Warren's head came up. "Eureka and *you*, Trix. Everyone got along just fine until you started fighting with my mother."

She silenced him with a look.

"Can you tell me where you were last night between nine o'clock and midnight?" Lupe asked.

The couple looked confused, and then Warren's face cleared. "You can't be serious."

"I'm deadly serious."

"You think one of us killed Eureka?" Trixie sounded indignant.

Her husband had turned a sickly pale. "We were, um . . ." He glanced at his wife, who narrowed her eyes at him. "At home," he finished.

"Both of you?" Lupe asked.

"Yes, both of us. Together." Trixie glared.

Lupe folded her arms. "I take it you didn't find it."

"Find what?" Warren asked.

"Dr. Sanford's will."

"We didn't have a chance to go—" Then Trixie realized I was standing right there, and I'd seen them come out of the house. "We didn't have a chance to look," she amended. "As soon as we realized the house had been broken into, we checked to see if anyone was hurt inside and called you guys."

That sounded fishy to me. Who would be inside besides Eureka? The person who broke the lock?

Lupe turned to me. "Would you be able to tell if anything was missing?"

I shook my head. "I've never been in Eureka's house. But I bet Maria could help."

She nodded. "I'll call her. Better call the chief, too. I thought this was a simple burglary but didn't realize until after the call came in that this was Eureka Sanford's residence."

Lupe pointed at the Perezes. "You two stay here."

Trixie huffed and went to stand by the porch railing. Warren, looking pensive, went to stand by her.

"Better check inside to make sure no one is in there," Lupe said to Officer Danielson. "Try not to disturb anything."

Danielson nodded and unsnapped his holster, then trotted up the steps and went into Eureka's house.

While Lupe called Maria and Chief Gibbon, I went back to my vehicle, opened the newly purchased bag of peanut butter treats, and gave a couple of them to Dash. After all, the poor guy had spent hours stuck in the Wrangler that afternoon. While he gobbled them down, I grabbed my phone and retreated to the far side of the street to call Maggie. As I waited for her to pick up, I noticed a few more people on the block had come out of their houses to see what was going on.

"Scents and Nonsense."

"Maggie, it's Ellie. I'm so sorry, but I've run into a situation, and I'm going to be late. Is there any chance you could stay until four? Or does your shift at the Roux start at three?"

"It starts at three," she said.

I groaned. It was five minutes to.

"But don't you worry," she said. "I'll make it work."

"No, no. I don't want you to get in trouble with Harris. Just go ahead and close the shop, and I'll get there as soon as I can."

"Don't be ridiculous. The restaurant will be dead until at least five, and this time of year things are slow even during happy hour, other than Fridays. I'll get someone to cover for me, and I'll make some excuse for Harris, so he won't be mad at you."

"I couldn't care less if he gets angry at me, I just don't want him making life difficult for you."

"Don't worry. I can handle Harris."

I thanked her profusely and hung up just as Maria arrived. I met her on the street as she got out of her minivan. "Hey. Welcome to the party. I just met Warren and Trixie, and they're as delightful as you might think." I surreptitiously pointed at the couple.

"Great," Maria muttered, and we went through the gate into Eureka's yard. Officer Danielson had come back out of the house and was looking around the perimeter of the front fence.

Lupe came over, still speaking into her phone. "Sure, boss. We'll take a look inside, and then I'll cordon it off. You can come take a look after your meeting." A pause. "Right, sir. I'll take care of it." She hung up and made a face. "Chief was in a sit-down with a county task force this morning, and a budget meeting all afternoon."

"Busy man. Must make it hard to investigate a murder," I said mildly.

"He's a good cop." Her tone was a little defensive. "And it's not like Max and I are sitting on the sidelines."

"Of course not," I said.

My friend was in a difficult situation. It was hard enough working with Max without Chief Gibbon slowing things down by trying to do the jobs of chief and detective at the same time—even if his intentions were good.

She nodded to Maria. "Thanks for coming on such short notice."

"No problem. My assistant can handle things at the library on her own for a while."

"Well, come on inside. Officer Danielson took a quick look, and the things most burglars would take—TV, stereo, smaller electronics—are still there. I'm hoping you can tell us if something else was taken during the break-in."

"I'll do what I can," Maria said.

I followed them onto the porch, and when Trixie saw we were going inside, she made as if to follow.

Maria stopped. "Detective Garcia? Are they coming in, too? I don't think Eureka would want . . ." She trailed off.

"Who the heck are you?" Trixie demanded. "And how would you know the first thing about what Eureka would want? She left us this house, after all."

The librarian drew herself up to her full height and raised her chin. "I was her friend. She told me all about you. And this house isn't yours yet!"

Warren put his hand on his wife's arm, but she angrily shrugged him off. She opened her mouth to retort, when Lupe held up her palm.

"I'd like you to stay out here." She waved over the

patrolman. "And I'm sure you won't mind if Officer Danielson takes a look inside your truck."

"What? You think we stole something?" Trixie spluttered. "You think we broke into Eureka's house? And then were stupid enough to call the police?"

"Trix!" Warren said.

She ignored him.

Lupe smiled pleasantly and called, "Officer? These people are going to open up their truck, so you can look inside."

"No, we're not!" Trixie said. "I know my rights, lady—"

"Yes, we are," her husband said wearily, and led Officer Danielson over to their vehicle.

"Warren!"

We turned and went inside the house.

Maria went into each room on the first floor, scanning the contents of each with care before moving to the next one. The kitchen still smelled vaguely of toast and the ripening bananas in a bowl on the counter. In the rest of the house, Eureka's furnishings were sparse and the dust bunnies profuse. It fit with her personality—laser focused on the things that mattered to her and not giving a hoot about the little stuff. I could tell her loss weighed heavily on Maria. When I saw her remove the essential oil blend I've given her earlier in the day from her pocket and take a sniff, I was glad.

On the second floor, we went into Eureka's bedroom. It smelled of Ivory soap and mothballs. Each of us contemplated the rumpled sheets for a long moment before moving into her office next door. There I smelled the familiar scent of fountain pen ink I'd come to associate with the dead woman.

Maria paused in front of her desk. "Her laptop is gone."

Lupe and I came to stand on either side of her. Sure enough, there was a square on the mahogany surface defined by the dust around it. We stepped back as Maria moved to look behind the desk and on top of the return that created an L-shaped work surface for the academic.

I looked around at the rest of the office. The bookshelves were packed, and a giant Boston fern arched over the deep window. A funny Charles Bragg print on the wall behind the desk was the only decoration.

"Did she work on it a lot?" I asked Maria, thoroughly puzzled. I hadn't ever seen Eureka with a laptop, and she'd still used a flip phone rather than a smartphone— rather pointedly, in fact.

"Some," Maria said. "At least, she brought it to the library to do research for her book. She didn't love technology. Maybe it was because she spent her whole life studying the past, but she was a bit of a Luddite. She used her computer for getting information off the Internet, but she took a lot of notes on legal pads, too."

Like the one she'd been taking notes on when she was killed.

"Did she tell you much about her book?" I asked Maria. "I know it was about everyday life during the gold rush."

"Specifically about everyday life for women," she corrected me. "She spent a lot of time in the library looking through our local reference materials. You'd think it would be fairly simple, but there were a lot of different types of women in Poppyville then, as now. Different religions, races, and cultures, and they all operated in a complicated social strata. Her academic focus was on Western US history, California history, and the gold rush in particular. That's why she was so interested in getting Heritage House up and running. She told me she'd published another book based on real-life events several years ago, and it was quite successful. She was happy to have the time to write again after retiring and hoped she could still leverage her earlier success for her new book."

We were silent for a moment, thinking about how Eureka would never be able to finish her project now.

"Do you think Warren and Trixie took the computer?" Maria wondered aloud.

I frowned. "Why? I mean, it wouldn't be worth enough to steal, would it? Not if they left the stereo and television downstairs."

Maria shrugged. "I don't see how it would be valuable to anyone but Eureka."

"There could be other things besides book research on it. What if there was something on it about her will? Or if they could get access to her bank account?" I wondered out loud.

Her eyes widened in alarm.

Lupe said, "We'll follow up on the bank accounts, but people don't typically keep a copy of their will online."

Maria's face cleared. "Tom Beagle was Eureka's attorney here. He'd have a copy of her will."

"Good to know." Lupe scanned the room again. "And

if Warren and Trixie did take her laptop, Danielson will have found it in their vehicle by now."

Unless they had taken it and came back later to report the burglary. Or hid it someplace to retrieve later. But why would they? Impossible to tell without knowing what was on the computer.

Then another thought struck me. What if Eureka had information about the Xavier manuscript on the computer? I'd done a little bit of research between waiting on customers that morning but hadn't found any reference to old manuscripts using multiple alphabets. Perhaps Eureka had had better luck. Perhaps she'd discovered something that impelled her to go look at it again at Heritage House.

Maria interrupted my thoughts. "Those two are Eureka's only family." Her expression soured. "I don't know what kind of arrangements they'll make for her, but I feel like we should have some kind of gathering in her memory. Something informal, like a party with some of the people who knew her and worked with her."

"Oh, what a good idea," I said as we went back downstairs. "When would you want to have it?"

"The sooner the better," Maria said. "How about tomorrow afternoon?"

I nodded. "We could have it in the Enchanted Garden in the late afternoon. Say, four o'clock?"

She smiled. "Thank you, Ellie! She loved spending time there. No videos or photomontages or eulogies. Just mingling and drinks and friends."

Lupe made a face. "You might need to wait. The morgue can't release—"

I held my hand up. "We're just talking about a friendly gathering, not a funeral."

"Yes," Maria agreed. The idea seemed to have given her a bit of peace.

We paused inside the doorway. Lupe looked thoughtful. "Are you going to invite those two?" She pointed out the window.

The librarian started to shake her head, but Lupe held up her hand. "Because I think you ought to."

Maria sighed. "Oh, all right."

I exchanged a look with the detective. She didn't care if the Perezes felt left out; she saw the gathering as a possible way to get more information about Eureka's murder. I didn't disagree.

When we went back outside, Warren and a still-fuming Trixie were waiting with the patrolman, who reported there was nothing suspect in their truck.

"I told you!" Trixie said.

Lupe thanked them for their cooperation, gave Warren her card, and said she'd be in touch if she had more questions. Maria told them about our plan for Eureka's memorial, implying they could come but not specifically inviting them. Trixie sniffed, but Warren straightened his spine and thanked Maria.

After the couple left, Lupe and Danielson retrieved yellow crime scene tape from his vehicle and began draping it around Eureka's front porch. Maria headed back to her minivan, and I hightailed it back to my Jeep and my patiently waiting corgi.

# CHAPTER 11

✿

THERE was an impromptu tea party in the Enchanted Garden when I got back. Three little girls and one little boy were gathered around the wicker table tucked into an alcove by the big, engraved boulder. Maggie had moved one of the chairs from the back porch to round out the three wicker chairs that were already there, and the kids sat on the edges, their feet swinging, sipping lemonade from teacups and munching on Astrid's chocolate crinkle cookies.

Two women looked on from the bistro set over by the retaining wall, and I could detect the tang of Darjeeling curling up from the hot tea in their cups. Nabby kept an eye on everyone from the bench by the hydrangea.

I told Maggie about Eureka's memorial the next day. She told me she'd try to make it, but she was scheduled to work at the Roux during the early Friday happy hour.

She offered to order a selection of appetizers and have them ready for me to pick up, though. I thanked her profusely and sent her on her way, thankful she'd only be an hour late for her shift at the restaurant.

After she left, I went out to greet the customers in the garden. I brought a pitcher of lemonade to refill the kids' cups, then took it over to where the women sat. The tall blond was Tessa of Tessa's Tea Room, so when she praised the tea blend they were drinking, I felt gratified. Her companion was Zoe Ward, the mayor's wife, who had come into Scents & Nonsense quite a bit during the first few months I was open.

"Glad you two stopped by," I said. "Haven't seen you for a while, Zoe. Did I miss you at the opening of the time capsule yesterday?"

Egad. Had it just been yesterday?

Zoe shook her head. "Delia had a dentist appointment."

"I missed it, too," Tessa said with a sigh. "I wish I'd been there, though. Sounds like the museum is closed indefinitely after what happened to Eureka Sanford." She shuddered, and Zoe and I nodded in silent agreement with her reaction.

Then Zoe nodded toward the table. "We thought they deserved a little treat after school today." She sighed, and I felt the exhaustion rolling off her.

Overworked, and not getting nearly enough rest.

She was mother to three of the kiddos at the table, plus known for taking on a pile of volunteer work. I could only imagine all the invisible stuff that must go along with being the wife of an ambitious mayor on the cusp of election season, even in a small town.

"Maybe you deserve a treat, too," I suggested gently.

"Oh, those cookies look yummy, but I just can't. The pounds just sneak up on me if I'm not vigilant."

"I wasn't talking about food."

"Ellie can give you something to help you sleep," Tessa suggested.

I turned my attention to her, but she radiated peace and calm. *Good.*

"There are a few things we might try," I said to Zoe. "Let me take a look. In the meantime, do you want more tea?"

They demurred, and I went back into Scents & Nonsense feeling as tired as if I'd run a marathon. Of course, I'd only managed four hours of sleep the night before, but I knew some of it was a reflection of Zoe's fatigue.

First, I selected a small bottle from the display case and sniffed the contents. It didn't contain perfume, but strands of saffron. The scent was delicate, but made me feel stronger. Zoe needed a bit more, though. To help her sleep, I selected a custom blend of oils I'd distilled the summer before from four different kinds of thyme that grew in the Enchanted Garden, along with a dose of soothing lavender.

Back out in the garden, I handed her the bottles and told her to open them by her bedside before she went to sleep at night. She accepted them with gratitude.

"I'm happy to help. Please let me know how they work."

Something was still missing, though. Then my gaze fell on the tumble of sweet pea vines twisting up from a carpet of spent crocuses. They were beginning to bloom on the trellis that hid the spigot and hose at the side of the shop.

Of course. Crocuses for cheer, but sweet peas for bliss.

I hurried over, picked two small bouquets, and inhaled the sweet, spicy fragrance of the delicate flowers. Instantly I felt happier. Back at the table I handed each of the women a nosegay. "A little something extra. I'll grab some bottles you can use as vases."

"Oh, Ellie. These are precious. Thank you!"

"Glad to help," I said with a smile, and left them to resume their conversation.

Back inside Scents & Nonsense, I started making calls to the Greenstockings to let them know about Eureka's impromptu memorial the next afternoon, and to ask them all to pass along the invitation to anyone they thought should know—and to ask everyone they spoke with to do the same. Anyone who wanted to honor Eureka should know about tomorrow's gathering in the Enchanted Garden by the end of the day. Heck, in twenty-four hours everyone in Poppyville would know about it.

Bless their hearts, everyone dove right in with offers of refreshments, too. Astrid promised cookies, of course, and Gessie would bring her famous guacamole. Thea, who didn't cook, offered to bring beer, and volunteered Ritter to pick up plates, cups, and utensils. I called Felicity last. She answered her cell with a distracted hello, then asked me to hang on for a sec.

"Yes, of course, Dr. Radcliffe," I heard her say. "I'll let housekeeping know. Oh, if you'd rather, I'll connect you to them now. Hold the line."

A few seconds later she said, "Ellie, are you still there?"

"I'm here," I said. "You sound like you're still at work."

"Front desk guy called in sick, so I'm covering for him."

"The glamorous life of a manager," I said. "Listen, Maria thought we should all get together to honor Eureka, and I agree."

"That's a great idea. When and where?"

I filled her in on the details and asked her to pass them along to anyone who might be interested. "In fact," I added, "Odell Radcliffe might want to come."

"Okay," she said. "I'll let him know."

I thanked her, hung up, and went to tidy the display of scented drawer liners. As I arranged the rolls, I inhaled the hints of cedar, citrus, and sage that escaped from the packaging and thought about my conversation with Dr. Radcliffe. He'd seemed quite fond of Eureka, as had Haley. How had Eureka reacted to them?

I racked my brain but couldn't remember anything unusual about their conversation in Library Park. They'd obviously been friends if she'd invited him to Poppyville, and he'd certainly seemed upset about her death. But the look in his eyes when he'd spoken of her made me wonder if he might have wanted to reignite their relationship.

T HE tea party finally wound down right before I closed the shop. In addition to the perfume and saffron, I sold them a box of cedar drawer liners, four packs of scratch 'n' sniff stickers for the kids, a lemon and sage soy candle, and a selection of spiced soaps.

I flipped the sign on the door to CLOSED, gathered all the teacups and saucers to wash in my own kitchen, tidied up stray napkins and tea bags, and returned the chair to where it usually sat on the flagstone patio. Then I went out and unloaded the back of the Wrangler and put everything away.

Ritter was going to pick me up at seven thirty for our reunion dinner at the Sapphire Supper Club, and I wanted to look especially nice. I cleared the register, locked up Scents & Nonsense, and hurried down the path to my waiting shower. Dash ran ahead of me and met me at the door, his doggy grin seeming to echo my own anticipation of my upcoming date.

*Date!* It had been so long!

I tossed a shower bomb on the floor of the round, high-sided Japanese tub, and soon the steamy air was filled with the scents of clove and cinnamon. Spicy, enticing scents that would linger subtly on my skin and hair. When I stepped out, I applied orange-scented body butter, donned my comfy robe, and carefully applied tinted moisturizer, eyeliner, mascara, and a swipe of lip gloss. A few minutes with the blow-dryer turned my curls into tame waves. I eyed them, knowing a single encounter with humidity would make them frizz right back into ringlets. On an impulse, I gathered my hair up, pinning it here and there and letting the ends flip down. If they curled as the evening went on, so be it.

Suddenly, my image in the mirror gave me pause. With my hair pinned up like that and the high collar of my robe, I looked even more like the woman in the picture from the time capsule.

*Who were you, Alma?*

My stomach growled as I went upstairs to get dressed. Once again, the day had whizzed by, and I'd skipped lunch, intending to grab something to eat at the grocery store—the one errand I hadn't completed. It was a good thing Spence had brought me the bagel earlier—even if it turned out his timing could have been better.

In my bedroom, I pulled out a dress with a blue hand-kerchief skirt I'd been told matched my eyes, a pair of black ponte pants, and a pinkish beige silk blouse with bell sleeves and a neckline that plunged lower than I was usually comfortable with.

"What do you think?" I asked Dash, who'd followed me up the stairs and now watched from the end of the bed where I'd laid out my choices.

He nosed the dress, looked up at me quizzically, then went over and lay down by the blouse.

"Really?"

He blinked slowly.

"You're right. The dress might be a bit more, er, innocent looking than I want tonight."

After I dressed, I slipped on a pair of patent leather pumps to dress up the pants a bit more and fastened my mother's pearls around my neck. They gleamed with the patina of age, which complemented the color and sheen of

the blouse—and perhaps distracted a bit from my décol-
letage.

Or not.

Small gold earrings completed the look, and I went
back downstairs to open the wine and tidy the living
room.

At seven fifteen, my phone rang. It was Ritter.

"Elliana, I'm so sorry. I'm going to have to put off our
dinner until tomorrow night."

"What?" It wasn't the most graceful answer, but he'd
surprised me.

"I'm sorry," he said again. "God, I'd never do this to
you if I didn't have to."

My stomach flip-flopped. "Is something wrong? Is
Thea okay? Are you okay?"

"No, no, nothing like that. It's the project."

"The . . ."

"The research project," he said. "They ran into some
issues, and they need my help to make sure the data
doesn't become compromised. It's important, Elliana.
The scientific results of the whole mission up there could
be invalidated if I don't step in."

*Mission*. It sounded like he'd been to the moon. Close
enough, from my side of things.

"I understand," I said. And I did. He loved his work,
and he'd come home sooner than he probably should
have—for me. I couldn't begrudge his breaking a date
with me to save almost six months' worth of work.

"I'd like to say it won't take that long, and we could
meet for a late dinner," he said in a defeated voice. "But
I'd be lying. From what I just learned on the phone, we'll

need several hours of videoconferencing to straighten things out." He swore.

Ritter never swore. This was bad.

"We'll have lots of dinners together," I said. "You go save your project and absolutely don't worry about me. I've waited this long. I can wait another day."

He groaned.

"I'm serious! That wasn't to make you feel guilty!"

"I do anyway," he said. "You are the best. I'll try to call you if it's not too late. Otherwise, I'll check in with you tomorrow morning."

"Deal," I said. "Now go save the tundra."

We hung up, and I looked down at Dash. "Well, buddy. Looks like it's you and me tonight."

Again.

Trying to tamp down the disappointment curling in my stomach, I went into the kitchen to find something to eat.

Except the cupboards were almost bare. I'd figured skipping the grocery store didn't matter since we were going out to eat. The plan had been to enjoy a glass of wine together before our reservations at eight o'clock. The thought that I could still go to the Sapphire flitted through my mind but didn't take purchase. This was to be a celebration, and it would be in time. Going by myself would only make me feel terrible.

I found a box of stale cereal but was out of milk. I'd eaten the last of the peanut butter with saltines for breakfast the day before. Even the eggs were gone, used in the pasta carbonara I'd thrown together the night before. A half-dried chunk of cheddar greeted me in the cheese bin.

Sighing, I pulled it out and sliced off the wrinkled part. Then I grabbed the few saltines that were left, a knife, and the lone apple in the fruit bowl.

*At least it will be a balanced meal.*

The wine stood open on the coffee table next to two goblets. I grabbed it and one of the glasses as I passed by on my way to enjoy my repast in the Enchanted Garden.

# CHAPTER 12

❧

THE evening had turned cloudy while I'd been inside primping. A damp chill enveloped Dash and
me as soon as we walked outside, and a stiff wind tossed
the oak branches above. The tulips had closed against
the dark, and now leaned toward the ground with each
gust. The chimes that hung from the eaves of the shop
clanged and pinged and rattled and rang, filling the air
with a cacophony of sound. Above, the rooster weather-
vane on top of the shop's roof peak spun to and fro like
a drunken square dancer.

Not a great night for a picnic.

Still, I didn't want to stay in my house. It felt depress-
ing after all the planning for the evening with Ritter. I
hurried to the back door of Scents & Nonsense and let
myself inside. Nabby regarded me with sleepy eyes from
his bed, now situated in the window, before turning his

attention to the storm brewing on the other side of the glass.

After flipping on the display case and office lights, I considered the cheese and crackers. Then I pushed them aside, climbed onto a stool, and called Astrid.

"Ritter stood you up?" she exclaimed after I'd offered to buy her a drink and a pot of her favorite bacon mac and cheese at the Roux Grill.

"How did you even know we had a date?"

"Duh. I talked to Thea. Everyone knows."

*Great.*

"Well, he didn't stand me up. He had to work."

She blew a raspberry.

"No, really, it's okay. At least he came back from Alaska early."

"Yeah, I guess. But I can't have dinner with you tonight. Sorry."

I sighed. "Let me guess. You have a date with Dylan Wong."

"Yep!" I could almost hear her grinning.

"Where are you going this time?"

"Willie's Pool Hall for pub grub."

"What? That place is gross. I think the health department almost shut it down last month—not to mention the clientele."

"Don't be a snob, Ellie. It doesn't suit you. And they mostly serve stuff from the Schwan's truck. Straight from the freezer to the microwave."

"Ugh."

"Don't knock it 'til you try it. The bagel dogs are half-awesome with enough mustard."

My stomach growled. I eyed the wine, then reached over and poured myself a glass.

"What do you know about this Dylan guy?" I asked.

"Let's see. He's an antiques dealer in San Francisco who's here to go to a bunch of estate sales. Bargain hunting, you know? He's thirty-nine, drinks tequila, is gluten intolerant, and, oh, did I mention *he's hot*?"

"I believe that came up," I said wryly, and took a big swallow of wine.

She laughed.

"All right. Have a good time playing pool and eating your bagel dogs and whatever else you have in mind."

"Okay," she said. "Don't be sad about Ritter."

"I'm not sad!"

"Yeah. Okay. Good night, Ellie."

We hung up.

I *was* sad. Not mad. Just sad.

I took another swallow of the expensive cabernet sauvignon from my big red wine goblet. The deep tannins mixed with plummy notes and chocolate tones and the tiniest hint of jasmine. I cut a piece of not-too-dried cheese, plopped it on a saltine cracker, and took a bite.

Better than nothing. Probably not better than a pool hall bagel dog, though.

Still, I felt better after I ate a little. When I'd finished the apple, too, I took my wine into the office, turned on the computer, and settled in. If Ritter had to work tonight, I could, too. I had e-mail to answer, orders from my online shop to process and get ready to fill the next day, and inventory to order for the summer crowds.

Only I didn't do any of that. Instead, I ran a search on Dylan Wong.

That turned out to be a fairly common name, and one that spanned the globe. A little more work narrowed it down to an insurance adjuster in Davenport, Iowa, a baseball player for a farm team in Colorado, and then, bingo: an import-export dealer who lived in San Francisco. Slightly different than an antiques dealer, but still.

I sat back in my chair, poured a bit more wine, and considered the screen. What did an importer-exporter do, anyway? Specifically, what was he importing and exporting?

Antiques? And if that were the case, he might consider himself an antiques dealer, which was exactly what he'd told Astrid.

That made sense. Right?

So, what was it about the guy that sent my hackles to attention? I'd felt that way the very first time I'd seen him.

At the time capsule ceremony.

Antiques dealers would be interested in the past, of course, just like historians. Well, maybe not the past itself, but *things* from the past. From what Astrid had said he wasn't in town because of the museum, but news of the time capsule had been circulating, so he probably heard about it at the Hotel California, where he was staying.

Nothing wrong with that.

I put down my glass and went back to the keyboard. There was only one picture of him when I searched images. It had been taken at a high school reunion a few years back.

A site that offered to do background checks kept showing up in my search results. I clicked on it. Had a sip of wine. Considered my options.

*Do I really feel that strongly about the guy? I mean, Astrid has dated some weirdos before. It never came to anything. She's a serial dater. He'll be gone in no time.*

I made a face at the cost of the background check. And not only did it cost more than I felt comfortable with, they wanted you to sign up for a monthly subscription with the fee taken directly from your bank account. Seemed like an awful lot just to see if there was evidence to back up my icky feeling about Dylan.

Opening a new window, I searched for estate sales in Poppyville. There was one recent one. It had ended the previous weekend, two days before the contents of the time capsule had been brought to light.

So why was Mr. Wong still in Poppyville?

Maybe for Astrid. After all, men loved Astrid. She was never at a loss for male companionship. Yet he'd just met her.

Could he have recognized the Xavier manuscript as being valuable—perhaps more than Eureka could have dreamed—and stolen it?

*You're overreacting, Ellie. He would have left town by now if he'd killed Eureka. Besides, he was on a date with Astrid.*

I thought of Max with his warrant for the names of people who had come to Poppyville to see what was in the time capsule and then left. Some would have taken off right after the ceremony, but anyone could have checked out of the hotel and then stayed out of sight until they could break into Heritage House that night. Only they wouldn't have had to break in, because Eureka was already there.

How to explain where you were to the police during that time, though? Dylan, on the other hand, had a great alibi. He was with Astrid that evening and hadn't left town afterward. So why would the police be suspicious of him?

If it was a deliberate alibi, then it was darn clever. Also, that would make Dylan a pretty scary guy.

Eureka had been killed between when Maria had seen her at nine thirty and when I'd found her a little after midnight. So when exactly had Astrid and Dylan met for drinks?

I took another slug of wine, eyed the background search one more time, then typed in "Dylan Wong, antiques, San Francisco." Then on impulse, I added, "arrest."

An article from the *San Francisco Chronicle* popped up in the search results.

"Uh-oh," I said to Dash, who was lying by my foot. He cracked an eye, then rolled onto his back to resume his nap.

I scanned the article, and my alarm grew with each paragraph. Dylan Wong had been arrested for selling stolen antiquities. Specifically, he'd offered a collection of Native American artifacts from the Ohlone tribe to an undercover agent of the California Bureau of Investigation. Most of the article seemed to concentrate on the person Dylan had received the items from, as the CBI had been watching that individual for a while. Dylan was quoted as saying he had no idea anything had been wrong, and that the man he'd brokered the deal for had lied to him.

Really? That didn't seem like something anyone with experience in the antiques business would stumble into.

So, had he or hadn't he lied to Astrid?

More Internet searching failed to reveal what had happened after the arrest. Had Dylan actually been convicted of a crime?

I went back to the website that sold background checks. That anyone anywhere could use that service felt downright creepy to me, but at the same time, I was sorely tempted to do so myself. But I had another option.

Loud pounding on the front door made me jump, and Dash flipped onto his feet in one smooth motion. The clock on the computer showed it was almost nine o'clock. Heart pounding double time, I crept to the doorway and peered around the jamb.

Spence was standing with his hands cupped around his face, trying to see into the dark shop. He saw me, waved, and stepped back. Puzzled, I threaded my way through the displays and opened the door. The scents of wet leaves and ozone swirled inside with him.

"What are you doing here so late?" I asked. "Is something wrong?"

"Not at all. I was just driving by and saw your lights were on. Thought maybe you were working late."

I gave him a look. "Seriously?" He'd known Ritter and I had dinner reservations.

He grinned as he looked me over. "You sure don't look like you're working. In fact, you look great." Then his gaze shot over my shoulder. "Am I interrupting anything?"

Feeling my face turning pink, I shook my head and backed up to let him in. Locking the door, I said, "Ritter's the one who had to work tonight."

"Stood you up, huh." He stooped to pet Dash, who had come out to greet him.

"Not at all." I walked toward the counter, my tone cool and my blush fading. "There was an issue with his research project that he had to attend to. We'll have plenty of time to catch up."

He followed right behind me and leaned against the display case. "Right." Sardonic. "Sounds to me like his work is more important to him than you are."

I tried to glare, and opened my mouth to defend Ritter, to point out that he'd cut his stay in Alaska short to come back to me, but my eyes filled up with tears, and what came out instead was, "Spence, that was just mean."

He blinked, then looked abashed. "I'm sorry."

"What is your problem today?" I asked.

We looked at each other for a few beats, and then he said, "You really don't know."

"I—"

My phone rang. It was Ritter.

"Hello?" I knew I sounded eager, but maybe this meant he'd be able to make dinner after all.

"Hey, Elliana."

"Oh, gosh. You sound tired," I said.

Spence took a step backward and folded his arms over his chest.

"I'll be okay. The team is taking a little break, and I thought I'd check in with you. I'm really sorry I ruined our evening," Ritter said.

"We'll try again tomorrow," I said, though I couldn't keep the disappointment out of my voice. Spence noticed and quirked an eyebrow.

I turned away. "We're planning a memorial for Eureka in the garden at four, but we can go out afterward."

"That sounds great, hon. What are you up to tonight?"

"Just catching up on some work in the shop," I said.

"Hey, Ritter," Spence called.

I spun around and gave him a dirty look. "And Spence saw the light on and dropped by. He was just leaving."

Spence smiled.

Ritter was quiet for a few moments, then said, "Well, give him my regards. I'll call you later if I can."

"Okay, I'll wait up."

"No need. Hard to tell how late this will go. Good night, Elliana."

"Night."

He hung up.

I put the phone down and gripped the counter with both hands. "Some friend you are. Now Ritter thinks there is something going on between us. Thanks a lot." I felt tears threaten again.

Too little sleep and too much wine.

Spence stared at me, then ran both hands over his face. "God, Ellie. You really love him, don't you? He's the one you want."

"I told you that!" I said, feeling flummoxed. Never mind that things between Ritter and me on his first day back had been fraught with awkwardness and a distance that felt all the worse since he wasn't off in the wilds of Alaska anymore.

"All this time, he's been out of the picture, and you've talked about him, but he never seemed real to me," Spence said. "He just seemed like your excuse for not wanting to get involved with me." He straightened, and his eyes met mine. "I thought as we got to know each other I'd have a chance. I mean, we get along, you and me. But Ritter Nelson has really been your guy this whole time."

"Yes!" I sighed. "I thought you understood that."

In a tight voice, he said, "Listen, I'll leave you to . . . whatever you were doing." He turned, walked quickly to the door, and twisted the lock. "See you around."

"Spence—" I began to protest but fell silent as the door closed behind him.

Slowly, I locked the door again and went back to the office. Those online orders still needed to be filled and e-mails answered.

An hour later, exhausted to my core, I shut off the computer and checked my phone for the billionth time only to find Ritter hadn't called again.

"Come on, Dash. Let's hit the hay."

Knuckles rapped on the glass of the door.

Ritter? Spence again?

I groaned to myself as I walked out of the office, Dash at my heel. A quick glance showed it was neither one; Astrid stood on the boardwalk, the wind tossing her copper hair in the glow of the streetlight.

# CHAPTER 13

OH, good! I thought I saw a light on in here!" Astrid exclaimed. "Brr. The wind is getting crazy. Let me in." She stomped her feet to warm them, then breezed past me into the dimly lit shop.

"Man, you look bodacious." She grinned as I shut the door. "I don't think I've ever seen that blouse before. Ooh la la!"

She was making a pair of jeans look amazing and had added a plain white T-shirt and denim jacket for her date at the pool hall. The scents of beer, grease, and yes, mustard, drifted to my nose. There was something else, too. Smarmy aftershave.

My estimation of Dylan lowered another half notch.

"What are you doing here?" I asked. "Aren't you supposed to be out running the tables or whatever pool sharks do?"

"Already did that." She grinned and tapped her watch. "Do you know what time it is?"

"Unfortunately, yes." Nearly eleven.

"Well, this girl has a date to walk a Great Dane at seven in the morning, so I left Dylan at Willie's."

"How did he like that?" I led her over to the rocking chairs by the back window and flipped the switch on the instant teakettle. I had a feeling I was going to need more caffeine.

"Oh, he's one of those guys who gets along with any-one and everyone, so he's having a great time." She plopped into one of the chairs.

I turned on a lamp and settled into the chair next to her. Dylan hadn't struck me as particularly personable, but I let it go.

She suddenly leaned toward me, eyes searching my face. "You look terrible."

"Funny. You just said I look bodacious."

"You do, except your eyes. Have you been crying?"

*Maybe a little.* "Nah. Just tired."

"Bull pucky. It's Ritter."

Sighing, I handed her a cup. "Well, sort of. We haven't had a chance to really spend any time together since he got back . . ."

"Which was just this morning," she pointed out.

"True. But then Spence threw a wrench into things." I told her about how Ritter had walked in on Spence holding my hand, and then how Spence had shown up after Ritter rain-checked our date—and had been happy to let Ritter know he was with me. "It looks like you might be right after all. Spence has been more interested in me than he let on."

Astrid rolled her eyes. "Of course he is. But it's not like he made a huge secret of it. You are so naïve, Ellie. You were with Harris, who has always been a complete putz, and then you believed Spence only wanted to be your pal."

"Naïve? I didn't know you felt that way."

She shrugged. "You weren't ready to hear it. You went through a time when your self-esteem was pretty much bottomed out. Now you have Ritter, and you know he's a good guy. So maybe you will listen when I say that, from what you've told me, Spence is in love with you."

"Astrid . . ."

"And as of today, he feels justified in taking the gloves off when it comes to winning you over. See, now Ritter is back in the picture and a real competitor. After all, you can't compete with a ghost, and for all practical purposes, that's what Ritter has been to Spence these last few months."

Even though Spence had said almost the same thing, I stared at her as a defensive anger began to rise. Then I thought of all the fun Spence and I had had. Hikes and hanging out. We'd gone to the movies a few times. He'd drop by the shop.

Come to think of it, he dropped by the shop a lot.

And then I thought of how often he'd touch my hand or my arm, how sometimes his hello or good-bye hugs seemed to last a little too long, how often he showed up wherever I just happened to be. How he always seemed to change the subject whenever I started to talk about my latest phone call or video chat with Ritter.

"I'm an idiot," I said, my anger fading to embarrassment.

Astrid laughed. "No, you're a nice person. A little gullible, but with a good heart." She leaned forward. "A really good heart, and as loyal as they come. You've waited all this time for Ritter to get back, and Thea told me he came home early because he missed you so much. Don't let that go to waste. You need to set Spence straight, and the sooner, the better."

"Oh, God. I think I did, but maybe I wasn't clear enough." I rubbed my eyes, which probably smeared what was left of my mascara into raccoon circles. "I'd had a little wine."

She quirked an eyebrow.

"A *little*." I took a deep breath. "Hopefully, I can make Ritter understand."

"Well, you send him over to me if you need backup. I'll set him straight about the whole Spence situation."

I flashed a grateful smile. "I think I can handle it, but thanks." I paused, then changed the subject. "So, you and Dylan had a nice time tonight?"

"Sure. He's such a flirt! Cracks me up. Plays a mean game of pool, too."

"So, uh, how did you guys end up going out last night?"

She waved her hand. "We got to talking after you left yesterday afternoon, and he asked me to meet him for a drink at the hotel." Her eyes twinkled. "Which saved me the trouble of asking him, you know?"

I forced a grin. "What time did you meet?"

One side of her mouth pulled back. "Kind of late actually. Ten thirty. I'd have liked to meet earlier, what with work this morning and all, but he said he had something to do."

Ten thirty. That would have given him an hour window in which to kill Eureka and steal the Xavier manuscript.

Astrid's smile had become tenuous. "Why?"

I hesitated, then dove in. "You know you're my best friend, right?"

"Yeah . . ." She drew the word out, her voice full of suspicion.

"Well, as long as we're being honest with each other, I have a little bad news about your new boyfriend."

The smile dropped altogether. "Dylan? He's not my boyfriend. He's a, you know, a fling."

"Honey, I hate to tell you this, but he's a crook."

Her forehead wrinkled. "What are you talking about?"

"Come here. I'll show you." I got up, led her into the office, and turned on the light. Dash blinked up at us from his bed in the corner, where he'd had the good sense to collapse.

Twenty seconds later, I'd brought up the article I'd found in the *Chronicle*. I got up out of the desk chair, and Astrid sat down to read. When she had scrolled down to the bottom, she sat back with a huff.

"I can't believe you did this, Ellie."

"Why not? You barely know the guy, and it's pretty suspicious that there was a murder right after he came to town."

She swiveled in the chair and gaped up at me where I stood by the filing cabinet. "Murder? Now you think Dylan is a *murderer*?"

I threw up my hands. "I don't know! But neither do you. I mean, you can't tell me that you know all about him in such a short amount of time. He might have wanted the Xavier manuscript for himself. Or maybe he has a client he knows would be willing to pay him a lot of money for it. He's done that kind of thing before, after all. You can't possibly trust him."

Her eyes widened. "That, my dear, is exactly where you're wrong."

"Now who's being naïve?" I asked.

She bolted out of the chair, brushed past me, and went out the door. By the register, she whirled to face me. "Okay, I can see how it might look like that. But sometimes I can just tell about people. I can *sense* that they're okay. You know how that goes, don't you, Ellie?"

"Yes." I took a step toward her. "Yes, I know exactly how that goes. And I've known there was something off about that guy since the first time I saw him."

She stared at me. "I think you're making that up."

"Why on earth would I do that?" I demanded.

"Then why didn't you tell me right away?"

I rolled my eyes. "Because when I tried to steer you clear of certain guys before, you ignored me. Or you get mad, just like you're doing now. You remember Greer Grissom?"

"Yeah," she mumbled. "But even I knew he was a loser. We only went out twice."

I held my palms up to the ceiling. "See?"

Her expression hardened. "But you're wrong about Dylan. He's not a crook. That article said he was hood-winked by the guy he was brokering the deal for."

"The article says that's what *Dylan* says—which is a little different."

"God, Ellie. I'm sorry you're having man trouble, but don't take it out on me." With that, she turned and stalked to the front door.

"Astrid!" I called, but the door had already closed behind her.

*What the heck*? Was she really falling for the guy so quickly?

Sighing, I locked the door yet again, grabbed the wine bottle, called Dash, and made my way through the garden to my little house.

My stomach was in knots. I'd known Astrid since college, and we'd been through a lot. She and Harris had disliked each other, so my marriage had put a strain on our relationship. Still, through it all, we'd never actually fought.

The wind rustled through the leaves, but the chimes had settled enough that I could hear the whispers rising from new growth, green shoots extending above the fertile earth, sprouts unfurling from their seed pods beneath the ground. Clouds scudded above, revealing the waxing gibbous moon and brightening the path before us. A late daffodil nodded to me as I went by, more to garner attention for itself than as a greeting, I imagined. A lingering giggle ebbed and echoed from near the apple tree, so high and faint it could have been my imagination but familiar enough that I was pretty sure it wasn't. It seemed the longer the fairy tableaus were in the garden, and the more of them I made, the stranger the things were that happened at night when the customers and clients were long gone.

I paused at the door before going inside. The primroses by the step had their little white faces turned up to me, looking so innocent and appealing in the cool light of the moon. Then Dylan Wong's image came to mind, along with the memory of one of Gamma's lessons in floriography.

*Primroses mean I can't live without you . . . so lovely, yes? But evening primroses are for inconstancy.*

As in changeable and capricious. And very probably lying.

My best friend in the whole world, who was so mad at me right now, might have a good feeling about Dylan for whatever reason, but the guy was lying about something.

Not long after that thought, I was snuggled beneath my down comforter, plunging into sleep with the speed of a skydiver who couldn't find her rip cord.


T HE next morning, I woke one minute before my alarm went off. The wind had wuthered around the eaves for most of the night, and I'd risen a few times from the firm grasp of sleep enough to hear the soothing sound of raindrops spattering against the skylight. Droplets still lingered on the glass above my head, glittering gems in the angled sunlight edging over Kestrel Peak.

Downstairs, I checked Gamma's journal while coffee

brewed, but it was cool to the touch. The drawings of the mystery woman and the marigold were still there, but no new information awaited. That was frustrating, but at the same time, I was a little relieved. It seemed like every time a new piece was added to the puzzle, it only served to confuse me more about what the overall picture was supposed to look like.

A gentle fog rose from the damp meadow when I let Dash out back. Not the heavy tule fog that sometimes rolled in during the winter months to snaggle traffic on the highways and make it hard to see even a few feet in front of you, but a light haze that cast everything with the sunrise glow of hope.

The steam from my mug curled into the heavy, humid morning as I considered the evening before. I needed to straighten things out with Ritter. I made a mental note to make reservations for dinner at the Sapphire again that night. I also needed to have a serious talk with Spence. Astrid had been right that I'd been ignoring the signs that he wanted to be more than friends. In love with me, though? I still had a hard time wrapping my mind around that.

It was ironic that when I'd tried to tell her about Dylan, she hadn't taken it well at all. I could only hope she was over it by now. Astrid was the type whose temper flared and then quickly extinguished itself. Maybe it would help if I could point to more than a single newspaper article to show her that at the very least Dylan wasn't good dating material and at the worst a possible murderer.

I thought about the online background check again. In

the light of morning, I would have happily broken out my credit card if that was the only way I could protect my friend.

However, calling Lupe would be easier.

I looked at my watch. Too early for that.

Astrid might get angry at me all over again if I brought Lupe in, but what if there were more things in Dylan's background than those stolen artifacts?

What if there was a murder motive?

If so, it had to be the Xavier manuscript. My heartbeat quickened at the thought. It could be in his room at the Hotel California *at that very moment*.

But why had Eureka's house been broken into and her laptop stolen? Had she found out something about the old manuscript? Or had the burglar been after something else altogether? Maybe the book she was writing? That was hard to fathom.

I shook my head, confused, and drank some more coffee. There had to be something else on that laptop that someone wanted. The clearest suspect—or suspects, rather—were Warren and Trixie Perez. I mean, looking for her will less than twenty-four hours after Eureka had passed? That was downright mercenary. Maybe Maria was right. Maybe they were the ones who broke into her house. If they hadn't, I could only guess they'd intended to, since they didn't have a key. Trixie's story about hoping someone would be there to let them in—like that would have happened—was as thin as my explanation to Chief Gibbon about why I'd been at Heritage House in the middle of the night.

And what about Chief Gibbon? How effective could

he be if he was trying to investigate Eureka's murder between meetings and budgeting and running his department?

I sighed. The peaceful frame of mind I'd begun my morning with had dissipated along with the fog. I turned to go back inside.

Movement in my peripheral vision made me stop and look toward the stand of evergreens at the edge of the meadow. I was hoping to see the white doe again, whom I'd started thinking of as a sign of encouragement and strength.

Instead, a mountain lion slowly prowled along the perimeter of the trees. I caught my breath, stunned, then said in a low voice, "Dash, come."

He trotted over from where he'd been sniffing the morning dew sparkling on a spray of bunch grass, oblivious to our feline visitor across the meadow. Bounding up the steps, though, he looked over his shoulder to where my eyes were glued to the big cat, and grew very still.

"Good boy."

The mountain lion paused midstep to regard us with flat golden eyes. It was a sculpture of muscle beneath tawny fur, front paw the size of a salad plate held off the ground, nose twitching and mouth slightly open to breathe in the scents around it.

Stepping to the edge of the porch, I called, "Keep moving," in a voice that was shakier than I liked. It was a magnificent beast, beautiful, and emanating power and grace. I felt awed and honored to be in his presence, but another part of me was terrified.

Not for me. For the white doe.

Its leg came down, and after one long backward look, the big cat disappeared into the undergrowth like smoke.

I let out a breath, closed my eyes, and sent a mental warning to the doe. Silly, I knew, but perhaps she was my spirit animal and would hear me. Besides, I didn't know what else to do.

# CHAPTER 14

꙰

BACK inside, I showered and dressed in jeans and a light sweater. As I slipped on a windbreaker, I played the image of the mountain lion over in my mind.

Another sign? And if so, of what?

Dash shot out of the tiny house when I opened the door, and raced straight for the back patio of Scents & Nonsense. When I saw why, I broke into a run, too. Ritter was sitting in a rocker, bundled into a puffy down sweater, wearing jeans and a wool hat that was jammed down over his ears.

He came to his feet, and I folded into his arms.

"When I didn't hear from you last night, I thought you were angry," I murmured into his shoulder.

"How could I be angry when I'm the one who bailed on our dinner date?"

I stepped back and examined his face. "You look terrible." He'd shaved off the beard, but a day's worth of stubble had replaced it. There were dark half-moons beneath his red-rimmed eyes.

"I don't doubt it. Haven't slept since I got back into town."

"Oh, Ritter!" I pulled him back to the chairs, and we sat down. "You had to work all night?"

He nodded. "Until about an hour ago. Then I headed over here."

"I wish I'd known. You could have come in and at least had some coffee. You look like you're chilled to the bone." I stood again. "Let's go inside the shop, at least."

"I need the fresh air," he said with a smile. "Though if I'd known you were awake . . ."

Reluctantly, I sat back down. "Did you save the project?"

"Looks like it. Had to access backups of the data after the computer corrupted it, and then cobble it all back together. At least we had the backups, though." Weariness threaded his voice.

"Let me get you some coffee," I tried again.

"No, thanks. I'm going to head back to Thea's pretty soon and crash."

"You should do that right now. You didn't have to come by. You could have texted. I would have understood."

He was quiet for several seconds, then said, "I was gone a long time, Elliana. Things can happen when you're apart that long."

My stomach clenched. What was that supposed to mean? Had something happened in Alaska? I knew there were several women on the research team, but I'd never gotten so much as a hint of him being interested in anyone else when we'd talked on the phone.

On the phone. God. Like I'd be able to tell.

I took a deep breath. "Are you about to confess something?"

He blinked. "No. Of course not. I'm just saying I understand about you and Tanner Spence."

I stood. "Oh, for Pete's sake. There is nothing going on between us. Turns out he might want there to be, but I set him straight last night."

Ritter searched my face, then seemed to relax. "I was just saying I understand—"

"Stop," I said. "There's nothing to understand."

"Okay."

Feeling like the clown in a jack-in-the-box, I sat back down.

"So, you're hosting a memorial for Eureka this afternoon?" Ritter asked.

Happy to change the subject, I nodded. "At four."

He looked at his watch. "I only met her a few times, but I'd like to come."

"Of course. Plus, your sister said you'd bring paper plates and napkins."

"Oh?" he snorted. "Good to know."

"And then we can have dinner after," I said.

Nodding, he reached over and took my hand. His skin was cold. Well, it would be—he'd been sitting outside waiting for me since dawn. "Have you heard if the police got a lead on the murderer?" he asked.

"Not that I know of," I said. "It's only been a day."

Then I gave him the short version of what I'd been thinking about that morning. I was about to tell him about the mountain lion, but then stopped. For some reason that felt like a secret.

"So you're investigating." His eyes searched mine. "Again."

"Not really. I mean, I guess I'm thinking about the possible suspects."

"And doing research online. And asking questions."

"Well, yeah. But Chief Gibbon thinks someone wanted to steal a gold nugget from the museum, even though the nugget was already at the bank. I don't know if he's even had a chance to interview Eureka's family, what with his busy schedule. And Max probably still thinks I hit poor Eureka over the head to get my hands on the Xavier manuscript."

Ritter raised an eyebrow. "You did say you were interested in that manuscript."

"I wouldn't kill anyone for it!" I exclaimed.

He rolled his eyes. "Of course not. But you still want to find it, don't you?"

"Of course. It made me feel so strange. Say, I'd like to show you something. Would you mind?"

He shook his head, curiosity breaking through his fatigue.

I went back to the house and retrieved the copies I'd made of Alma's photo—front and back. After a few seconds of hesitation, I grabbed Gamma's garden journal, too. Back on the porch, I handed him the copies.

He took them and frowned when he saw my likeness. "Where did you have this taken?"

I shook my head. "That's not me."

"Huh." He looked up at me, then back at the photocopy. "She looks just like you. Where did you get this?"

"It was in the time capsule." I held up my hand at his surprised expression. "It was in the glass case with the Xavier manuscript and the other items that were in the butter churn. Whoever took them apparently dropped it outside the museum. That's where I found it." I grimaced. "I shouldn't have taken it, but it was late, and I was tired, and well, look at her." I sighed. "Honestly, I wanted to take a closer look. After I made those copies, I took the original to Chief Gibbon."

He raised one eyebrow. "I bet he wasn't very happy with you."

"Not so much, no."

"So, who is this woman? She could be your twin."

"Look at the other copy—back of the photo. You can barely make out the name Alma there."

"Yes, I see it."

"Now, I don't know who Alma is, but look at this." I held out Gamma's journal, open to the page with the rough sketch of the woman on one page and the drawing of the marigold on the other. He made as if to take it, but I drew back a little. No one besides me and Gamma had ever touched that book, and I felt protective of it. He gave me a puzzled look but put his hand down and leaned forward to see it better.

"She looks like you, too," he said.

I checked it again. "You think so?" Honestly, the sketch did seem a little clearer today. Something about the angle of the jaw. And yes, she did look more like me than I realized.

"Um, yeah. What's up with that? Did your grandmother draw that?" He knew I often consulted her garden journal, but he didn't know the information in it had a tendency to appear when I needed it.

How do you tell your boyfriend something like that?

"I guess so," I said. "I, er, never noticed it before. Have you ever seen a symbol like this?" I pointed to the brooch at Alma's throat and its mirror image in Gamma's drawing.

Ritter squinted. "Can't say that I have. I bet Maria could help you find out more about it."

*Mental facepalm.* "Of course she could."

He yawned.

"Oh, gosh! I shouldn't be making you look at this stuff right now. You go get some sleep. I'll make reservations at the Sapphire for our rain-check dinner—I don't want to take any chances—and I'll see you around four. Or come later if you need to. I want you well rested for tonight." I waggled my eyebrows.

He laughed, then stood. "Sounds good." He drew me back into his arms. "I've really missed this."

"Me, too," I sighed, then emphasized my words with a nice, long kiss.

Ritter left, and I heard Thea's big, mint-colored, stepside pickup start out on the street. I busied myself for the next hour and a half tidying the Enchanted Garden for the get-together that afternoon. Thankfully, the rain and wind hadn't caused any lasting damage, but I needed to sweep the paths, remove the stray leaves from the fairy gardens, and wipe down the tables and chairs. Then I pruned the hydrangeas, deadheaded the bleeding hearts, and checked the rosebushes for signs of rust or black mold.

When everything looked shipshape, I went in and opened the shop.

I hadn't seen Astrid, but that happened often enough. When she had to get to work or had an early dog-walking gig, she let herself into the shop and left the daily cookies on the front counter or over by the coffee urn.

But today there were no cookies.

It was the first time she hadn't brought any in over a year.

I sank down on a rocking chair by the back window and put my head in my hands. A feeling of loss and dread settled into my stomach. I was pretty sure I'd lost Spence as a friend, and now my BFF was even angrier than I'd imagined, though I'd had her best interests at heart when I told her about Dylan's legal trouble.

I sighed, rubbed my eyes, and lowered my hands to find Dash gazing up at me with worried brown eyes.

"Hey, boy." I patted my knee.

He rose on his hind legs, put his paws on my knee, and nosed my hand. I ran my fingers between his foxy ears, then bent down and buried my face in his fur. Inhaling the scent of dog overlaid with the sage he must have brushed against in the garden, I fought the urge to cry.

After several seconds, I took a deep breath and straightened. "Thanks, buddy."

When he broke into a doggy grin and let out a low *woof*, I couldn't help but smile.

\* \* \*

HOPING against hope, I called Maggie later that morning to see if she was interested in coming in before her bartending shift. Normally, I'd have asked Astrid to cover for an hour while I went to the library to research the tree symbol. Today that didn't seem like such a great idea, though.

"Sorry, Ellie," Maggie responded regretfully. "I'm watching my granddaughter, and then Harris asked me to come in early for my shift at the Roux. Folks are starting to respond to the early Friday Afternoon Club before the regular happy hour. And if I'm late again today . . ." She trailed off.

"Say no more." I hurried to assure her. "I'll figure something else out."

"I might not be able to make it to the memorial, either," she said apologetically.

"I'm sorry about that, since you knew Eureka. I don't suppose Harris would—"

She laughed.

"Right. Well, I'll stop by the Roux later to pick up those appetizers. Thanks for setting that up with Raleigh." Raleigh was the chef at the restaurant.

"No worries. I'll see you later."

I hung up and thought for a moment. *Of course!* Quickly, I dialed Larken Meadows' number.

I was in luck. She picked up on the second ring and said yes before I'd finished making the request.

"Colby is gone for three more days, and I'm going

stir-crazy out here with nobody but the dog and the chickens to talk to."

"I'll pay you," I said.

"And I'll take it. Turns out creating a passive irrigation system isn't as cheap as you might think. In fact, I'll help out at the shop as much as you want, Ellie."

I made a happy mental note of that. "Thanks!"

"And I heard there's going to be a party there this afternoon."

"Party? Sort of. For Eureka."

"You need some help getting ready?"

"Well, the garden space is in pretty good shape, and the weather should be okay," I said. "We might need to move some chairs and tables around, though. Then there's coffee and tea . . . yeah, I could use your help. And as long as you're offering to cover for me, I need to make a trip to the grocery store this afternoon, too."

"Deal. I'll be there in an hour. Does that work?"

"Bless you, Larken. You deserve a raise already."

"Why, thank you! But I don't know how much I'm getting now," she teased.

I laughed. "We'll talk."

I checked my e-mail next. There was nothing but a sales ad from my favorite essential oil company and an invitation to subscribe to a soap-making newsletter in my inbox.

While customers browsed, I gathered items to fill four orders from the Scents & Nonsense online shop so Larken could create packing lists and pack boxes for a UPS pickup. Then I placed orders for ingredients that I used to make some of the items tourists bought like crazy in the summer—lavender room spray, natural zinc sunblock scented with rose hydrosol, and lemongrass, citronella, and clove essential oils for herbal insect repellent and mosquito candles.

I'd just finished printing out invoices when Larken came in. She smelled like sunshine and lanolin, and exuded earthy healthiness. Her tanned skin was flawless, her peanut-butter-colored hair was plaited into matching Laura Ingalls Wilder pigtails, and her slightly crooked teeth gave her infectious smile character. She wore jeans and a hand-knit sweater over a chambray shirt.

We hugged, and she gave me a dozen extra-small eggs from her newly laying pullets.

"Oh, my gosh. These are fantastic," I said, admiring the white and blue and brown orbs.

"You just wait," she said with a happy grin. "I'll keep you in eggs and veggies all summer. I planted more potatoes this morning, and the tomato seedlings are a foot high in the greenhouse."

"Mm. Garden tomatoes. I'll supply the basil."

"Deal," she said, and went to stash her sweater in the office.

Handling the carton as if it contained precious jewels, I carried them to my house and put them in the barren refrigerator.

Back in Scents & Nonsense, I reminded Larken about the basics of the register and showed her how to make packing lists for the online orders. Then I called the Sapphire Supper Club. They weren't open yet, but the owner answered.

"I'm sorry, Ellie. We have a private party tonight. A wedding reception. The dining room will be closed."

Glad I'd thought to call, I thanked them and considered. Should Ritter and I have dinner at the Roux Grill or the Empire Room in the Hotel California? Because the only other choices were bagel dogs at Willie's Pool Hall or a mess of chicken-fried steak at the Juke Diner. The Juke had scrumptious home cooking, but the atmosphere was a bit Formica-centric for a celebratory meal. Plus, they didn't have a liquor license.

My stomach growled, and I remembered that I'd had a terrible dinner and not so much as a defrosted breakfast cookie to soak up my morning coffee.

Harris spent almost all his time at the Roux, and I really didn't want to have to deal with him while on a date with Ritter. The Empire Room it was. I called and made reservations for eight o'clock, assuming the memorial would have wound down by then.

Larken was helping a man find a gift for his wife's birthday when I waved to her and went out to the boardwalk. Dash had seemed content hanging out in the garden with Nabokov, so I'd left him there. The copy of Alma's picture was tucked into the daypack slung on my shoulder.

# CHAPTER 15

※

T HE scent of oven-fresh bread that rolled out of the
Kneadful Things Bakery as I crossed Corona
Street nearly made me swoon. Vowing to make a trip to
the grocery store immediately after talking to Maria, I
headed inside the bakery. As soon as the door closed
behind me, the heady aromas of caramelized sugar,
browned butter, and all manner of brightly spiced and
earthy herbal notes hit me like a cartoon anvil. I slowed
as I approached the counter, savoring each inhalation
and feeling invigorated simply by the anticipation of eating one of their overloaded sandwiches.

I chose the daily special: two halves of a giant oozing
ball of burrata mozzarella, grilled pancetta, slices of
purple and orange heirloom tomatoes, and a thick slather
of bright green pesto redolent with basil, garlic, and
roasted pine nuts, all sandwiched between two slabs of

Texas toast that had been drizzled with a balsamic reduction and truffle-infused olive oil.

I took it with me and ate the whole dang thing sitting on the bench in front of the library, washing it down with sips of steaming French press coffee.

Full to groaning, but feeling utterly rejuvenated, I headed into the library with a list of questions for Maria.

The assistant librarian, Brigitte Jessup, looked up from behind the information desk when I came in. "Hey, Ellie."

"Hey, Brigitte. Maria around?"

She pointed toward the librarian's office at the rear of the building and opened the thick bodice ripper she'd flipped closed when I approached.

I wended my way past the new releases, the staff picks, and the holds shelf. The door was open a crack, and when I didn't hear any voices, I tentatively pushed it open. The smell of toner, Pine-Sol, and orange blossoms greeted my nose. The fluorescent tubes above hummed ever so softly beneath the strains of Thelonious Monk drifting from the speaker on the file cabinet.

Maria was head down over a small volume that lay open on her desk. She must not have heard me come in, because she jumped when I asked, "Is it considered an occupational hazard or a bonus when librarians read on the job?" I dumped my pack on her guest chair as I spoke.

After her startled reaction, she sat back with a half smile. "A little of both."

Then my gaze fell on the book on the desk. "That looks old."

Maria nodded, her forehead wrinkled with puzzlement. "It appears to be. This morning, Chief Gibbon asked if I'd take the more valuable items from Heritage House and store them here while it's closed to the public. Said they were technically done processing the crime scene but didn't want to release it quite yet and didn't want to tempt thieves. Of course I said yes. I put a few of the papers in the California history room, but most of the stuff I grabbed is in the basement." She sighed. "It was hard to determine what might be considered valuable. I hadn't thought about the museum being a target for burglary before, but we really do need to put in a security system."

"I can't imagine the town council wouldn't approve the funds for it after what happened to Eureka," I said. "You moved it all over by yourself?"

"Mostly. Lupe was there to document what I took, and she helped."

"I wished you'd called the Greenstockings. Someone would have been free. It must have been unsettling to go into that place." I stopped myself before I said something that would upset my friend.

However, she offered a gentle smile. "You know, it *was* unsettling, but I didn't really even want Lupe's help. As I chose what to bring here, I kept thinking of what Eureka would have said and used that as my guide. Oddly, it felt like I was honoring her."

I came around the desk and leaned down to give her a hug. Standing again, I looked over her shoulder at the book. "I don't remember seeing that in the museum."

"I hadn't seen it before, either. It was stuffed behind

the old school materials on the shelf behind the reception desk," Maria said with a frown, and closed the volume. "I was gathering some of the other items and dislodged it. There was no reason for it to be there, and I know it wasn't part of any displays. It just seemed to call to me."

"What do you mean, 'call to you'?" My pulse quickened.

She shrugged. "Nothing weird. I'm a librarian. It's a book. I wanted to know what was in it."

Her reasonable answer slowed my pulse almost back to normal. "Is it interesting?"

Maria stroked the cover with her fingertips, making me think of Eureka's admonition not to touch old paper with bare skin. But Maria knew what she was doing.

"It's the journal of a young man. So far, he's written about paying a dollar for a pound of potatoes, visiting a saloon, and writing to his mother back home. He worked odd jobs around town and helped out at the stables."

"What was his name?" I asked.

"The name Charles Bettelheim is inscribed in the front. He's quite literate for the time. His mother apparently lived in Pennsylvania, and he left her at a young age. He must have had some schooling before coming west, though." She tipped her head to the side and pushed away from her desk. "This isn't why you came to see me, though. Is there something you were looking for?"

Nodding, I grabbed my pack, opened it on her desk, and drew out the copy of Alma's picture.

Her eyes widened when she saw what it was. "Ellie! How did you get this?"

"I found the picture in Library Park the night Eureka

was killed, and made a copy before I gave it to Chief Gibbon," I said, and gave it to her.

Her eyes glinted. "And the woman in that picture looks just like you, so you couldn't resist."

I made a face. "Sort of, I guess. I wasn't thinking very clearly right then."

She grimaced. "No kidding. Neither was I." She examined the black-and-white copy of the black-and-white photo. "Amazing. I wonder who she was."

"Alma," I said.

"Who?" She looked back up at me.

I lifted one shoulder and let it fall. "Look at the copy of the back of the photo."

She did.

"There." I pointed. "In the corner."

Holding it at an angle as I had, she squinted. "I see. Alma. Nice, old-fashioned cursive penmanship."

"Any idea if we could figure out who she . . ." I began, but stopped as she suddenly whirled and grabbed the old journal.

Quickly, she flipped it open to one of the early pages. "Oh, Ellie, look!"

I joined her and peered down at the page she held out.

*I believe Mother would approve of the young lady I met yesterday afternoon. She was delivering her horse to the stable, a bay mare of quiet disposition, after a ride into the foothills, and we began talking. Such a charming creature. I have decided to begin courting her in earnest. Her name is Alma Hammond. She and her brother are from Pennsylvania, where it is said their*

*parents are quite well-to-do and very respected. It is*
*even possible Mother has heard of the family name. I*
*shall ask her in my next letter. The brother is a bit of a*
*firebrand, but decent to all men regardless of station,*
*and my hope is that he will not only allow, but encour-*
*age, my friendship with his sister.*

"Ohmagod," I breathed. "Maria, that's why she looks
so much like me. Or I look like her. Either one. Let's
see." I did some mental math, and it seemed to come out
right. "Alma must be Zebulon Hammond's sister. Probably his younger sister. No one ever talked about a sister.
But they wouldn't, would they, the times being what they
were and her only being a girl." I couldn't help my lip
curling a bit as I thought of the legions of women lost to
history merely because of their gender.

"Um, Ellie? Perhaps I should know this, but who is
Zebulon Hammond to you?"

"He's my great-great-great-grandfather," I crowed.
"So, Alma would be my aunt!" As I peered at the photo
again, I again felt the connection to the woman in it—the
same connection through time that I'd felt ever since first
seeing her image.

Then something registered. Something in Maria's
voice.

My head came up. "What's wrong?"

"Nothing," she said, a speculative look on her face.
"It's just that Eureka was interested in Zebulon. Not just
him, though. All the founders of Poppyville."

"It was called Springtown back then, because of the
hot springs," I said.

"Right." She motioned me toward the door and continued talking as she led me to the reference room. "And then the town changed it in honor of Poppy Thierry. She must have been quite a woman—madam or not."

And she had a special relationship with Zebulon, as I understood it. But ancient family scandals didn't seem relevant at the moment. Unless . . .

"Was Eureka interested in Poppy?"

Maria shook her head. "Not other than her essentially being one of the founders, too."

"Poppy must have known Alma," I said, and my thoughts went to the collection of historical documents my distant cousin's father had left her. But she'd offered to let the Greenstockings look at all of it—except for a few items that I knew about—when we were gathering content for Heritage House. Eureka had been with us and had identified a couple of handbills as worthy of the museum. She hadn't seemed all that interested in anything else in the minutiae of my family records, though.

Of course, that had been before we found the time capsule.

Brigitte barely looked up from her book as we went into the reference room. A few people were in the stacks, and a man was working on his laptop at one of the long tables.

My friend unlocked a cabinet and put the journal into it. Then she pulled out a couple of books from a top shelf. She brought them over to the table where she'd set the copy of Alma's photo. As I looked at it, I could almost smell the marigold petals that had been saved with the original. I settled into a chair and put my chin in my hands. "I wish I knew what Eureka thought about the Xavier manuscript," I mused. "You know how you said you were drawn to the journal, but that was normal because you're a librarian?"

Maria nodded, a slight wariness in her gaze.

"Well, the desire I felt to look at the Xavier manuscript was not normal. I've never felt anything like it."

She nodded thoughtfully. "I could tell there was something bothering you. Even before the capsule was opened. And now it's gone with all the rest." She nodded at the copy of Alma's photo I clutched in my hand. "Well, almost all the rest."

I said, "One of the reasons I'm here is to see if—"

"You can find out anything more about the manuscript."

"Yes!" I leaned forward.

"Well, I looked it up already," she said. "Or at least I looked up old vellum manuscripts written using more than one alphabet."

*Of course she did.* My heartbeat quickened.

"What I could find, at least. There's not much, even online. A Wikipedia article, and another article suggesting that it's a relic from long lost Atlantis."

I stared at her. "*Atlantis*? I didn't see that in my search."

"That's because it's in a thirty-year-old article buried in an obscure, pay-only database that libraries have exclusive access to."

"Could it actually be . . . ?" I trailed off.

She rolled her eyes. "Oh, for Pete's sake, Ellie." Her tone was crisp. "The manuscript that was in the butter

churn is not from Atlantis. Plato posited the utopian is-
land kingdom of Atlantis existed a full nine thousand
years before his time. First off, that's pretty dang old, as
in *way* older than any bunch of vellum with written language on it could be. Secondly, Atlantis *was a metaphor*
for the perfect state, which he created as part of his
teachings." She shook her head. "So that stuff about Atlantis is a bunch of hooey."

"Gotcha," I said, half reeling from the blitz philos-
ophy lesson.

Maria shrugged. "Anyway, we're getting off track."
She gestured to the small pile of books she'd removed
from the locked cabinet. "Eureka said she'd finished the
research for her new book, but during the week before
she was killed, she started up again. This is what I
helped her with."

"Huh." With a quick glance at Maria to make sure it
was okay, I pulled the topmost one toward me. "A Bible?"

"From the church. There was only one in town at the
time, no particular denomination, just a general bulwark
against the debauchery in the saloons and brothels."

I looked at her from under my brows, but her face was
placid and her tone mild. She was simply stating the
facts.

"It's interesting from a historical perspective because
of the list of births and deaths of the townspeople."

"Ooh." I flipped it open to the back. Pages had been
glued in at the end, and cramped, spidery handwriting
crammed the narrow lines. Skimming the page, it soon
became apparent there were a great many more deaths
recorded than births. I remarked on it to Maria.

"Sure," she said. "Most of the people in the community came from other places, and in comparison, there weren't that many babies being born in the rough old days of the gold rush."

I nodded. "So, for the most part, it's a list of deaths. Some are just names and dates, but it looks like a few entries include how people died."

She scooted her chair closer to mine. Reaching over, she flipped a page and ran her finger down a column without actually touching the page. "Here. This seemed to catch Eureka's attention."

Turning the Bible to better catch the light, I read,

*Alma Hammond, disappeared May 16, 1850*

# CHAPTER 16

MARIA and I looked at each other then back at the Bible. "Disappeared?" I asked. "I don't see any other record where someone disappeared. They died from dysentery and influenza, or fell in ravines or off horses, and some died of bullet wounds, but . . ." I paused, flipped the page, and examined more entries. "Nope. No one else is listed as disappeared."

"Eureka thought that was pretty strange, too. I mean, there had to be some disappearances, right?"

I tipped my head, eyes still glued to the old handwriting. "Of course. But I bet they weren't related to a major mover and shaker in town." I tore my gaze away. "Zebulon probably made quite the stink if his sister just up and vanished."

"Especially if her disappearance was never solved," Maria noted.

I leaned back and looked at the ceiling as if it could give me answers. "Why didn't Alma and her disappearance make the annals of history? There are so many records from that time and place, and here I'm just learning Zeb had a little sis."

And that she looked exactly like me.

Sitting up, I asked, "What other research did Eureka do?"

Maria lifted one shoulder and let it drop. "Here in the library, she spent most of her time looking at what we've got on the history of Poppyville and whatever information she could find on the gold rush in this area. She had hopes of reading old copies of the *Picayune*, since the newspaper was established in 1847, but they didn't start keeping a morgue until a couple of decades after that."

She tipped her head to one side and looked into the distance as if trying to remember something. Then she snapped her fingers. "You know, Eureka did mention that last week she'd come across a mention of a tragic death at the stables back then. She was going to go talk to Gessie, see if she knew anything about it since she owns the stables now. I don't know if she managed to get out there before she died, though."

I made a mental note, then sighed. "Does Charles say anything else about Alma?"

"Not so far," Maria said. "I'll let you know if I find anything."

"I don't suppose I could take that journal with me . . . ?"

She hesitated, then made an apologetic face.

"You're right. I shouldn't have asked," I said.

She smiled. "Of course, it would be okay if you read it here, though."

I grinned. "Right!" Then I sobered. "Unfortunately, I'll have to come back. I have another errand to run, and I need to get over to the Roux and pick up the food Maggie arranged for Eureka's memorial party."

Maria stood. "I'll come early to help set up."

I followed suit. "Thanks. It should be pretty low key."

"Good. Eureka would love a bit of a party, but she wouldn't want to be fussed over."

I started to walk away, then stopped. "Oh, wait. I have something else to ask you. Before I go, would you take another look at Alma? Specifically, her choice in jewelry."

Maria shot me a puzzled look and reached for the photo I held out to her. I pointed to the tree-shaped brooch. Squinting, she examined it for several seconds, then lowered the hand that held it. Her eyes were dancing when she met my gaze again.

I grinned. "You recognize it, don't you?"

"Sort of."

"And . . . ?"

"You'll see," was the librarian's cryptic response.

Impatiently, I watched as she put everything away and locked the cabinet. I grabbed my pack, and she closed the reference room door behind us. I noticed it had a lock on it, too, and the library itself had an alarm system because it was a public building.

If only the Xavier manuscript had been safe in here instead of in that old log cabin.

That wasn't fair, of course. No one had broken into Heritage House.

Wait a minute. Did that mean Eureka had let someone in? Or had she simply left the door unlocked because she thought of Poppyville as a sweet little town with a next-to-nothing crime rate? Because if she'd let her killer in, she'd probably known that person.

I let out a huff of frustration. That wasn't necessarily true, either. If Dylan Wong, for example, had knocked on the door of Heritage House, my bet was that Eureka would have opened the door for him. But would she have opened the door to Trixie or Warren? Hard to know.

"Here you go, Ellie. I set this aside for you," Maria said.

My ears perked up at that. When Maria had a book for you, you'd better pay attention to it.

"Brigitte, have the returns from the book mobile been re-shelved?" she asked gently as she went behind the information desk.

Her assistant looked up and blinked, then grinned. "Nope! Haven't done a darn thing since I picked this up. I'll get right on it, boss." She tucked her book under the desk and strode away.

"How long has she worked here?" I asked, trying to remember.

"Since before I moved here from San Diego," Maria said. "That was fifteen years ago."

"Really? And she's still your assistant?"

My friend nodded. "She likes it. She's good at it. Despite what you just saw, I really don't have to tell her what to do. She knew I just wanted a little privacy." Reaching below the desk, my friend pulled out a book and handed it to me.

The title was *Celtic Myths and Symbols*.

"How do you do it?" I asked, flipping through the pages. I stopped when I saw a picture of a tree with arcing branches echoed by the web of roots below. I touched it with the tip of my finger.

"That's the tree of life," Maria said.

"It's very close to the one on the brooch." I looked up at her. "And I don't know if you noticed, but there was a drawing of it in the Xavier manuscript, too."

And the drawing in Gamma's journal.

Maria shook her head. "I didn't get to look at it for very long, and mostly I remember that weird language."

Indeed. But all I said was, "How odd that the same symbol showed up both places."

"Not really," Maria said. "The tree of life symbol has been around for a long time, and in various cultures. And both the picture and the manuscript were in the time capsule. Maybe it was a popular motif at the time."

I frowned. "The manuscript was much older than anything else in the time capsule." Turning the page, I scanned the text. "The tree of life has all kinds of meanings, including strength, wisdom, and longevity. It says here that the Celts believed people originally came from trees, so trees were magical to them. The tree of life not only represented immortality but also connected the heavens and the underworld."

"And then there are those spirals around the one on the brooch," Maria pointed out."

I looked down again. "Yeah, that's the main difference. This picture in the book shows the circle around the tree as made up of a tangle of roots and branches.

The tree on Alma's brooch was surrounded by . . ." I turned a few pages and stopped. "By these." I was looking at the linked spirals that created the border of the motif.

Maria nodded, a slight smile on her lips. "Keep reading."

I did. The symbolism of the spiral was also old and universal. However, I was drawn to the descriptions of its symbolism in ancient Celtic tradition. The idea of holistic growth combined with a connection to cosmic energies resonated with me the most.

I flipped through a few more pages. "I don't suppose there's any mention of someone named Kell in here."

"Kell?" Maria asked. "As in the Book of Kells in Dublin's Trinity library?"

My head came up. "The illuminated manuscript of the Bible! Of course!"

"Not the whole Bible. Just the four gospels."

"So, who is Kell?" I asked eagerly.

"Not Kell. *Kells*. And not who. Where. It was written—or at least partially written—at the Abbey of Kells. There is no one named Kell associated with that codex."

Well, so much for that idea.

I closed the book and stood in silence for a few seconds to let all the new information swirling around in my head settle a bit. Maria climbed up on the stool behind the desk and waited.

"Huh," I finally said, then, "how exactly do you do that thing?"

"What thing?"

"Figuring out what book someone might need before they know."

Her head tipped to the side. "I don't know what you mean." Her eyes were smiling, though.

"Right. Don't mess with a good thing. At any rate, thank you for your help. I have a lot to think about." I turned to go. "I'll see you later this afternoon."

"Glad I could help," Maria called as I reached the door.

I stopped and turned. "Oh, and I'll be back to take a look at that diary as soon as I can find a little time. In the meantime, let me know if Charles has anything else to say about dear, disappeared Aunt Alma."

WHEN I left the library, it was nearly two o'clock. People would start showing up in the Enchanted Garden in two hours. The grocery store didn't seem quite as important after eating a sandwich as big as my head, and I needed to grab the food Maggie had arranged at the Roux Grill. Still, my cupboards were bare, so I decided to swing by the restaurant on the way back from the market.

But first, I wanted to check in at Scents & Nonsense and see how Larken was coming with the online orders.

She'd been the picture of efficiency. Boxes were stacked unobtrusively by the storeroom door awaiting pickup, neatly taped and addressed with custom Scents & Nonsense labels that showed our logo: a blue butterfly in midflutter above an elaborately scrolled perfume bottle sporting the name of the shop.

She came out from behind the counter and joined me by the coffee urn, where there was fresh brew on offer but a disturbing lack of cookies. Keeping an eye on a teenaged boy—certainly not our usual clientele—browsing in the bath products section, Larken said, "Did you find what you were looking for at the library?"

"Sort of," I said.

However, she obviously had something else on her mind. "While you were gone, Gessie King called and said one of her horses has been skittish lately. She said you gave her an aromatherapy mist for it a while ago, and was wondering if she could get some more."

I nodded. "No problem."

"What's in it?" she asked. "If you don't mind telling me."

"Not at all. The combination that seems to work the best for him is Roman chamomile, vetiver, and ylang-ylang. At least if it's for the horse I'm thinking of."

"Cool. Anyway, someone also called about an order."

"One of those?" I pointed to the boxes.

"No, one they haven't placed yet. It's a boutique hotel in Silver Wells, and they heard about your lavender room sprays. They wanted to know if you'd make a smaller version for them to stock in their rooms. An added benefit for their guests."

Lowering the mug that I'd been sipping from, I felt a wide smile spread across my face. "What a great idea. I wonder if I could talk Felicity into doing the same thing at the Hotel California."

Larken waved her hand. "Of course it's a great idea, and of course I told them yes. But I couldn't give them pricing, so I told them you'd call them back. Then I went to check out the online shop to see if you had anything like that on there, and, Ellie—" She stopped and looked down at the floor.

"And, Ellie . . ." I prompted.

Her expression apologetic, she said, "It's terrible."

"What is?" I asked.

"Your online store! It's difficult to navigate, and only half of what could be for sale is listed."

"I haven't had time—" I started.

"Let me do it."

I blinked. "You?"

"Yes! I'm pretty good at stuff like that, actually. I could revamp the site, add whatever you want me to, make sure people know that you do custom orders. Ellie." She frowned and shook her head. "That's not even on there. You have a potential gold mine that you're just not tapping into. Retail doesn't have to be local anymore, you know. Online is the way to go. Don't you want to take advantage of that?"

"Yeah," I said slowly.

"I know you're doing okay here, but you're not exactly raking it in. So I know you can't really hire me."

I shook my head. "If more sales come in from the website, then I can certainly hire you to maintain it. How long do you think it'll take to make the changes you're thinking of?"

"Oh, a couple of days to a week. Depends on how much I have to change the basic design. And if I can do it from home."

"You can do it wherever you'd like." Pursing my lips, I considered. "How about a flat rate for the update?" I named a figure, and her eyes lit up. "And then we can decide on an hourly rate for future updates and maintenance once it gets going."

Eagerly, she nodded. "That sounds great!"

Her gaze shifted behind me. "Hang on. I'll be right back." She hurried behind the register, where the young man was waiting with a big bottle of vanilla-scented bath oil.

"It's for my mom's birthday," he said. "She loves this place, but I don't think she has any of this stuff. Do you think she'll like it?"

"Like it? She'll love it," Larken said. "Here, let me wrap it in a gift bag with some tissue and a ribbon. Then you just have to get her a card, and you're all set!"

"A card," he repeated.

"You'll find a nice one at Rexall Drugs, I'm sure." Larken tidied the bow she'd made on his gift bag and handed it to him.

He took it with a grateful smile and left.

"Ellie, you might want to think about carrying cards," she said as she rejoined me and poured a cup of hot water over a peppermint tea bag. "Just a small rack of carefully selected ones. I mean, people come in here all the time for gifts. You might as well offer one-stop shopping."

"That's a good idea," I admitted.

I'd avoided carrying anything in the shop that wasn't scent oriented in some way, but there was the "Nonsense" part of the shop, too. As for her indictment of my online store, it was true that I hadn't given it much attention. That was probably why there were only four orders for the whole week. But I disliked spending time in front of a computer screen when I could be out in the garden or whipping up fragrant products to sell, plus I helped people find the scent they needed best when we were face-to-face.

"I'll think about the cards," I said. "In fact, maybe I'll have you pick them out."

She grinned. "I'm glad to help. There are some by local artists that the tourists would love."

"Perfect. And I have links to some online catalogs you can look at from home. Just keep track of the time you spend." I tipped my head and watched her over the rim of my mug as I polished off its contents. "How are things with the farm?"

It might have sounded like an unrelated question, but we both knew it wasn't.

"Good! I love it, I really do. And Colby does, too, despite how afraid he was to be tied to a piece of land like that. Still . . ." She hesitated, then flashed her infectious smile. "As much as I would like to be completely self-sustaining, Colby and I are both going to need to work—at least part-time. That's just a simple fact."

I nodded, unsurprised. "Well, I can obviously use your help with the website, as well as a bit of part-time work here in the shop. Thea was complaining about the kid she hired, so maybe she could use some help, too. And Gessie has a basic website for the stables, but she might be willing to pay you to make it more appealing and easier to book hayrides and cookouts and such." I was just brainstorming by then, but Larken had moved to the counter and was happily jotting notes.

I glanced out the window to check on Dash. He and Nabby were contentedly sunning in the middle of the flagstone patio, and I let them be. "I'm going to the store now, then by the Roux to pick up food for the gathering."

"Right!" She smiled. "I'll keep the home fires burning here at the shop."

I STEERED the Wrangler north on Corona Street toward the county road that would loop me around to the supermarket. I put together a mental grocery list as I drove. The farmers' market wouldn't open for a couple of weeks, with new greens and tender asparagus, baby carrots, radishes, and pea pods just begging to be stir-fried. In the meantime, I'd grab the makings for a few salads in the produce section. I needed chicken and mushrooms for coq au vin, and granola and yogurt since I didn't know whether I'd ever get another cookie from Astrid, and I needed to eat *something* for breakfast.

That thought made me sad.

Sighing, I went back to my list. Pasta and rice and potatoes. A slab of salmon, maybe a couple of steaks— just to have around since I hoped to have plenty of dinners at home with Ritter in the next few weeks . . .

A block ahead, a familiar Peugeot pulled out and headed the same way I was going.

Speak of the devil.

Across from the Roux Grill, it veered into a parking spot, and Astrid got out. I slowed and saw her go around and open the passenger door. A Great Dane leaped to the sidewalk, its leash firmly in Astrid's hand. She led him over to the metal fence that surrounded the outdoor seating, and tied the leash to one of the standards. The dog bent to drink from the big water bowl that was always there, then lay down like a regal Sphinx to watch passersby. My friend didn't notice me drive by as she pushed the front door of the restaurant open and went inside.

I pulled around the corner and parked. After all, stopping by the Roux was on my list of things to do. If I happened to go in when my best buddy happened to be there, well, that would just be a happy coincidence—and hopefully one that would allow for me to apologize. Or at least to try to explain. I still didn't think I'd been wrong to check into Dylan Wong's background. After all, she barely knew the guy.

# CHAPTER 17

My steps slowed as I came around to the front of the Roux Grill. I'd spent plenty of long days and late nights inside that building. Harris and I had worked our tails off to get the place up and running, starting with his mother's recipes and doing the work of four people ourselves when we couldn't afford to hire the help we needed. We'd worked so hard for so long that I hadn't even noticed that our marriage wasn't the best.

However, I was still proud of the place, and the kitchen still served some of the best food for miles around. I wasn't sorry to be done with the heavy lifting of running a restaurant, though. Starting Scents & Nonsense had been hard work, but far more of a labor of love than the Roux had been. At least for me. It was still Harris' first love, and probably always would be.

The umbrellas over the outdoor tables were furled,

but two couples basked in the sunny afternoon warmth. Perky pansies smiled up from where they tumbled around Oregon grape in the half-barrel planters on either side of the big wooden door. I pushed it open and stepped inside.

As always, the smell of garlic hit me first. It was the warm, round fragrance of whole cloves slowly heated in butter for two hours before the golden liquid was poured directly into the bowls of bite-size rolls that were brought to each table when customers sat down. Despite my earlier sandwich, my mouth started watering. That reaction was as Pavlovian as it got, and the anticipation of those garlicky rolls affected most repeat customers the same way.

The hostess station was empty, so I was surprised when I rounded the corner from the foyer into the main dining room and saw so many people. Nearly half the booths that marched down the wall to my left were full, and so were a few of the tables in the middle of the long room. Three customers sat at the heavy, dark mahogany bar on the right, which was colorfully illuminated by the light shining through jewel-toned liquor bottles lined up in front of the window.

Maggie moved back and forth, mixing drinks for the stony-faced waitress who waited for them. She was a new hire, and my lips parted in surprise when I realized who it was. She was certainly pretty, so Harris might have hired her with or without waitressing experience. Still, it was the last place I thought I'd see Trixie Perez working.

Harris stood at the end of the bar, watching Trixie

with a pleased expression. I wasn't sure why, since she radiated resentment. Hardly an invitation for customers to hang out.

A man who was sitting at the bar turned so that I could see his face, and I realized it was Odell Radcliffe. Beside him, Haley leaned over an electronic notebook in her lap. Her hair formed a curtain that hid most of her face, but I could make out the edge of her thick glasses. A cup of hot tea sat on the bar in front of her.

Her father, however, apparently had no compunction about drinking at three in the afternoon. Odell held up his empty margarita glass to Trixie, who ignored him. Maggie was busy and didn't notice right away, but Harris did and sauntered over.

"Another one?" he asked, taking the glass.

Odell nodded. "Please. Your bartender makes a mean one. Not too strong, and not too sweet."

I wasn't surprised. Maggie not only made the best dirty martinis, she was renowned in Poppyville for her awesome margaritas and Sunday morning Bloody Mary bar.

"Certainly, sir," Harris said. He took the glass back to the sink and said something in a low voice to Trixie as he passed by. She nodded, but once she turned away from him, she rolled her eyes. Then she saw me watching, hesitated, and shrugged.

I looked around for Astrid, and realized the place was really busy, even for a Friday afternoon. The Friday Afternoon Club Maggie had told me about must be a great hit.

Well, good for Harris.

Detective Max Lang lounged in one of the booths, a beer in front of him when he should have been out trying to find Eureka's killer. Thea and Gessie were chatting at a back table, and I gave them a wave. Astrid hadn't joined them, though. Instead, she slid into a booth, facing me.

My wave attracted Harris' attention. He gave Odell his drink and came around the bar and over to me.

"Ellie."

"Harris."

He was a handsome man, with dark hair worn long on top so it artfully flipped over his forehead. He had a brilliant smile when he deigned to display it, but more often his upper lip was curled into a slight sneer. I'd once made the mistake of telling him it made him look like Elvis Presley, and the idea that it was sexy must have stuck. And I had to admit he attracted a lot of women. Always had—married or not.

"I thought you'd be selling your little perfumes this time of day," he said.

At one time that comment might have bothered me, but now his condescending reference to the shop slid right off my back. After all, I *did* make a living from doing my dream job, so who cared what the man I'd increasingly come to think of as "the jerk" thought?

Of course, it was Astrid who'd helped me realize that.

"I hear your boyfriend is back in town," Harris said.

"Ritter is hardly a boy," I started, then stopped myself. I had almost forgotten what a challenge it was to let his comments float away like so many dead leaves, a tactic that kept me sane and made him crazy.

"How does he feel about his little woman playing Herlock Holmes?"

"Oh, that's a good one," I said sweetly.

"Max says you were obsessed with that old bunch of papers in the time capsule." He shook his head.

I smiled. "How nice of Max to take an interest."

"Say what you will, he has the chief's ear." He pointed, and I saw Chief Gibbon had joined Max in the booth.

Trixie stopped and set a cup of coffee in front of the chief. He smiled and said something to her. She turned away to another customer without smiling back.

"Looks awful busy in here," I said. "You sure you have enough help?"

"Got a new waitress," Harris said.

"I see that. Looks like she's great with the customers." He didn't seem to notice my sarcasm.

She stumbled right then, and nearly dropped her tray—and the pitcher of beer on it.

"Does she have any experience?" I asked.

"Of course!"

"Bull pucky," I said, borrowing from Astrid. "She doesn't know anything about waiting tables."

"Well, I'll make sure she gets *plenty* of experience here," he said.

"You're an idiot and a pig," I said evenly. "And she's married."

I didn't think I needed to worry about Trixie being able to handle my ex-husband. That woman could take care of herself. However, she obviously hated working at the Roux. So why was she?

Money. It had to be. Maria mentioned there were rumors about their financial situation. Warren must be having trouble at his dealership. No wonder they were so determined to get Eureka's house as soon as possible.

I made a note to check with Lupe about Warren and Trixie's finances. If she'd tell me, that was.

Were they desperate enough to kill Eureka and try to make it look like a robbery? And if so, what had they done with the Xavier manuscript?

"You always think the worst of me," Harris said.

"Trixie might be cute, but she won't last a week."

He smiled. "We'll see. You know her, then?"

"Not really." I changed the subject. "Your early Friday happy hour looks successful."

"From three to six well drinks, wine, and beer are two dollars. By the time the dinner hour rolls around, people have to stay and have a big meal to soak up the booze."

"Classy," I said.

He nodded happily.

Movement drew my eye, and I saw Astrid waving at me.

"It's been lovely," I said to Harris, and started toward her.

I was halfway to her booth when I saw she had a companion in the opposite seat. Dark hair cut short, longish sideburns, slight build, tall.

Dylan Wong.

*Dang it.*

Not in the mood for a happy hour confrontation, I picked up my pace a bit and breezed by their table with a quick, "Gotta pick up some food for the gathering this afternoon."

"Ellie Allbright, you sit down right now," Astrid said.

I slowed. Turned. Saw she was smiling at me, and it appeared to be genuine. I took a breath, nodded, and slid into the seat next to her.

Trixie came over. "You want anything?"

"Maybe later," I said.

She drifted back toward the bar. I watched her for a few seconds, then brought my attention back to my companions. Both appeared to be drinking iced tea.

*Not everyone will have to stay for dinner after drinking your cheap booze, Harris.*

"You remember Ellie, don't you, Dylan?" Astrid asked her date.

"Sure. Nice to see you again."

"Thanks," I said. "You, too."

She beamed at us both. Something was going on.

"Astrid tells me you have a terrific garden behind your perfume shop. Sounds cool. Maybe I'll come with her to your friend's memorial this afternoon, so I can see it."

I blinked. "Um, I'll give you a tour if you'd like. Another time." It hit me sideways that he wanted to attend our gathering to honor Eureka as if it were just another date with Astrid.

"Oh, that's okay," he said easily. "I'd like to see your shop, too."

I gave him a tight smile, ready to bolt for the kitchen and my waiting appetizers.

"Honey, I'm so sorry I wasn't able to bring cookies by

this morning," Astrid said. "I made up a batch of lemon sour cream cookies first thing, but then had to get right to work. So, I decided to bring those this afternoon." Her smile was open and affectionate.

I felt my angst and anxiety about our argument the night before melting away. "I was a little worried," I admitted. "But you know you don't have to bring goodies to the shop every day."

"She's an amazing baker, isn't she?" Dylan asked. "And I can testify that those lemon cookies are to die for."

He'd sampled them? In the morning before she went to work? Even after I'd warned her?

I felt my hackles rise again.

"Dylan, you remember that manuscript that was in the time capsule?" Astrid asked out of the blue.

I barely managed not to gasp. What was she thinking?

He frowned, then his face cleared.

"Oh, sure. I guess I've been thinking of that as a palimpsest—since it was so old and written on vellum."

"Right," she said. "You'd know the particulars of what to call something like that since you're in the business of buying and selling old things."

I bristled internally. *As if Eureka wouldn't know?* Not to mention that Dylan had supposedly seen the Xavier manuscript only on Wednesday afternoon, just like the rest of us, but he sure seemed to remember an awful lot about it.

"It's missing," Astrid said. "And since you're in that business, Ellie and I were wondering if you could tell us how easy it would be for the thief to sell it."

Dylan considered me for a long moment. "And are you and Ellie wondering *where* said thief might be able to sell it?"

"Well, sure, if you know!" Astrid said. "That might give the police another way to find Eureka's killer."

My eyes were still locked with Dylan's. He looked away first. When he did, I glanced over at Max and Chief Gibbon sitting a few tables away. They were both watching us.

Dylan sat back and spoke in a clipped, professorial tone. "It would be next to impossible to sell that palimpsest to a reputable dealer. They would require evidence of the provenance, and as a matter of course the authorities will have already contacted organizations like the Art Dealers Association of America to let them know it had been stolen." He looked toward the ceiling, thoughtful. "Of course, there are private dealers who are not so concerned with ethics, or it's possible whoever took it had a collector waiting for it who wouldn't ask any questions." His gaze returned to Astrid. "Whatever the thief was thinking, that piece is unlikely to be found."

"Ever?" I asked without even trying to keep the horror out of my voice.

He nodded. "Think about it. After what happened to Dr. Sanford, anyone found with the manuscript would be assumed either to be a murderer or to know the murderer."

He made a face and suddenly put his elbows on the table and snagged me with his eyes again. "Listen, Ellie. Theft is one thing, but murder is so much worse. I, uh . . ." He trailed off. Looked at Astrid. She smiled at him. He smiled back and put his hand over hers on the table.

I watched them, baffled.

"I made a mistake one time," he said. "I once brokered the sale of something very old and valuable even though the provenance was a bit sketchy. It was a small collection of onyx artifacts from the Ohlone tribe. I should have known better, but I trusted the guy who wanted me to set up the deal. It turned out that I shouldn't have." He took a deep breath. "He got caught, and I got in a boatload of trouble." A shudder ran through his body, and Astrid squeezed his hand. "I can't even imagine how awful it would be if there had been a murder involved."

Astrid tore her gaze away from Dylan to give me an *I told you so* look.

"Good information," I said neutrally, checked the time, and rose. "I'm afraid I really do have to grab the food for this afternoon's gathering and get back to help Larken set up. I'll see you there."

"Okeydoke," Astrid said, turning back to Dylan.

I nodded to Chief Gibbon and Max as I hurried by on my way back to the kitchen, pretty sure they'd both been listening. I hoped so, just in case they'd learned something new—especially about Mr. Dylan Wong's illegal past. Because even though I wanted to give him the benefit of the doubt for Astrid—at least she had managed to convince me he wasn't a killer—beneath the savory scents of the restaurant, I still smelled a lie of some kind.

Chief Gibbon nodded back with a perfect poker face, so I didn't know if he was upset with me or not. Max was far easier to read. His eyes were narrowed, and with a start, I realized he looked a little nervous.

Was he afraid I'd show him up again?

Well, it wasn't my fault if he wasn't a very good detective.

# CHAPTER 18

ONCE again, I'd been sidetracked and hadn't managed to get to the grocery store before having to get back to Scents & Nonsense. However, there would be food at the memorial, and Ritter and I would head to the Empire Room afterward. I was already looking forward to their Guinness beef stew and colcannon as I parked in the lot across the street from my shop.

As I crossed Corona Street, a bundled-up figure several yards away raised a hand in a tentative greeting. Lowering my sunglasses, I saw it was Bongo Pete. He was heading into Raven Creek Park, where he could often be found walking the fitness trail or spending time down by the water. Quickly, I waved back, not wanting him to think I was ignoring him or hadn't seen him. Most thought Pete Grimly strange, but he demonstrated a sensitivity I found both philosophical and otherworldly.

*I wonder what he thought of the stuff in the time capsule*, I thought as I continued across Corona Street. Though perhaps he'd lost interest and wandered away. I didn't remember seeing him after the mayor had finished.

Inside the shop, the boxed orders had been picked up, and Scents & Nonsense was clean and tidy. I found Larken on the patio, where she'd dragged out a set of canvas directors' chairs from the storage closet. Dash and Nabby supervised from under the birdbath in the Enchanted Garden.

"Oh, I'd forgotten I had those," I said, setting down the containers of food the chef at the Roux had had waiting for me. "Let's put a few in the greenhouse. People might want a little time alone or to have a more private conversation."

She pointed at me. "Good idea. A hidey-hole for the introverts." She picked up a couple of the folded chairs and headed toward the back of the property.

I followed behind with another chair. She pushed open the unlocked door of the greenhouse, and we went inside.

The space was a bit over fifteen feet deep and twelve feet wide. Thea had helped me install wooden planting benches on either side of the gravel-strewn center aisle, and now they boasted flats of herb starts, along with baby heirloom vegetables for Larken and Colby to put in their garden. The distinctive scent of tomato leaves twined around the licorice-like smell of tiny basil leaves, and as I breathed in the miasma, I automatically thought of Gamma.

*Tomatoes for love and for poison, two sides of a coin.*

*Basil for best wishes but also for hatred, so carefully judge.*

The Victorian language of flowers was a convoluted one, indeed.

Among the flats were the more delicate plants from the Enchanted Garden, overwintered and ready to return to their places outside within the week. There were jasmine and moonflowers, oleander and oxalis, hanging begonias and fuchsias. Near the door, I'd placed the *Brugmansia*, or angel's trumpet, opposite the *Datura*, aka devil's trumpet, in an ironic nod to their names. Both were highly toxic despite their sweet fragrances.

I left the chairs for Larken to set up and went to retrieve platters for the food.

Fifteen minutes later, a few new seating areas had been added around the garden, and two tables were covered with bright blue tablecloths that a wedding party had left behind the previous summer. I set out the deviled eggs, caprese toasts, spinach and queso dips, cheese platter, chicken wings, and a big bowl of the Roux's special red potato salad with bacon, sunflower seeds, and buttermilk dressing.

In the open air of the garden, the scents of dill, cheddar, vinegar, and onion mixed with the sweetness of wallflowers and the earthier fragrances of hydrangeas and tulips. Larken had propped the door of the greenhouse open with an etched rock that read *Breathe*, and soon the perfumes of those plants joined the aromatic fray.

Leaving Larken to greet the first arrivals, I headed down to my tiny house to change out of my jeans and sweater into something more respectful—and suitable for my long-awaited reunion dinner with Ritter later that evening.

I decided on the skirt Dash had rejected the evening before. Looking at myself in the mirror, I debated whether to create the same updo that had made me look so much like Alma Hammond, then shook my head and brushed my curls into waves that fell below my shoulders. I didn't need to look any more like Alma. I already shared her blood.

I STOOD by the back door of the shop with Ritter. He was clean-shaven and appeared refreshed after finally getting a few hours of sleep at Thea's. His cinnamon-colored shirt, so crisp it crackled beneath my fingertips when I touched his arm, matched his eyes and the highlights in his longish hair. Trying not to be too obvious, I breathed him in, thankful that he was finally there in the flesh and not just a voice on the phone.

The impromptu Poppyville phone tree had done its job, and dozens of people milled and talked in the Enchanted Garden. All the Greenstockings except Gessie were already there, along with most of the members of the Poppyville town council. Sure enough, Dylan had accompanied Astrid. There were a few locals I recognized but didn't know very well. Odell and Haley Radcliffe sat side by side on the bench by the north fence. Warren Perez stood by the front gate as if ready to bolt, and there was Trixie, right next to him.

Surprise, surprise. Harris let her off work, but not Maggie.

A flare of anger at my ex ignited for a few seconds, but I pushed it away. This was supposed to be about Eureka, not how easily Harris could drive me nuts.

Mayor Ward moved from one group to another, a sad look on his face. It was an opportunity to glad-hand, but I wanted to give him the benefit of the doubt. Like the council members, he'd come to know Eureka during her fight to start up Heritage House. His wife, Zoe, broke away as he went to talk to someone else, and I watched as she went to the trellis of sweet peas, drew a few blooms toward her face, and took a deep whiff. Her shoulders dropped a fraction, and I imagined the tension draining from them. I could only hope the saffron, thyme, and lavender I'd given her had helped her sleep better.

Detective Max Lang stood alone by the oak tree, blatantly surveying the scene. When I looked around, I saw Lupe standing up by the corner of the shop, nearly as far away from him as she could get. I gave Ritter's arm a squeeze, then sidled over to her.

"Hey." She didn't look at me but continued to scan the crowd.

"See anyone acting suspicious?" I asked, half teasing.

"Trixie doesn't want to be here," she said, utterly serious. "I get the feeling Warren wanted to come, and she didn't want him here alone."

"She's waitressing at the Roux," I said.

Lupe turned to look at me. "Really?" Then she looked back at her. "Huh."

"Did you find out anything about their finances?" I asked.

Her lips pursed.

I waited.

"Let's just say that inheriting a house sooner than later would give a much-needed boost to their bank account," she finally muttered.

Short on details, but it was enough to know Eureka's nephew and niece-in-law had a motive for killing her.

"The will?" I asked.

"We checked with the attorney, and Maria was right. Eureka left her house to them. Trixie will probably be quitting her job at the Roux pretty soon."

"And maybe going to prison. In which case they can't benefit from Eureka's death, right?"

"Well, there's that."

Harris would be so disappointed.

"You check into that guy?" I asked, pointing with my chin to where Dylan stood with his arm around Astrid.

"He's on the list, along with everyone else that was here from out of town during the ceremony," she said.

"But he's here right now." I couldn't keep the frustration out of my voice. "And he has a record. Well, sort of."

Lupe frowned at me. "It you're talking about his arrest for trafficking in stolen goods, we know all about it. He cooperated with the district attorney and wasn't charged." She tipped her head. "Why are you getting involved with this, Ellie? We've got it under control."

I didn't answer. "Where's the chief?" I asked as if I were changing the subject, but we both knew I wasn't.

"In a meeting," she said shortly.

"Another one, huh. Okeydoke." Then I nodded toward the Radcliffes, who were talking with the mayor now. "What about him?"

The detective's lips twitched. "What about him?"

"Lupe," I growled.

A subtle shake of her head, then she relented. "He was in his suite at the Hotel California during the time of the murder. His daughter was there, too."

"She seems kind of lonely, though she and her father are obviously close."

"Her mother is deceased," Lupe said.

"I know. Died when she was a little girl, just like mine did." I sighed. "But I had my stepmother to take me shopping and show me how to use makeup and give me advice." I gave a little laugh. "Whether I wanted that advice or not. Still, I don't think Haley had anyone like that. I mean, look at her."

As we watched, Odell rose and went to talk to Larken by the greenhouse. Haley remained on the bench, the cardigan she'd been wearing the day before now wrapped around her button-down shirt and dark slacks. Her hair was held off her face with a headband, and I could sense her shyness and discomfort among all these people she didn't know.

Astrid, bless her heart, must have seen the same thing I did, because she broke away from Dylan and went to sit by Odell's daughter. I felt my lips curve up as she said something that made Haley snort and cover her mouth.

Lupe gave me a puzzled look. "Some people are just shy. You don't usually seem like the mothering type."

"Yeah. I'm not. There's just something about her that feels needy."

I saw Max was watching us.

"I better move around," Lupe said, eyeing him. "Later."

Thea was talking to Ritter when I turned back. I waved and joined them by the rose trellis. Just then Gessie came through the gate, juggling bowls of guacamole and chips. Thea quickly excused herself and went to help.

I slipped my arm around Ritter and gave him a kiss on the cheek. The skin was still a little pinched around his eyes. I'd been hoping for a big night, but perhaps it would be better for him to go home and get more rest right after dinner.

Then he smiled down at me, and I decided he could get as much rest as he needed that night—right by my side.

Together, we went to commune with the others who were mourning the loss of Eureka Sanford.

S HE came to my classroom to talk about the gold rush, and the kids loved her!"

". . . never seen anyone so determined to get the town council to see things her way . . ."

". . . a temper, but it was short-lived."

"Came in every Tuesday for dinner. Great tipper . . ."

Snippets of conversation reached my ears from all over the Enchanted Garden. As Ritter and I passed Odell Radcliffe, he said to the mayor, "I think the head of the department was terrified of her, but she was always on the side of right. And Eureka didn't change a whit after the success of her first book. She was a mentor and an advocate for her students."

I moved away and heard Warren telling Trixie, "She

told the silliest jokes. Kid stuff. I loved the one about why elephants paint their toenails red. Because—"

She cut him off. "I don't care about her stupid jokes." She was about to say something more but saw me and clamped her mouth shut.

Ritter raised his hand in greeting to an old high school friend standing by the front fence. "I'm going to say hi."

I nodded and stepped back to scan the garden. Clusters of people murmured together, their voices combining to form a soft buzz among the flowers. The branches of the oak and apple trees arched over them, protective and listening. A few visitors meandered into the greenhouse, where Larken stood by the door looking earthy and serene. As I watched, Maria joined her, and I wondered whether she'd had a chance to finish reading Charles Bettelheim's diary.

"Ellie! How are you?"

I turned to see Dr. Eliza Scott from the Poppyville Clinic. No white coat today. She wore tailored tweed slacks with a wide-necked cashmere sweater, matching vest, and boots. She was a tall African American woman pushing fifty with gray-streaked hair in a thick braid over one shoulder, and always seemed to smell faintly of strawberries.

She smiled at me from behind her glasses. "This was a nice thing for you to do."

I gestured toward Maria, who was telling Larken that Eureka wore her newsboy cap because she couldn't be bothered to mess with her hair when there were so many other things that were so much more important. "It was her idea, actually."

Dr. Scott looked around the garden. "But this is the perfect place. It's relaxing here. Calming, you know?"

I nodded.

"It's open to the public?" she asked.

"Of course. Anytime the shop is open," I said. "No purchase required."

"I should take a break and come here during the day. I often forget to have lunch, and there are times my job is a bit, well, stressful."

"I can imagine," I said, not mentioning how often I forgot to eat lunch as well. I'd snagged a deviled egg and a chicken wing when people had begun trickling in, though. "Did you know Eureka well?"

"We were getting to know each other," Dr. Scott said. "We got along. I'm sorry we never had the chance to spend more time together." She sighed, and I felt a pang of the same regret. "Mostly our conversations were about the gold rush and my family history here."

My forehead wrinkled a little. "Oh?"

"I went to Cornell, but I was born here. My family has deep roots in Poppyville. Eureka wanted to interview me for a book she was writing."

My eyes widened. "Really? What did she ask about?"

"My great-great-great-grandfather. He was a slave who came west with the son of a Louisiana plantation owner during the gold rush. He bought his freedom with the gold he mined for himself, and my family has been here ever since."

"Dr. Scott, I knew your family had been here a long time, but I didn't know that story."

"It's not an uncommon one. There were a lot of African

Americans who were caught up in the gold rush for various reasons, not to mention the Indian tribes that were run roughshod over by the stampede of prospectors and dreamers. I was glad to see the Greenstockings included some of that history in the educational materials at Heritage House."

"Thanks to Eureka," I said. "She was the expert."

The doctor nodded her head. "She wanted to know about the stables back then. My family ran that stable until a generation ago, but my parents weren't much on sentiment, so I didn't really have anything to give her. I sent her to talk to Gessie King."

I frowned, then looked around. "Gessie was just here, but I don't see her now. Do you?"

"She left a few minutes ago," Dr. Scott said. "Told me she had to get back to check on a horse that's been acting colicky."

I nodded and went to find Ritter. Talking to Gessie would have to wait.


PEOPLE began to trickle out of the Enchanted Garden around six o'clock, and almost everyone was gone by seven. I shooed Astrid out when she tried to help clean up.

"I left you all to deal with the aftermath of the time capsule ceremony the other day. I've got this," I said.

"*We've* got this," Ritter emphasized. My hopes for the evening had kindled again.

"Deal," Astrid said, munching on one of her own

lemon sour cream cookies. "I'll be by in the morning. Oh, and I'm thinking brookies for tomorrow."

"Brookies?" I asked.

"Half chocolate chip cookie, half fudge brownie."

The thought made me half swoon. "Yum," I managed.

She grinned and grabbed Dylan's arm.

"Nice garden," he called as she dragged him through the gate.

There was still something off about the guy, but I couldn't help laughing a little at their antics.

Larken approached. "I'm sorry. I have to get back to the farm. The critters are all waiting for their dinner." She rolled her eyes. "It'll be easier when your brother gets back, and I won't have to do everything by myself."

"No worries," I said. "And the website update? I'll e-mail you the information, so you can dive in whenever you want to."

She grinned. "Excellent! Ellie, you are going to love what I come up with for you."

After she left, Ritter asked me what Larken meant, and I filled him in as we packed up the few leftovers, put away chairs, closed the greenhouse against the coming chill of night, and otherwise cleaned up.

When we were nearly finished, he went in to shut off the lights in Scents & Nonsense, and I did a check of the garden one last time to make sure we hadn't missed a paper cup or stray napkin. As I came around the oak tree, a flash of orange caught my eye. I walked over and kneeled by a fairy tableau that featured a sweet set of wee white wicker chairs and table, complete with tiny embroidered pillows on them and potted succulents arranged on the white pebble floor.

A single orange marigold had free-seeded at the edge of the pebbles, pushing a few of them aside with its dark green leaves. One bloom had unfurled, and now it stood winking at me in the gloaming as night approached.

*Marigolds for malice.*

A low moan carried down through the budding leaves of the oak, barely audible but ebbing and flowing like a wailing tide against my senses. I reached down and yanked out the marigold by the roots.

Suddenly, a gust of wind blew through the garden, carrying with it the scents of mountain mahogany and fountain pen ink. I knew that combination from only one source.

Eureka.

Had her spirit tried to warn me of something? And if so, what?

# CHAPTER 19

I TOSSED the marigold plant on the compost pile before coming inside, but the scent remained on my skin. At the kitchen sink, I scrubbed at my hands with pine-scented soap, then grabbed a dish towel and looked down at Dash.

He was not so patiently waiting by his feeding station, which was under the end of the counter—easily accessible with his short legs and out of traffic in the small space. I dished out a bit of kibble and added half a left-over deviled egg from the memorial. He tucked in with glee, crunching and slurping as if he hadn't eaten in a week, despite all the food I'd seen people giving him in the Enchanted Garden.

Glancing at the clock on the stove, I saw we had a half hour before we had to leave for dinner, so I grabbed a couple of glasses and the two-thirds-full bottle of wine I'd opened the night before.

Ritter stood by the back door in the living room. The jacket he'd been going to hang on the wall hook was still in his hand. As I approached, he glanced up at me, then pushed the door with a fingertip.

Silently, it swung open.

"Did you mean to leave this open?" he asked.

I shook my head, still smelling the bitter hint of marigolds that I'd dragged inside. "It was definitely closed."

"Locked?" Now he sounded concerned.

My lips pressed together as I replayed the afternoon in my mind. "I don't know."

"Maybe someone came in during the gathering for Eureka. To get a drink or use the bathroom." He lifted one shoulder and let it drop, apparently willing to let the subject of my open door do the same.

I frowned. "Through the back door? They'd have had to go outside the fence. I deliberately locked the front door so no one would decide to explore inside. There were plenty of drinks, and I made the restroom in the shop available."

He took the wine from my hand and set it on the low table beside the love seat. "Does it look like anything's missing?"

My eyes widened. "Oh, no. You don't think . . ." I trailed off and whirled around to check the spiral bookcase.

Gamma's journal was still there, right where I'd left it. I felt my shoulders relax a fraction as my gaze flicked around the living room. A quick trip into the kitchen and bathroom revealed no disturbance, either. I started up to the loft, and Ritter quickly joined me on the stairs.

I turned to look at him.

"If someone came in, they could still be here," he said.

"Oh!" My eyes widened. There had been a murder, after all. And I'd been asking questions.

He grinned. "It's probably nothing. You want me to go first?"

I gave him a look. "Why do I get the feeling you're just trying to get me into the bedroom?"

He shrugged, the grin still on his face. "Fine. You stay here. I'll go up and check."

"Let me check my jewelry box," I said. "And then we'll put the mysteriously open door out of mind, have some wine, and you can regale me with tales from the tundra."

"Nice try," he said with a smile. "I'd much rather you fill me in on what your sleuthing has unearthed."

I grimaced. "Woefully little."

Ritter shadowed right behind as I padded up the circular staircase. Everything in the bedroom looked to be as I'd left it, and my few pieces of jewelry were exactly where they were supposed to be. When I checked the cupboard where I kept the ancient copper alembic I used to distill essential oils from the garden, it sat, squat and gleaming, in the shadows waiting for the next time I needed to create a custom perfume.

Back downstairs, Ritter took my hand and led me to the love seat. "Everything good, then?"

"Yep," I said. "Maybe I just left the door unlocked, and the wind blew it open." Even as I said the words, I knew it sounded like something a stupid heroine in a slasher movie would say. But I honestly couldn't think of any other reason for it to be unlatched.

Ritter uncorked the bottle and poured the wine. His eyes flashed as he handed me a glass, and I felt my face grow pleasantly warm at the prospect of what the rest of the evening held. For the first time, things felt like they had before he left for Alaska.

I lifted my glass and smiled, and Ritter did the same before bringing the wine to his lips.

Then the scent hit my nose: slightly sweet, yet deeply earthy and similar to the tannins in the wine. But it wasn't the wine. It was something else. In the split second after detecting it, my neurons lit up with all the knowledge that years of honing my senses had developed, and a single picture flashed into my mind.

The botanical drawing of *Datura stramonium* in Gamma's journal.

"Ritter! No! Don't drink that!" It felt as if my hand was moving in slow motion as I reached for his glass.

Fear stabbed through me as his Adam's apple bobbed.

Knocking the glass out of his hand, I sprayed wine across the ottoman and hardwood floor.

"Elliana! What the—"

"It's poison. You didn't drink any, did you? Tell me you didn't drink any," I demanded, hoping against hope that I hadn't just seen him swallow.

"Well, yeah." He frowned at the stain spreading across the fabric of the footstool. "A little."

I reached over and picked up the bottle. Held it up to the floor lamp. Sure enough, there was plant material in the wine. Squinting, I made out a tangle of leaves.

If I checked the greenhouse, I was sure I'd find they'd been removed from the plant I'd overwintered there.

"It tasted fine," Ritter said. He was concentrating on the maroon pool on the floor, so he hadn't seen what I had.

Pointing to the bottle, I said, "That's why the door was open. Someone came in and put *Datura* in the wine. *Datura*, Ritter. Jimsonweed." He was trained in botany. I didn't have to explain how poisonous is was.

His head snapped up. "Oh, Elliana, how do you—"

"I smelled it. I still can." I grabbed my phone and searched for the number for the Poppyville Clinic.

"You can?" He shook his head. "What am I thinking? Of course *you* can." His eyes widened. "Wait. You're saying I drank wine with *locoweed* in it?" Yet another name for that beautiful plant. "That stuff's bad."

Reluctantly, I nodded. "It might be. Better to be safe than sorry."

I dialed. It rang four times before going to voice mail. Everyone had left for the day.

I switched on the flashlight feature on the phone and shone the light in Ritter's eyes.

His head jerked back. "What the . . . ?"

Ritter's pupils should have contracted with the sudden light but hadn't. He blinked at me like a stunned rabbit. A wave of dizziness moved through me as I tuned into what he was feeling.

There wasn't a scent combination I knew of that could counteract the effects of the tropane alkaloids that made jimsonweed a dangerous hallucinogenic—not to mention deadly. Quickly, I dialed 911.

"Hello, Nan? It's Ellie Allbright. Listen, I need you to call Dr. Scott and get her over to the clinic right away. Ritter has ingested some *Datura* . . . some jimsonweed. Tell her that. I'll meet her over there."

"You got it, Ellie." I heard typing. "You want the cops, too?"

I hesitated, but only for a second. "Yes. I think you'd better send them over, too." I hung up and turned to Ritter. "Come on, big guy."

He blinked at me again, and my stomach sank. The effects were already settling in.

I helped him with his coat and grabbed my own. "Dash, come."

The corgi whined.

"It's okay, sweetie. But I need you to stay in the shop for a little while." I didn't want him in the house with poisonous wine on the floor, and I also didn't want him alone in the Enchanted Garden if the person who had sneaked into my home could still be nearby. If I was going to be gone for too long, I'd call Astrid and have her come get him—even in the middle of the night, and even if she was with Dylan. She was my bestie at heart, and I knew I could count on her.

Dash trotted beside us as we started down the path toward Scents & Nonsense, glancing up at me every few seconds with worried brown eyes. Ritter kept looking around, his expression veering from confusion to delight to alarm. My heart sank. *Datura* caused hallucinations, and his behavior so soon after ingesting the plant scared me.

*What is he seeing?*

A sparkle of light in my peripheral vision made me

turn my head, but nothing was there when I looked. A wind chime tinkled in the still air. I smelled roses, though none were in bloom. Faraway laughter giggled at the edge of my perception.

I hadn't been poisoned, but strange things were always happening in the Enchanted Garden, especially at night.

My lips pressed together. *Great. This is a fine time for the plant spirits to tease me.*

Ritter's steps slowed, and he rubbed his eyes with his fingertips.

"Here." I put his hand on a sturdy trellis. "Hold on to this for a second."

He watched his own fingers curl around the metal bar as I sprinted to the back of the shop, twisted the key in the lock, flung open the sliding glass door, and urged a reluctant Dash inside to join a startled Nabokov. Quickly, I closed the door again and relocked it. Back at Ritter's side, I grabbed his arm and urged him toward the street.

All the while, a part of my brain was scrambling to make sense of how this could have happened. The plant matter couldn't have been soaking in the wine all that long. At the most, someone had added the *Datura* after I'd opened it, and that had only been twenty-four hours ago. Who could have—?

By the front fence, Ritter stumbled again. All thought of who had poisoned the wine flew out of my head, and I focused on getting my wobbly boyfriend into Thea's mint green step-side pickup.

"Here we go," I said cheerfully, and pulled open the gate.

My heart was pounding, and panic scratched at the edge of my thoughts. I pushed it away. I couldn't afford to panic. The gate swung closed behind us. Thankfully, the truck was parked right in front of Scents & Nonsense. I half pulled, half pushed Ritter toward it.

When we reached the passenger side, I said, "Just lean against the bed here for a second." I tugged at the door handle.

"Locked." The word came out slurred.

"Oh. Okay. Where are the keys?" I kept my tone as light as I could, though my throat was tight with worry.

He blinked at me.

"Ritter, honey, I need the keys. Did you leave them back in the living room?"

He took a deep shaky breath, and he shook his head. "No. They're in my pocket." He fumbled with his coat. "Elliana, I don't feel so great."

I pushed him against the truck with one hand and fished in his pocket with the other. "Let's just get you to the clinic. Ah! Got 'em," I said, holding up the keys.

"How much locoweed do you think I ingest . . . ingested?" He sounded truly frightened, and I didn't blame him. He knew very well what the effects of the poison were.

Shaking my head, I unlocked and opened the door of the classic old pickup. The hinges moaned. "You only had the one swallow. Right?"

"Um."

"Of the wine?"

"I think so," he said slowly.

Too slowly. One look told me how confused he was, and fear arrowed through my chest all over again.

"Can you get in the truck? We're going to see Dr. Scott."

He swayed, then gave a nod and pulled himself around the doorframe and lunged into the truck. I tried to help, but he was about twice my weight. A few adjustments later, and he was settled. I reached for the seat belt, then saw he was sitting on it, and thought better of it.

No time.

I slammed the door and ran around to the other side. Boosting myself behind the wheel, I fumbled for the seat adjustment. Not finding it immediately, I scooted to the edge of the seat, started up the old truck, and put it in gear. A car honked as I started to pull out onto the street, and my heart stuttered. Inhaling, I closed my eyes for a moment to regroup. It wouldn't help Ritter if we got into a wreck.

Looking carefully over my shoulder, I tried again. Once we were on the street, though, I couldn't help but break the pokey twenty-five-mile-an-hour speed limit.

Ritter swept his hand over his face. "Sweating. That fits. Skin feels clammy, even to me. The light's way too bright, so my pupils are dilated." Despite the fact that he was listing his own symptoms, the solid, scientific tone in which he was doing it reassured me.

I took a corner a little too fast. "Don't worry. The doc will fix you up."

"What else? Elliana! I can't remember what else!" Panic threaded his tone.

"What else what, Ritter?"

"What the other symptoms are!"

I reached over and grabbed for his arm but caught his wrist. Holding it firmly, I said, "Stay calm. You're going to be fine." I infused my voice with determined confidence, but I could feel his pulse racing beneath my fingers.

"Ooh." He breathed out the word like a mantra, then clamped his other hand over mine. "You are my gem, Elliana."

"Um, thanks." A small smile tugged at my lips. "That's very sweet."

"No! It's not sweet. It's the *truth*. You said you waited for me. Thank you for waiting for me, Elliana."

"You're welcome." I tried to pull my hand back, but he wouldn't let go. "Honey, I need my hand to shift gears."

His grip didn't loosen.

"And to steer. This puppy doesn't have power steering, you know."

"You waited for me," he said again, staring out the window.

Forcibly yanking my hand back, I downshifted just in time to make the next turn. When I glanced over again, he'd turned his head and was staring at me with big dark eyes. In the dash lights, I could see his pupils mostly eclipsed his irises.

"I waited for you, too," he said. "You don't know how long."

"Oh, yeah?" I said, thinking back to our discussion

that morning. Had something happened in Alaska that he was going to tell me about after all?

"For years. I waited for years and years and years to find someone that I love like I love you, Elliana." He sighed, and his eyes drifted closed. "So much."

Even though I knew he was high as a kite on loco-weed, his words still made my heart expand to fit my entire body, my entire *being*, and tears pricked at the corner of my eyelids. At the same time, that warmth met a jumble of worry and angst and fear that Ritter could be really sick or even die, guilt that it was my fault because the poison had no doubt been intended for me because of my questions about Eureka's murder and the missing manuscript, and finally, a fierce protec-tiveness.

Like, lioness fierce.

My foot pushed down on the accelerator a little more.

"I told them no," he said dreamily. His eyes were still closed. "No, no, no. Not again. Not going to lose my El-liana. Came too close this time."

What?

The sign for the Poppyville Clinic lit up the end of the block. A car pulled into the small parking lot from the other direction.

"Told who no?" I asked in a casual voice.

"The institute. Got 'nother grant. Glacier National Park. But no, no, no. Gotta stay with Elliana."

"Wait, what? Ritter, you got another grant? But you're not even done with the tundra project. When does the new one start?"

"Not gonna start at all. Said no. No, no . . ." He trailed off.

"Honey, I don't want you to say no." At least I didn't think so. "But I'd like to spend some time together before you have to leave again."

Truthfully, I wanted to spend a *lot* of time with him before he left, but I'd known from our first date that the nature of the work he loved would sometimes take him away from me.

"No, no . . . ," he repeated. I reached over and patted his wrist. "Okay. We'll talk about it later, okay?"

"Hate that sonofa . . ." His voice faded.

"Who do you hate?" I asked.

He rallied and spoke with the careful precision of a drunk. "Tanner. Spence. After my girl. Not gonna happen." He shook his head.

The truck bumped into the clinic's lot, the old shock absorbers lending an extra bounce to our arrival. I grabbed Ritter with one hand, but he had sunk into his seat like a contented sloth.

I shook him, and his eyes blinked open. "Are you telling me you were offered another research project, and you didn't take it because you thought there was something going on between Tanner Spence and me?" I demanded.

He blinked, then gave me a high-wattage, if bleary, smile.

His door flew open, and Dr. Scott stood on the other side of him. She wore a gray sweatshirt and hiking pants, and her face was scrubbed clean.

"Hey, Ellie," she said, climbing partway into the truck

and peering into Ritter's face by the light of the sign outside. "Nan thought you said jimsonweed. But that can't be right. It's too early in the season."

"Not in my greenhouse, it isn't," I said grimly as a Poppyville patrol car veered into the parking lot.

# CHAPTER 20

OFFICER Danielson was just in time to help us manhandle Ritter into the clinic. Moments later, Dr. Scott's nurse, Carla Higginbottom, barreled in the door. Soon my boyfriend was situated on the bed, and the doctor was reaching for a stethoscope.

"Ellie says Ritter ate some jimsonweed," she said to Carla, then looked up at me. "How much?"

"Just a little. Actually, he didn't eat it. It was soaking in some wine."

She stared at me. "I know you're a nature girl, Ellie, but why on God's green earth would you do that?"

Vehemently, I shook my head. "I wouldn't!"

"Are you saying it was an accident?"

"No, I don't think it was. I think someone put it there on purpose. The point is, he didn't drink very much, but

I don't know how strong it was. Please," I begged. "Just take care of him."

She glanced at Officer Danielson, who was standing by the wall taking down everything into his notebook. "Okay," she said. "I'll leave the hows and whys to you and the police." She turned her attention back to Ritter. "Heartbeat and respiration appear slow, but not seriously compromised." She leaned over and flashed a penlight in his eyes.

He knocked it out of her hand, and I ducked as it flew over my head. It broke into several pieces as it hit the wall behind me. "Don't do that!" He sat up and glared at her, then looked around the room with wide eyes before sinking back down to a prone position.

"Ritter!" I moved toward him.

"Stay back," Dr. Scott barked. "He's suffering from scopolamine and atropine poisoning. Carla, see if we have any Antilirium. And grab the lorazepam while you're at it." Her gaze softened as she looked back at me. "Sorry, Ellie. I'm going to sedate him. Jimsonweed can make people combative, and I'm not taking the chance."

I felt the blood drain from my face as I whispered, "Okay." Then: "Do you need to pump his stomach?"

She came over and put her hand on my shoulder. "That won't be necessary. Ellie. He's going to be okay. Really. I can tell this is a mild case. But the poison has to wear off, and he's going to be here for a while."

Tears threatened, and I set my jaw. "So am I, then."

"Of course. Why don't you wait in the other room while Carla and I get him settled?" She and Danielson exchanged glances. "Maybe you could give the officer your statement about what happened."

I nodded reluctantly. I didn't want to leave Ritter but knew it would be better if I got out of the way.

"Good girl," she said. If anyone else had said that to me, I might have been offended, but coming from Dr. Scott it somehow made me feel better.

Danielson followed me down the maroon-carpeted hallway to the waiting area, where he flipped on the lights. The room smelled faintly of antiseptic, toner, and a whiff of Jean Naté perfume over by the receptionist's desk. We settled into a couple of boxy, peach-colored chairs.

He quirked an eyebrow. "So? You've certainly been busy since I saw you yesterday afternoon at Eureka Sanford's house. Asking questions around town, I hear."

I sighed.

"So how did your guy in there manage to ingest jimsonweed? You said something about wine?" He sounded skeptical.

"That's right." I took a deep breath. "Well, not right, but correct. Someone stuffed leaves from *Datura stramonium* in an open bottle of wine. Ritter drank some before I could stop him."

"So, you noticed it first?"

"Yes." I didn't elaborate.

"Saw it?"

"Smelled it."

He stared at me.

I shrugged. "I'm a perfumer. I have a fine-honed sense of smell."

"Ah." He made a note.

"Wine is one of the best ways to extract the chemical compounds in plants," I explained. "Because some are soluble in water, and others in alcohol. Either someone knew that, or they got lucky."

"I see. And have you and Mr. Nelson been getting along okay?"

"Of course . . . what? You don't think *I* poisoned him, do you?" Even as the words tumbled out, I could suddenly see how someone might think that.

My wine.

My jimsonweed.

My herbal expertise.

And I'd known better than to drink the wine myself.

*Dang it!*

"Just gathering the facts," he said in a neutral tone.

"I'd never, ever . . . Listen, whoever did this probably took the jimsonweed from my greenhouse. Yes," I said pointedly. "I know that doesn't look good. But I'm pretty sure it was intended for me, since the wine was in my house and, as you said, I've been asking questions about Eureka's murder. I'm supposed to be the one in there." I gestured toward where Ritter lay, probably knocked out by now. Tears threatened, and I looked away.

"Any idea who could have done it, then?"

Who'd had access the night I opened the wine?

Someone who had been at Eureka's memorial gathering and come through the open back door. The greenhouse had been open. People had been going in and out and all over the garden, chatting and connecting as they told stories and shared recollections about the deceased professor. And while I'd been careful to make sure the front door of my home had been locked so no one would take it upon themselves to explore the cute little tiny house, I probably had left the back door, with its only access from the meadow, unlocked.

I told Officer Danielson as much, and he dutifully took notes. He did not offer his own opinion, however.

"I'd like to follow you home," he said. "It sounds like it could be a crime scene, and I need to collect evidence."

Appalled, I stared at him for a few seconds. "I'm not going anywhere until I know Ritter is okay." I thought, then dug in my pocket and took out my key ring. Removing my house key, I handed it to him. "Feel free to go in and do whatever you have to do. You know where I live?"

He nodded and took the key.

"Some of the wine landed on the floor and ottoman when I tried to stop Ritter from drinking it, but there should be plenty still in the bottle for testing."

A brisk nod, then: "I'll take that to check for fingerprints and see what else I can find."

"My fingerprints are going to be on it," I said matter-of-factly. "And Ritter's. The back door was open when we got home, so check that, too."

"Your prints are on file?" he asked.

I nodded. "They took them last year. Will you be calling one of the detectives to help?"

One eyebrow flickered up. "Probably. Give me your cell number."

I did, but when he left, I felt more relieved that he'd

stopped quizzing me than confident that they'd find the person who'd put Ritter in Poppyville's version of the emergency room.

O NCE Ritter was settled and dozing, I went out to the reception area to call Thea. I could hear the television on in the background when she answered. There was a stunned silence after I told her what happened.

Then she said, "He's going to be okay?"

"Dr. Scott says he will be," I said. "Though she's going to keep him at the clinic overnight."

"I'll come right down."

"He's sedated, so he won't know you're here." I left out that Dr. Scott had put him under in case he became violent.

"But he'll be fine," Thea said.

I understood her need to know for sure. "He didn't swallow very much, and I got him to the doctor immediately. He gave me a scare, but I believe Dr. Scott."

"Idiot," she said.

"What?"

"Not you. That brother of mine. He has a degree in botany, for heaven's sake. He should know better than to eat jimsonweed."

"Oh, no, Thea. He had no idea. Someone got into my house and put it in an open bottle of wine. I think the *Datura* came from my greenhouse."

"Someone poisoned my brother on purpose?" She sounded outraged, as well she should have.

"Er, I think someone meant to poison me, not Ritter. But I smelled the *Datura* and didn't drink it."

She swore. "Is this because you've been asking questions about Eureka's death?"

I sighed. "Probably. Thea, I'm so sorry."

"Oh, honey. I'm not blaming you. You must feel horrible enough already. I just want to know who did this."

"Well, I think it was someone who was at the memorial this afternoon."

Silence.

"If the jimsonweed came from my greenhouse," I went on. "It isn't growing this early around town yet, so it either came from the plant I've been overwintering in my greenhouse or . . . It's a popular ornamental. I don't suppose you have any at the nursery right now?"

"No. I don't typically carry it, anyway. If someone wants it for a landscaping project, I special order it. So, let's see. Who was there today?"

I listed everyone I remembered. She added a few names, then asked, "Who out of those people are on your suspect list?"

"My . . . ?"

"Don't be coy, Ellie. My brother's been poisoned." Her voice was hard.

"Right. Well, I don't know anything for sure, but there are a few people that I wonder about."

Dylan Wong. Odell Radcliffe. Warren and Trixie Perez. Who else?

Before Thea could ask for particulars, I said, "Ritter was a little loopy on the way to the clinic. He said some, er, interesting things."

"Like what?" she asked.

"Some really nice things," I hedged. "But also something about a research project at Glacier National Park."

"Right. I'm surprised he hadn't already told you about that. He was pretty excited. It has something to do with tracking the flora and fauna in the areas where the glaciers have been receding. It starts in July."

"Oh, Thea."

"What?" Alarm rang from the word.

"He said he told them no."

"He said . . . no, he didn't. He wouldn't. That project is perfect for Ritter. He loves Glacier, and it taps into his botanical expertise and his passion for the environment."

"It sounds perfect for him! But he said he turned them down, so he could stay here with me."

Silence, then I heard her let out a disappointed whoosh of air.

"I didn't ask him to do that, Thea! I didn't know anything about it until he was talking on the way to the clinic! I know how much he loves his work. Dang it!" I closed my eyes. "Why didn't he talk to me about it?"

"I don't know," she said.

I sighed. "I do. Because of Tanner Spence."

"Ah."

"Jeez, you, too? I've been true blue as could be while Ritter was gone, but he doesn't trust me not to dump him if he leaves again."

"And you won't?"

"Of course not. Listen, your brother and I are figuring some things out, but we really care for each other. I'd never ask him to choose between me and his work—just as I know he'd never ask me to make that choice, either." Anger surged through my next words. "He should have at least talked to me before turning down that project. It might be his decision, but it affects both of us, and that's not fair."

"You're right. Maybe he can call them back," she said.

"Maybe. He's not in any shape to talk to anyone right now, though. I'll have him call you in the morning, okay? I'm sure he'll be feeling better then."

"Are you going to stay there all night, Ellie?"

"I don't want him to wake up alone, especially if he's still feeling the effects of the jimsonweed."

"That makes me feel better," she said. "I'm happy to come spell you, if you'd like."

"No need. Keep your phone nearby, and I'll call if anything happens. But I've got this."

"All right. Thanks for letting me know. And, Ellie?"

"Yeah?"

"You're good for my big brother. I'm glad you two are together."

"Me, too, Thea. Me, too."

I called Astrid next. She was happy to go pick up Dash and keep him for the night. When I asked if she was home, she hedged.

"Not at the moment, but I'm on my way, and I'll just swing by your place. Don't you worry about a thing, Ellie. And I'm so sorry to hear about Ritter. He's in good hands, though."

"I know. Thanks. I'll check in with you in the a.m."

* * *

THE tranquilizer had done its work, and Ritter was deep asleep when I went back in. I stood by his bed for several minutes, watching his sleeping face and listening to his slow breath as his earlier words replayed in my mind.

*I waited for years and years and years to find someone that I love like I love you.*

My stomach was clenched with worry, my heart welled with tenderness, and beneath it all, a tight fury burned. I'd wanted to find justice for Eureka, and I'd wanted to learn more about the Xavier manuscript, but now someone had gone and hurt the man I loved. Come hell or high water, I was determined to find out who.

And to see that they were punished.

Dr. Scott brought me a blanket and said I was welcome to sleep on the sofa in the reception area if the chair by the bed became too uncomfortable.

"I'll be in my office if you need me." She side-eyed Ritter and perched on the edge of the other chair in the room. "I have a cot in there for times like these when I want to stay close to a patient overnight. I'll check on him every hour and a half or so."

"Thanks, Dr. Scott."

"Eliza," she corrected. "Did you and Officer Danielson figure out what happened?"

I shook my head. "I'm pretty sure it has something to do with Eureka Sanford's murder, though."

"And with you investigating it?"

I made a face. "Does everyone in town think I'm doing that?"

"Pretty much," she said, not unkindly.

"Well, of course I want her killer brought to justice," I said, not elaborating on my earlier thoughts of punishment.

She nodded and stepped to the bedside and looked down at Ritter, then longer at the monitor at the head of the bed. Finally, her gaze met mine. "There's nothing you can do here. You sure you don't want to go home?"

I shook my head. "No, thanks. I'd rather stay."

She smiled. "Okay."

When she'd left, I called Lupe's cell. She didn't answer, so I left a message. "I told Officer Danielson what happened, but I wanted to let you know. I can't say for sure that it has anything to do with Eureka's murder, but, well, it probably does, don't you think? Anyway, I'll talk to you later. Bye."

# CHAPTER 21

A LITTLE before six the next morning Dr. Scott's voice wended into my consciousness, and I struggled awake on the sofa in the reception area. It took me a few seconds to realize it was coming from the other room, where Ritter had slept through most of the night, only waking twice.

The first time, he'd been disoriented and didn't seem to know who we were for several seconds. The second time, he'd sighed and murmured my name before his breathing deepened and he drifted off again. That, along with his heartbeat and respiration returning to normal, had reassured me, and I'd abandoned the chair beside his bed to spend the rest of the night on the sofa in the reception area.

I swung my feet to the floor and padded toward his room in my stocking feet. Dr. Scott stood over him, checking his vitals and murmuring into a recorder. Ritter was still out cold. She looked up and smiled when I came into the room.

"He's doing well. Did you get any sleep?" Her expression was kind.

"More than I thought I would," I admitted. "That couch is deceptively comfortable. How about you?"

"It's been a while since I've had to stay all night with a patient," she said. "Most emergencies we treat and then ship off to the hospital in Silver Wells."

"But not Ritter."

"We had the drug to counteract the poison here. After that, he just needed some time. Still needs a bit more, actually. Go home, Ellie. I'll call you if there's any change."

Rubbing my eyes, I nodded. "Okay. I need to shower and get ready to open the shop." Dropping my hand, I snagged her gaze. "Thank you, Dr. Scott. I was really scared last night."

She smiled. "I know. Getting him here so quickly was key. You did good, Ellie."

I kissed Ritter's forehead. His skin was soft against my lips, not too cool and not too warm. I put my hand on his chest and felt his steady heartbeat beneath my palm.

He was really going to be okay.

Relief calming some of my angst, I said good-bye to Dr. Scott and walked out to Thea's truck. The doctor's words made me feel better for a few steps, but I couldn't help thinking how close Ritter and I had both come to serious illness or even dying.

And whoever had tried to kill me was still out there.

\* \* \*

I GUIDED the Wrangler toward Astrid's house. A few
early risers were getting in their daily walks and runs
in the thin dawn light, but it seemed most of Poppyville
hadn't woken up yet. I gambled that Astrid would be up
and busily baking already, and when I pulled to the curb
in front of her white craftsman-style house, sure enough,
the lights were on.

The small square lawn had been recently mowed, and
the smell of freshly cut grass filled the air around me as
I hurried up the front sidewalk. Bright red tulips waited
for the sun to touch them, a few of the blooms nibbled by
rabbits during the night. Rubbing the back of my neck, I
absently took in the fact that the hyacinths in the pot on
the porch needed to be watered.

Astrid called for me to come inside when I rang the
bell, and the smells of sugar, chocolate, and melted butter about knocked me over when I pushed the door open.
Dash ran out of the kitchen, greeting me by jumping up
and putting his front paws on my leg. Stooping, I dug my
fingers into the thick ruff around his neck.

"Hey, buddy. How was spending the night with your
favorite vet tech?"

"It was great. We watched *Lady and the Tramp*," Astrid said from the kitchen, where she was pulling out a
baking sheet covered with cookies that were half light
brown, half dark brown. Her apron read I COOK AS GOOD
AS I LOOK.

I laughed. "One of his favorite movies."

Astrid's house was a one-bedroom, one-bath cottage

with a small room toward the back that she used as an office for her pet-sitting business. The carpet needed to be replaced, but with the myriad of animals that came and went, she'd kept putting it off. A sprawling sofa dominated the living room, flanked by overflowing bookcases. Art prints of dogs and cats decorated the walls. Perhaps the most notable thing about the room, however, was the fact that there was no television.

In the kitchen, I settled onto one of four vintage vinyl-and-chrome chairs arranged around the Formica table and gratefully accepted the mug of steaming coffee she offered.

"How's Ritter?" she asked.

"Better," I said.

"You didn't have a chance to tell me exactly what happened last night."

So, sipping coffee and sampling one of her half-cookie, half-brownie confections, I filled her in on the details.

When I was finished, she slid onto the chair opposite and regarded me with concern. "Ellie, if that jimsonweed came from your greenhouse, then someone grabbed it during the memorial for Eureka."

I nodded. "I think you're right. Of course, I don't keep the greenhouse locked, so a customer could have sneaked out there anytime in the last few days, but why would they? I don't feel like I've found out anything all that useful during my so-called investigation. And how did the poisoner get into my house? They'd have to go around to the back."

"That wouldn't be that difficult. What have you found out?" Astrid asked.

For a few seconds, I gathered my thoughts. Then I

started ticking off items on my fingers. "One, Eureka's nephew and niece-in-law inherited her house upon her death, and apparently they're strapped for cash enough that Trixie is waitressing at the Roux Grill. They also may have broken into her house. Or not. Either way, they had a motive to kill her. If one or both did, they might have taken the Xavier manuscript thinking they could sell it for a chunk of money."

I held up a second finger and smiled apologetically. "Dylan Wong is supposedly here in Poppyville for estate sales, but there aren't any listed in the paper, and he has a record of dealing in illegal antiquities—which would give him a motive for stealing the Xavier manuscript."

Astrid rolled her eyes and made a derisive noise. "Ellie, Dylan already admitted to making a mistake about those Indian artifacts," she said. "And for the record, he's been using Poppyville as a base in order to attend several estate sales in the area. He's going to one in Silver Wells this morning, and then to one over by Placerville tomorrow."

"Okay, that makes sense. And your little show in the Roux Grill did convince me that he's not a killer, so there's that." I held up another finger. "Odell Radcliffe said he came for the time capsule ceremony, and to see his former teaching colleague, but I think there might be more to it than that."

"Like what?"

"I think he might have still had a crush on Eureka. They were actually a couple over a decade ago."

Astrid whistled, which brought Dash running from the other room. She absently gave him a treat from the endless supply in her pocket as she asked, "No kidding? But what's his motive for killing her?"

"I don't know. Something to do with the book she was writing? He seems to bring it up a lot. Or maybe he killed her in a fit of passion after she turned down his advances."

She frowned. "He and Eureka did talk for quite a while in the park after you left that afternoon."

I leaned forward. "Did you hear what they were saying?"

"Nah. They were off by themselves. Probably chatting about old times. They seemed friendly enough."

I sat back. "Yeah, he certainly appeared upset about Eureka's death. Besides, Lupe told me he has an alibi for the time of the murder."

"It's his daughter I feel bad for," Astrid said. "She seems so lonely. Did you see her sitting all by herself at the memorial?"

"Yeah. It was nice of you to go talk to her. I think she'd be okay if her father would cut the apron strings, so to speak. She's smart, but needs to make a life away from Odell."

"If Odell has an alibi, why does he get a finger?" my friend asked, looking pointedly at my hand.

I dropped it and picked up my coffee mug. "He shouldn't, I guess. But there's something about him . . ."

"Like there's something about Dylan?" Luckily, she seemed to be teasing.

"There is something about Dylan," I said in all seriousness. "Please be careful."

She started to wave that away, then paused. Nodded. "Okay. I know you're just looking out for me."

Gratified, I went back to thinking about murder suspects.

"What about the chief's idea that someone wanted to steal the gold nugget, ended up with that old palimpsest, as Dylan called it, and then had to kill Eureka to cover their tracks?" she asked.

I gave a facial shrug. "It's not impossible. And that could have been anyone in town. Even someone who left right after the ceremony and then came back in the dead of night. The police are following up with everyone who was staying at the Hotel California during that time."

"What about bed-and-breakfasts or the Holiday Inn on the edge of town?"

"I don't know. Probably. But Astrid, if the killer was one of those people, why would they try to poison me?"

"Maybe the jimsonweed is unrelated to the murder."

Now I stared. "Great. That's a big help. Now someone wants to poison me out of the blue?"

She grimaced. "Sorry."

Taking a deep breath, I checked the time. "Listen, I'm going to run over to the stables. I've got an aromatherapy blend for Gessie's skittish horse."

*And while I'm there, I might as well ask whether Eureka talked to Gessie about her book research.*

"Here," she said, rising. "Take her some brookies."

"Gladly. But don't be surprised if I sneak another one."

N ow the streets were beginning to bustle with families heading out for Saturday morning breakfast. The bakery, Juke Diner, and Roux Grill would be packed soon, while the hotel guests filed into the Empire Room for more upscale fare. That made me think of their eggs Benedict, and I grumpily wondered for a moment if I was ever going to get a real dinner again. Then I thought of Ritter stuck in bed and felt bad. Not only had he missed dinner the night before, but also it had been my fault.

I shuddered, thinking what might have happened if I hadn't smelled the *Datura* in the wine. Another shudder ran through me as I considered again that someone wanted to kill me.

Still, the smell of the warm brookies filled Thea's pickup, and I couldn't help slipping one out of the container as I drove. Dash watched with avid eyes.

"Sorry, buddy. These have too much chocolate in them for puppies to eat."

He huffed and lay down on the seat.

I swung by Scents & Nonsense to pick up the chamomile, vetiver, and ylang-ylang combination for Gessie's horse. Telling Dash to stay in the shop, I went out back and through the Enchanted Garden to the greenhouse. Expecting to find several leaves had been pinched off the *Datura stramonium*, I discovered instead that the whole plant was missing. Had the poisoner taken the whole thing, or did I have Officer Danielson to thank for its absence?

I grabbed the spare key from under a pot of sprouting basil . . . and paused.

What if someone found this and returned it after using it to get into my house?

But wouldn't I or someone else have seen them if it had been during the gathering for Eureka?

Shaking my head, I let myself inside to change out of my wispy blue skirt, which was looking a bit worse for wear after I'd slept in it all night.

However, before going upstairs to dig out a pair of jeans and a long-sleeved T-shirt, I paused in my postage-stamp living room to survey the damage. The wine stain on the ottoman would never come out, and I didn't want to be reminded of what had happened every time I used it. Grabbing it, I went to the back door to put it out on the deck. That's when I saw the fine dusting of powder on the knob and doorframe.

There wasn't any police tape in or around the house, so I went ahead and carefully opened the door. After depositing the offending ottoman temporarily out of sight, I went back and saw the stain on the wood floor wouldn't be so easy to dismiss. A dark splotch had soaked into the wood. I could scrub and scrub, but it would always look like blood to me. The boards would have to be replaced. In the meantime, I'd cover it with the throw rug from the kitchen.

I found a note on the counter. A receipt, actually. It listed the wine bottle, an intact wineglass, and the pieces of the other, as well as the potted jimsonweed from the greenhouse. It was signed by Detective Lupe Garcia.

That made me feel better, not only because Danielson had involved a detective, but also because it meant that even if he'd been there, Max Lang hadn't had the run of my house by himself.

As I ran up the stairway, I checked my phone and saw Lupe had left me a text. I'd been so discombobulated when I awoke at the clinic that I hadn't even checked. It said she'd call me in the morning.

Dressed in soft warm clothes, I relocked the house, pocketed the key, and went to grab Gessie's aromatherapy blend and my corgi. I took Thea's Terra Green pickup, hoping she might be at the nursery so I could return it. I caught her about to go check on Ritter in her personal hatchback. We left the truck parked in front of the retail shop, and she drove me back to my Wrangler, which was still in the parking lot across the street from the shop. I updated her on her brother's condition on the way. Then she left for the clinic, and I boosted Dash into the Jeep so we could head to our next stop.

The stables were on the far north end of Corona Street, near a curve in the river. Back in the day, it had been the heart of transportation in Poppyville, before the railway had been added to the mix. Now Gessie offered trail rides to visiting dudes, along with hayrides complete with bonfires and chuck wagon feeds. In addition to catering to tourists, she boarded horses, gave both Western and English riding lessons, and occasionally hosted hunter jumper and dressage competitions.

Hay dust and horse musk greeted my nose as we pulled into the parking lot and got out of the Jeep. Gessie was in the outdoor arena with a young helmeted woman on a bay gelding. It appeared the rider was having difficulty with her mount, which would pause every few steps to crow-hop to one side. She was frustrated, and even from where I was, I could see her tension wasn't helping the situation.

Suddenly the horse bucked, and I saw sunlight between the rider's posterior and her pancake saddle. She landed back on the horse without falling but was half splayed across its back and tugging hard at the reins.

Gessie stepped directly in front of the horse and held out her hands to each side, low and with her palms facing the animal. Everything about her radiated calm. I could hear her quiet, wordless murmur to the horse before she said flatly to the rider, "Get off."

The horse hopped to the side again as the young woman swung her leg over and swiftly dismounted, but she made it to the ground. Her eyes were wide as she handed Gessie the reins.

Immediately, the horse quieted. Gessie murmured again, then approached it and rubbed it along the withers. Her hand continued to the cinch that went under the horse's chest to hold on the saddle, and she frowned. Quickly, she loosened the leather strap and turned to her student.

"This is pushing against the grain of his hair. Bob here is sensitive, and if he's uncomfortable after you tack him, he'll try to throw you when you've been working him awhile. Next time make very sure the hair is lying smoothly under the leather. But don't let him bully you. Believe me, he'll try it." She patted the horse, and his lips pulled back from his teeth in a comical smile.

She grinned and handed the reins to the woman, who took them with a nod.

"Okay, I'll remember," she said. "Come on, Bob. We're going to be friends yet."

Gessie came over to the fence where Dash and I waited. "Ellie! Bit early for you, isn't it?"

I briefly explained about the previous night's adventures as I dug out the bottle of essential oils from my bag and handed it to her.

"Good lord," she said when I'd finished telling her about Ritter's ordeal. "That's horrible. I've got coffee on. You look like you could use a cup."

"Another cup. Yes, I could. And Astrid wanted me to give you these." I handed her the container of brookies.

Her eyes lit up. "Well, this is a treat!"

I followed her while Dash went to romp with Gessie's Bernese mountain dog. Her office was a crowded space across the barn aisle from the tack room. The shuffle of horse hooves and whuffle of their breath joined the strong flavors of leather and saddle soap in the air.

Over my second steaming mug of caffeine, I settled onto a folding chair across from her desk and asked about Eureka.

# CHAPTER 22

☙

"Yes, Eureka was here," Gessie said. "She was asking about a death that occurred here in the stables back in the gold rush days."

Half-jittery from sugar and caffeine, I scooted to the edge of my chair. "A death?" That fit with what Maria had said Eureka was researching at the library—only she'd called it a *tragic* death.

She gave a little nod. "Said Eliza Scott told her to check with me, but I'm afraid I wasn't much help. Nothing I've found here referred to anything like that."

Frowning, I considered for a moment. "Did she give any details about the death? Was it an accident?"

"Suicide."

I blanched. "Oh." *Tragic indeed.*

"What else did she say?"

"She wanted to see my safe."

My forehead wrinkled. "Whatever for?"

"Because it's old, I guess."

Gessie got up and squeezed past me. I rose and followed her into the tack room. Bypassing the cubbyholes stuffed with grooming tools, bits, rope halters, and leg wraps, she shoved aside a pile of brightly colored saddle blankets to reveal a huge, four-foot-by-four-foot safe.

It was black, with a combination smack-dab in the middle of the door over the words *Thayer & Edwards*. It looked as old as the Heritage House cabin. She grabbed the door and it swung open easily to reveal a pile of paperwork.

"This thing was here when I bought the place a couple decades ago. Lock was busted then, but the door closes, so it's still fire safe. Mostly, I keep vet records, breeding papers, sales records, and things like that in it."

"Wow. It looks like it should be in Heritage House," I said. "Is that why Eureka wanted to see it?"

She shook her head. "I'd told her about it when we were putting together the displays, and she said it was just too big for the space. It's not in very good shape, either, as you can see." Her eyebrow quirked up as she looked over at me. "No, Eureka wanted to measure the inside of the thing. Said she wanted to see if something would fit in there."

I blinked. "Like what?"

Gessie closed the door and replaced the blankets. "I have no idea. She acted very mysterious about the whole thing, but she seemed quite pleased after measuring it."

Baffled, I followed her out to the barnyard.

Her Bernese mountain dog and my corgi had been

joined by a broad-faced man who smelled of tobacco and earth.

"Hey, Bongo Pete," I said.

"Hey, Elliana Allbright. Thanks for bringing Dash to see me."

"He likes to visit," I said.

Pete smiled at me, a sweet, gentle expression that was part quiet innocence and part unease. I knew I wasn't making him uneasy, and neither were Gessie or the dogs, whom he loved. Pete was extremely sensitive to the world around him, to the point where it grew painful and overwhelming at times. At least, that was what I'd gathered from our conversations.

Today, however, I was getting a strange feeling from him. A shiver ran down my back like a mouse. It was familiar in a way. With a start, I realized it was the way the Xavier manuscript had made me feel.

And then I remembered seeing Bongo Pete going into Raven Creek Park right before Eureka's memorial. He could have easily come around the back side of my fence to the back porch of my house. Come inside. Found the wine.

But why? He wouldn't hurt a fly. And it wouldn't explain how he got the jimsonweed from my greenhouse. He wasn't at Eureka's memorial.

Though I'd just told Astrid an hour earlier that it would be easy for anyone to go into the greenhouse from the Enchanted Garden. It was never locked.

That still didn't explain why. No, Bongo Pete wasn't my poisoner. So what was this feeling I was getting from him?

"Hey, Bongo Pete," Gessie said in the same easy, low tone she used with her horses. "You want to help me muck stalls this afternoon?"

His face lit up. "Can I?"

She smiled. "You bet."

"You like to muck stalls, Pete?" I asked.

"*Bongo* Pete," he said, just as he always said it when you forgot to call him that. And sure enough, he turned around to show the back of his T-shirt, which read KING OF THE BONGOS. He had a collection of them, gifts from Biddy's T-Shirt Emporium. "I love it. The horses say thank you, and Gessie always makes me a big ol' pile of sandwiches to take down to my tent."

I wasn't really listening anymore, though. When Pete had turned around, I'd seen something unusual sticking out of his pocket.

Parchment.

"Pete?" I started. "Sorry—Bongo Pete? Can I see what's in your back pocket?"

"Sure." He strode over, pulled the folded pages out of his pocket, and handed them to me.

It buzzed against my skin like a gentle live wire. Oh so carefully, I unfolded the roughly bound book.

Gessie looked over my shoulder. "Uh-oh."

I raised my head and met her eyes, then looked back down at the Xavier manuscript Pete had unaccountably been carrying around in his jeans pocket.

"Pete . . . Bongo Pete? How do you happen to have this?" I asked.

He looked alarmed for a second, but when I just

smiled and waited, he relaxed. "Found it. It doesn't say much."

It fell open to the same page I'd seen briefly after the mayor had taken everything out of the time capsule. It showed the marigold and the now familiar depiction of the tree of life.

Pete's voice deepened as he said, "Cruelty. Grief. Jealousy. Malice."

My head jerked up. "You can read this?" Because he'd just recited the words that spiraled around the marigold. Words that neither one of us should have been able to read.

"Nah. I can't read. Least not very good." He leaned over and looked at the page in my hands. The smell of tobacco grew stronger as he said, "Violent death."

I started. There was something like that on the page. And I remembered those words in my grandmother's spidery penmanship in her journal.

Gessie put her hand on my arm. "No one can read that, Ellie. Don't pay him any attention."

"Well, I can't read, but I can *see*. I can tell," Pete said, obviously insulted.

"I believe you," I said, ignoring Gessie. "See this symbol?" I pointed to the tree circled with spirals.

"Kell," he said.

I involuntarily took a step back.

Gessie caught my arm. "Ellie?"

*Violent death times three*
*Will summon thee*
*Daughter of Kell*

"This is Kell?" I asked, pointing to the picture of the tree again.

He responded with a sweep of his arm. "It's *all* Kell." He smiled widely and leaned his head back, so the sun shone directly into his face. "All of it. The trees, the grasses, the plants. You know, Elliana Allbright."

And somehow, I did.

Could it be true? Bongo Pete was talking about nature, the whole of the natural world, but not just that. Could it be true? Could he also mean Kell included the plant energies I'd always been able to sense, like my mother and her mother before her?

Still, that didn't explain what "daughter of Kell" meant.

"Bongo Pete, I'm not sure I understand. Who is Kell's daughter?"

He shrugged and grinned at me.

"Oh, now," I said. "Come on. I bet you know."

He frowned, and I could see he was becoming agitated.

"Ellie, what is wrong with you?" Gessie muttered at my elbow. "You know this is all nonsense."

Bongo Pete looked over my shoulder, and his eyes grew wide.

"Oho! I come to ask Ms. King here about a note we found in Eureka Sanford's house about some old safe, and this is what I find."

I whirled to Detective Max Lang approaching from the parking lot. He stopped beside me, gazing down at the Xavier manuscript I held in my hand like it was manna from heaven.

"Well, lookie here. It's the missing parchment from the time capsule that you were so *very* fascinated by. Right there in your hot little hands." He laughed, and it wasn't a pleasant sound. "I *knew* you took it." He grabbed it away.

"She didn't take it!" Pete said, stepping forward. He was shaking, and I could feel his combined rage and fear.

"It's all right." Gessie stepped to his side and put her hand on his arm.

He shrugged her off. "You leave Ellie alone!"

"Got a new boyfriend, Allbright?" Max sneered, the manuscript crinkling in his fist.

"Please be careful of that," I begged. "None of us should be touching it with our bare hands. The oil in our skin—"

"So, she didn't take it," Max said, ignoring my plea. "Does that mean you took it, Pete?"

"Bongo . . . ," he began, then stopped. He shook his head. "I found it."

Sudden hope soared in my chest. "Where?" I demanded. "Where did you find it?"

"I'll ask the questions here," Max said, sounding like a caricature of himself. He turned to Pete. "So? Where'd you find it?"

Pete glared at Max and clamped his mouth shut.

*Thanks a lot, Max.* I wanted to pummel the idiot.

"Tell me," he demanded.

Pete shook his head.

"Well, then, I guess I was right about Ellie. Come on, Allbright. Let's go to the station."

"No!" Pete said.

Max smiled that joyless smile again. "Then maybe I should take you to the station instead."

Gessie stepped forward. "Oh, for heaven's sake, Detective Lang. Stop badgering the man."

"I need to know where this was."

Her eyes narrowed. "Give us a minute." She led Pete several feet away and began speaking to him earnestly.

"What did you find at Eureka's?" I asked Max.

"What?"

"You said you came here to ask Gessie about something you found at Eureka's."

He gave me an unbelieving look. "You think I'm going to tell you?"

"Why? Are you afraid I'll solve her murder before you do?" I regretted the words the second they were out of my mouth. This was not the time to poke this particular bear.

"Careful," he warned. "I don't think you'd want Chief Gibbon to know you said that."

I bit back my retort and looked away.

"Now, don't start crying."

"Don't be ridiculous." I blinked rapidly. I was running on too little sleep and food, and too much caffeine and worry about Ritter. I couldn't help it if I felt a little . . . fragile.

Gessie and Pete returned to where we stood. "Bongo Pete," she said. "You can go ahead and tell them what you told me."

He looked at the ground. "By the dumpster at the Grill."

"The Roux Grill?" I asked. "You found the manuscript by the dumpster in the alley."

"Allbright," Max gritted out.

"Oops. Sorry."

But Pete was nodding.

"Maybe the rest of the stuff from the time capsule is still there!" Gessie said.

"Behind the Roux Grill," Max said.

Pete nodded.

"Okay. I'm taking this"—he held up the Xavier manuscript in his hand—"as evidence. And, Pete? Don't you leave town, you hear?" Max turned on his heel and strode toward the parking lot.

Bongo Pete's brow furrowed as he looked between Gessie and me. "Why would I leave Poppyville? I like it here."

# CHAPTER 23

I BROKE the speed limit all the way to the Roux Grill, but Max beat me there. So did Lupe and Chief Gibbon. They were all standing around the dumpster as if they were waiting for a bus. Harris was with them.

Leaving Dash in the Wrangler, I hurried to join them.

"What are you doing here, Ms. Allbright?" Chief Gibbon asked.

Max squared his shoulders and said in a respectful tone, "She was there when the homeless guy told me he found the papers from the time capsule here, boss."

"Mm." Gibbon regarded me dispassionately for a few moments.

"Just have to stick your nose it, don't you?" Harris asked.

I ignored him. "Are the rest of the items from the time capsule here?"

Lupe glanced at the chief, then shook her head. "No. Nothing is."

"What do you mean?"

"The trash was taken away this morning. Pete must have found it yesterday," Gibbon said.

"Are you telling me it all could be in the landfill?"

Lupe nodded. "Looks that way. We were hoping there might be some video footage back here, but Mr. Madigan"—she nodded toward Harris—"explained that he's seen no need to install security cameras in the alley."

"It's Poppyville!" he protested. "The only nefarious things going on in this alley are my busboys sneaking out for a cigarette and the local cats prowling for scraps."

I leaned my back against the brick wall, suddenly tired and very sad. Running my hands over my face, I sighed. At least the Xavier manuscript had been recovered. Even if it was in a police locker someplace, and I couldn't get to it, I was still thankful.

When I looked up, everyone was watching me.

"What?" I asked.

"Do you have any ideas about how the manuscript might have found its way into the trash?" Chief Gibbon asked me.

"Well, I sure didn't put it there."

"I wasn't implying that you had. But you were talking with Mr. Wong about it yesterday." He nodded toward where the smell of bacon and onions wafted from the back door of the restaurant. "In there. Detective Lang and I witnessed it."

"He's an antiques dealer," I said. "We thought he

might know something about how a thief would get rid of a rare piece of stolen property like that."

Gibbon and Lupe exchanged looks.

"And I was particularly curious because Dylan Wong was arrested for doing just that a few years ago. Which you apparently already know."

Max and Harris looked at each other and smirked, but the chief simply nodded. "Is there anything else you can tell us to help the investigation?"

*He wants my help? Really?*

Too bad there wasn't anything I could tell him. "Nothing you don't already know." After all, Lupe knew about Warren and Trixie Perez, and I didn't want to bring Trixie up in front of Harris in case he didn't know he'd hired a murder suspect.

"I don't suppose you've made any progress toward finding out who tried to poison me last night and ended up sending Ritter Nelson to the clinic," I said.

Harris' eyes widened.

Lupe grimaced. "Sorry, Ellie. Nothing so far. There were only two sets of fingerprints on the wine bottle Danielson and I took from your house. One matches yours, and the other matches the set Ritter submitted for a background check for a grant application years ago. The wine is being tested, but given what you told us and what Dr. Scott confirmed, there's little doubt that the poison was jimsonweed. We also found a set of fingerprints on your back door." Her gaze cut to the chief then, and she fell silent.

I sighed again and pushed away from the wall. "Speaking of Ritter, I need to check on him." Turning, I waved my hand in a general farewell as I left.

"Hang on, Ellie." Lupe trotted to join me, and we walked toward my vehicle together. "How's he doing?"

"Okay, so far. The doc gave him something to counteract the jimsonweed poisoning, and then tranquilized him so he'd sleep all night. She seems to think he'll be fine in another day or so."

She let out a breath. "That's good news." She was silent for a few beats. "Who do *you* think did it?"

I stopped by the door of the Wrangler, and Dash jumped over to my seat to hang his head out the window. Lupe obliged by scratching his ears.

"I don't know. You were at the memorial, so you know who was there . . ." I trailed off. "You know, Chief Gibbon said he heard Astrid and I talking yesterday afternoon at the Roux about how the thief might sell the manuscript. Dylan said it would be dangerous to keep it. He spoke fairly loudly." I paused, remembering. "There were an awful lot of people in the restaurant who might have overheard him, and many of them ended up at the memorial, too."

"Like who?" Lupe asked.

"Well, Dylan himself. Could you please tell Astrid to be careful? She doesn't listen to me." And then, one by one, I counted off the same people I'd listed to Astrid that morning: Warren, Trixie, and Odell. "Who has an alibi," I finished. "So, really, we're down to the Perezes and Astrid's latest fling."

Lupe nodded. "You won't be surprised to learn Warren and Trixie are our prime suspects. Warren's business is in serious trouble, so they have lots of financial motive—which also fits with the chief's theory that whoever killed Eureka really wanted that gold nugget to start with. But they also benefit from her death, and their alibis for each other are a bit sketchy."

Relief whooshed through me, followed by anger when I thought of Ritter still lying in bed at the clinic. "You really think they did it?"

She gave a slow nod. "We're building the case." She put her hand on my shoulder. "We'll find out if Trixie or Warren knows anything about jimsonweed, and I've submitted the prints we got from your door to the state lab. They'll get back to us within a week."

"That long?"

"That soon."

"Oh."

"Be careful and give Ritter my love." She hugged me. I hugged her back, hard.


IT was nearly nine o'clock by then, and I had just over an hour before I had to open the shop. I drove home and took a quick shower, keeping an eye on Dash to make sure he wasn't tempted to explore the wine stain under the rug. He completely ignored it. When I was dressed, I scrambled up three of the little eggs Larken had brought me, and ate them out of the pan over the sink. Then I hurried out toward the Wrangler again.

Halfway through the Enchanted Garden, I paused, eyeing the stalks of wallflowers growing near the mosaic retaining wall. On an impulse, I went over and grabbed a set of pruners from my supply near the faucet and cut several stems. Inside Scents & Nonsense, I rummaged under the counter until I found a vase the right size, and quickly arranged the multicolored blooms in it.

Leaving Dash in the shop, I went out and wedged the flower container behind the driver's seat, then headed to the clinic.

Nurse Higginbottom was keeping an eye on Ritter between helping Dr. Scott with patients. She waved me back to his room, where I found him sitting up. He'd changed out of the clothes he'd worn for the memorial and our dinner date, and now wore an examination gown tied in the back.

I grinned. "Best hold that thing closed if you wander out of here."

"Thanks for the advice." His tone was wry.

I put the flowers on a counter and perched on the side of the bed. "How are you feeling, big guy?"

His pupils were normal, and the color had returned to his face.

He took my hand. "A little confused, actually."

"What about?"

"I don't remember what happened."

"On the way here?" I asked. "Well, for one thing, you told me you turned down a research project in Glacier National Park."

His eyes widened. "I told you that?"

"Yep. And you are going to call them back and say that you'll do it."

He made a face.

"I mean it, Ritter. I want you to call them. You can't give up your work because of me. And, Ritter . . ." I paused. "You have to trust me, okay? I love you, too."

He hesitated, and then, God help me, he blushed.

"Say okay."

"Okay."

I smiled. "Good."

"But I still don't remember what happened. Not since I got up after sleeping all day yesterday."

"What? You don't remember any of yesterday afternoon?" I asked, appalled.

"Ellie, don't panic," Dr. Scott said from the doorway. "It's not uncommon for people to have a period of temporary amnesia after ingesting jimsonweed."

I took a deep breath and tried to quiet my heartbeat. "You sure?"

She nodded. "But I want to keep an eye on Ritter for at least the rest of the day."

"Yes. Okay. Of course."

"Oh, Doc," he protested.

"No," I said. "You'll do as you're told."

A smile tugged at his lips. "Okay, boss."

I kissed him, adjusted his covers, and kissed him again.

"I have to go," I murmured.

"I know. I'll be fine. Don't worry about me," he said.

I nodded, loath to leave him there, but stood anyway. "I'll check on you soon."

When I was in the doorway, he said, "Elliana?"

I turned.

Gesturing toward the bouquet of flowers I'd brought, he asked, "What do those mean?"

I smiled.

"Come on. I know they mean something," he insisted. "All your flowers mean something, right?"

"Wallflowers mean fidelity in adversity," I said.

He held my gaze for several seconds, then said, "I like that."

"Me, too," I said.

B ACK home, I showered and took another whiff of the energizing peppermint, rosemary, and eucalyptus blend. It worked its wonders, and soon I'd brewed coffee, set out Astrid's delicious brookies, and fed Nabby and Dash. Right before opening Scents & Nonsense, I returned the call to the boutique hotel owner who wanted lavender air spray for her guests, and we came to a lucrative agreement.

Next, I tidied the shop and was on the computer researching greeting card companies when the phone rang.

"Scents and Nonsense," I answered.

"It's Maria." There was something in her voice.

I put down the mouse and turned away from the computer screen. "What's up?"

"A couple of things. One is that Professor Radcliffe is here, and he wanted to know what Eureka had been looking at. Ellie, I think he's trying to replicate her most recent research."

"Why?"

"He didn't say."

"Well, we can't really stop him, can we?"

A few beats of silence, then: "No, I suppose not. And

for all I know, Eureka would have wanted him to continue her work. But her work is related to the other thing I wanted to tell you. Actually, I wanted to show you."

"I've got something to show you, too. I'm at the shop."

"It needs to be here. It's Charles Bettelheim's journal. Ellie, it's not what we thought."

My ears perked up at that. "Maggie will be here in about an hour. I'll come over then."

"Okay. And, Ellie, this is something I'm not telling Professor Radcliffe. At least not yet. Not until you see it and tell me what you think."

Thoroughly curious, I hung up. Abandoning the computer, I went out front to soothe myself by mixing everyday essential oil blends to sell off the rack.

I HEARD a rumor they may have found Eureka's killer," Maggie said as she breezed into the shop at eleven.

I raised my eyebrows.

She tsked as she tied on an apron. "Not that I know who . . . wait, do you know who it is?" she asked with a sharp look.

*Warren and Trixie Perez. I wonder if they've heard the rumor.* Slowly, I shook my head. It was just a gesture, after all. Not an outright lie.

"Well, I must say, whoever it is, I'm glad they are going to be heading to trial and prison." She bustled over to the coffee urn and poured herself a cup.

I smiled. "Me, too. Listen, I have to go over to the library. Maria wants to show me something. Oh, and apparently, someone else might end up writing the book Eureka was working on when she was killed."

She grabbed a couple of dirty mugs and took them into the bathroom to wash. "You mean that Dr. Radcliffe?"

"The very one. You know him from the Roux, I take it?"

She came out with the mugs and went behind my work counter. Grabbing a dish towel off the pile tucked under the counter, she bobbed her head. "Lord, that man loves my margaritas. A little too much, if you ask me."

"Oh, does he now?" I grinned. "I saw him at happy hour the other day. Yesterday," I corrected myself.

"Yep. His daughter drinks tea, and he drinks tequila. Had three Cadillacs on Wednesday night, and he didn't start early, either. I bet he wasn't too chipper the next day." She waggled her eyebrows. "Because you know how I mix a Cadillac margarita, and most people never dare more than two."

I laughed.

Then I suddenly stopped.

"Hang on. You said Wednesday night?"

She nodded.

"What time?" I asked, my pulse beating a little faster.

"It was ten o'clock, at least, when he came in. Hardly anyone in the bar. If it completely empties out, some-times Harris will let us go home. But not that night. The professor didn't leave until after midnight."

Then understanding dawned. "Oh! So, you're part of his alibi."

She looked confused. "What are you talking about?"

"Lupe said Odell had an alibi for the time of the murder . . ." I trailed off. Lupe had said Haley was her father's alibi. She hadn't said anything about him being at the Roux Grill.

Maggie blinked. "I don't know anything about that."

I forced a smile, my mind racing. "Oh. Well, maybe I've got it wrong. Anyway, I'm going to head over to the library now."

"What would you like me to do while you're gone?" She rubbed her hands together as if she couldn't wait to get to work.

Distracted, I said, "It's slow. Take it easy. Hang out in the garden if you want. Just listen for the bell over the door."

"You are the worst boss ever," she joked as she settled onto a stool and pulled a magazine out from under the register.

O N the way to the library, I called Lupe. For once, she answered instead of letting it go to voice mail. "Hey, Ellie. You'll be relieved to know Chief Gibbon is working with the district attorney in Silver Wells to make that case against the Perezes."

"Don't be too sure it was them," I said as I dodged a woman pushing a baby stroller.

"Meaning?"

"What was Odell Radcliffe's alibi during the time of Eureka's murder again?" I asked.

"His daughter, Haley. She said he was in their suite that evening."

I blew out a breath. "Lupe, that's not any better than Warren and Trixie vouching for each other!"

"But they don't have the room service call."

"Oh?"

"He called at eight thirty, and the Empire Room delivered dinner to him and his daughter at nine. One of the waiters came and got the dishes from outside the room at ten and heard the television."

"Just one problem, Lupe. Odell Radcliffe was in the Roux Grill drinking Maggie Clement's margaritas from ten o'clock until after midnight. She told me. If Haley's claiming her father was with her at the hotel the whole evening, she's lying."

There were a few beats of silence, then, "Crap. I'll be by your shop in an hour."

"I have a better idea. I'll meet you at the Hotel California in an hour. I'm, uh, running errands right now."

She sighed. "Fine. See you then."

# CHAPTER 24

B RIGITTE pointed toward Maria's office when I came in the door of the library. As I passed the reference room, I saw Odell Radcliffe poring over some of the same items the librarian had shown me the day before, including the Bible.

*Did you kill Eureka to get to her research? Did you hit her over the head with a shovel, then go break into her house and steal her laptop with her research on it, then top it all off with tequila and lime? No wonder you had three drinks.*

I shuddered and kept going.

Maria was sitting at her desk with Charles Bettelheim's journal open in front of her. She looked up when I knocked and let myself in. I sat down across from her.

She shoved the diary over to me without so much as a hello. "Start on page sixty-eight."

I began to read. Page sixty-eight was a litany of every-day life on a Sunday. Taking a bath, doing laundry . . .

Wait. Laundry on a Sunday? I suddenly remembered Mayor Ward saying something about Sunday being laundry day. He'd just taken a single page from a diary out of the time capsule.

A shiver ran down my back. I looked up at Maria, who was watching me with quiet intensity. "I'd forgotten there was a page from a diary in the time capsule," I said.

She nodded very slowly, a small smile playing at her lips. "And if you look toward the front of that journal in your hands, there's a page missing."

Stunned, I flipped back a few more pages and saw where a shred of paper still adhered to the stitched binding.

I ran my hand over my face. "How could there be a page in the time capsule while the rest of the journal ended up stuffed behind some old school primers?"

But I was already thinking hard as I asked the question. Remembering how easily the lid of the butter churn had come off at the ceremony even though Officer Danielson had been prepared with a chisel and hammer. In fact, he'd seemed puzzled at how easily the seal was broken.

"Eureka and Felicity took the time capsule to the po-lice station, right? We saw them leave," I said slowly.

Maria didn't look happy. "I know what you're thinking."

"I'm thinking Eureka couldn't wait to see what was in that butter churn, and somehow managed to get into it before the ceremony?"

Her lips pressed together, and then she sighed. "Yeah."

"Hang on a sec." I retrieved my phone from my day-pack and brought up Felicity's number.

She answered on the second ring, and I heard voices in the background.

"Hi," I said. "I have a quick question for you."

"Fire away," she said.

"Did you and Eureka make any stops on the way to the police station with the butter churn?"

"Um, no. Where did you have in mind?"

"And you were together the whole time?" I asked.

Across the desk, Maria leaned forward.

"Sure," Felicity said. "Well, sort of. I mean, I left her to take the time capsule into the police station while I went to talk to the mayor."

I gave the librarian a triumphant look and said, "So Eureka was alone with the butter churn for a little while."

"Well, jeez. Not very long. I left her in front of the police annex. She must have taken it right inside."

"Okay," I said. "Thanks."

"Ellie, why are you asking—"

"I'll be by the hotel in a while," I said.

"Wait a sec—oh, heck. There's a problem with a reservation I need to take care of." She was already talking to someone else as she hung up.

"What did she say?" Maria asked.

"Eureka was alone with the butter churn after Felicity went to talk to the mayor. She must have opened it, looked inside, and taken this journal. Either the page fell out then, or it had already come loose, and she didn't notice it."

Maria rubbed both hands over her face. "Why would she do that?"

I shook my head. "Curiosity? Scholarship? I bet Eureka was willing to break the rules here and there. Dr. Radcliffe told me she didn't much care for authority."

"Yes, I guess I can see that." Maria hesitated, then said, "Do you think someone knew she'd opened the time capsule early? That it might have something to do with her death?"

Eyeing the old journal that sat in the middle of her desk, I said, "There must be something in there worth more than gold."

She smiled. "Literally, to Eureka. She removed this book but left the gold nugget worth a quarter of a million dollars in the time capsule." She bit her lip, then nodded to the journal. "You need to keep reading to see why."

I started in again, skimming the boring bits about what Charles had had for dinner or what horses he'd tended to at the stables that day. I slowed when I came to another passage that mentioned Alma.

*Alma agreed to share a meal with me at the hotel last evening! I immediately visited the barber, yet could not help feeling trepidation as I shaved and dressed, afraid that my meager wardrobe might offend her sensibilities. She was graciousness personified, however. Her brother warned me to have her home by eight thirty and to come straight back from the dining hall, and to that end I delivered her to him at precisely that hour. I have hopes of another meal with her soon.*

"So they dated," I murmured.
Maria said. "Keep going."

I skimmed some more until I reached another entry about my distant aunt.

> *My dear Alma is known to heal those who dare come to her with teas and tinctures made from the plants she gathers outside of Springtown. I'm coming to realize she has a reputation for more than doctoring, however. Some think her a witch, and she tells me she's met with threats in the street on more than one occasion.*

Hands shaking, I paused in my reading to take a deep breath. Had something happened to Alma Hammond because of her knowledge of plants? Seriously? I thought about how different it would have been for me to live in this place, but at that time. I felt a surge of gratitude that my talents and abilities were appreciated by my friends and customers rather than reviled out of superstition and fear.

The next mention of Alma again gave me pause.

> *Alma tells me she is tired of the way the townspeople treat her, and the tight reins her brother keeps on her. I told her about my gold nugget, which I've kept hidden in hopes of it funding a solid future. I asked her to be my bride, to come away with me. My gold will give us a decent beginning in a life together. I await her answer.*

Charles' earnest love for the young Alma saddened me since I knew something must have happened to destroy his hopes. In the next entry, I found out what it was.

*Alma Hammond has broken my heart. She told me she is in love, not with me as I'd dared to dream, but with Rolly Crump, a cad and a thief. My gold is of no matter to her. She intended to run away with him. To leave me alone and without succor.*

*Dear God above, I know I will never be forgiven for what I have done. I lost all my wits when she told me good-bye. The devil himself possessed me, and I did a terrible, terrible thing.*

*Alma was different than anyone I've ever met— man, woman, or child. At the same time strong and delicate, wise and silly, she could read those around her like Indians read the signs of passing game. Her affinity for plants and their essences was mystical, a gift beyond measure. One of her most prized possessions was the ancient stitched book in the language no one but she could understand. They said she was a witch, but if there was magic in her, it was that of the faeries and elementals, not the evil of which they speak.*

*I robbed the world of her magic, and for that there is no forgiveness.*

*After long thought, I have collected all remnants of our time together and placed them in a butter churn I stole. The menu from our first meal at the hotel. The picture she deigned to give me in the envelope with the crushed orange flowers. The photo of the building on the main thoroughfare where she lived with her brother while their house was being built. Her precious book. The heavy piece of gold meant to start our life together but which I used to end hers. This diary to explain what*

*I've done, and, finally, a map to show where I buried
her sweet, lifeless body in the foothills.*

    *I will seal the churn, place it in the safe, and direct
it be delivered to her brother, Zebulon, who searches
for her so frantically. I will have taken my own life by
the time he receives this confession, so he will not be
burdened with having to do so himself.*

When I was finished, I set the diary down and closed
my eyes. When I finally opened them again, Maria was
sitting with her elbows on her desk and her chin in her
hands, watching me.

"It wasn't a time capsule at all," I said. "It was a murder confession."

"And a suicide note," Maria added.

I nodded. "Sad."

"She was your aunt. Even so removed, it must hit
home. I'm sorry."

"How do we tell everyone?" I asked.

She lifted her shoulders and let them drop. "We just
do. I don't think it'll be a problem. This is one of those
cases of truth being stranger than fiction. I always
thought it was kind of odd that there were no notes or
letters in that butter churn. Real time capsules tend to
contain that kind of thing."

I remembered the dark smear of what I'd assumed
was dirt on the gold nugget when the mayor held it up for
us all to see. Now I wasn't so sure. "I wonder if her blood
is still on that chunk of gold over at the bank."

Maria paled.

"We'll tell everyone once the gold has been tested for blood," I said.

"It will be quite the display in the museum—grisly and tragic at the same time. The tourists will love it," Maria said with a grim expression.

I leaned back in my chair. "And Eureka knew what kind of appeal Charles' story would have."

She gave a little nod. "And that was the book she was researching before she died. The one Odell Radcliffe is researching now, apparently."

"Do you think she told him?"

"She must have told him something. But she didn't give him this." She pointed at the journal.

"She hid it," I said slowly. "So he took everything from the time capsule after he killed her."

And apparently tried to kill me—and Ritter—as well.

Abruptly, I stood. "He's not going to get away with it. Maria, make sure that diary is locked in your desk overnight."

"Okay." She watched wide-eyed as I marched out of her office and beelined to the open doorway of the reference room, where Odell Radcliffe was still poring over the birth and death entries in the back of the Bible.

"Hi, Dr. Radcliffe," I said brightly.

Startled, he peered up at me. "Ellie! Hello. And remember—call me Odell."

I smiled. "Odell. Right. I see you've discovered our old town Bible. You know, I heard Eureka found something really interesting in it the week before her death."

He straightened. "I heard that, too. Do you know what

it was? See, she asked me to come to Poppyville to work on a new idea she had for a book. A true-crime story, don't you know. I'd love to be able to carry on with her work."

Something must have shown on my face, because he hastened to add, "In her honor, you understand. I'd like to find out whatever I can before my daughter and I leave tomorrow. Unfortunately, all vacations must come to an end." He smiled.

I smiled back through gritted teeth. "I see. Well, gosh, I'm not sure exactly what she was researching. But I think it had something to do with a diary we found over in Heritage House. She said there was a crazy story in it, one that would be unbelievable if there wasn't evidence to prove it's true. It's too bad the police have shut the museum down and you can't get in there." I took a few steps into the room. "Honestly? I think she might have pilfered that diary from the time capsule before it was opened. But I don't want to tell the police that because I don't want her to get in trouble."

His eyes flashed. "Is that so? Well, we'll just keep that to ourselves, then. For Eureka."

I nodded, gave him a little wave, and walked away.

For Eureka indeed.

Once I was outside the library, I called Maria to tell her what I'd told Odell and that I'd check in with her after I talked to Lupe.

Charles' revelations haunted me as I slowly walked the rest of the way to the Hotel California. However, the last paragraphs in the diary haunted me more than the others.

The book written in a language only she could understand.

Alma Hammond had been like me.

* * *

THE big covered veranda of the Hotel California was empty. I climbed the steps and went inside. Pausing just inside the threshold, I looked around. Straight ahead, the wide staircase led to the second floor. The traditional welcome motif of pineapples adorned the columns that flanked the stairs, as well as the ornately carved crown molding near the high ceiling.

Clusters of sofas and brocade-covered wingbacks waited for guests to gather, and gas fires burned behind glass doors at each end of the lobby. A woman plinked out something unrecognizable on the grand piano. A combination of cooking smells from the Empire Room down the hallway, cheap aftershave, and rug shampoo swirled through the air.

Lupe was standing at the reception desk. Felicity stood on the other side. They were deep in conversation. The looked up when I joined them.

"So, we're trying to figure out how Odell could have made the room service call if he wasn't in the room," Lupe said.

"Are you sure it was him? Or just the room calling? As in, could Haley have covered for her father by making the calls to room service and then acting like her dad was in the room?"

"Maybe," Felicity said. "The staff aren't stupid, but they wouldn't be expecting her to try to establish an alibi for her father, either."

"Have you asked her about it?" I asked Lupe.

She shook her head. "Can't find either of them."

"Well, I can tell you where Odell is. The library. Apparently, he's going to write the book Eureka had planned. Which, by the way, is a different book than what she had been working on for the past year. He says she asked for his help with it. I think he might have killed her so he could write it himself."

"Really?" Lupe looked skeptical. "Seems Warren and Trixie Perez would have a better motive than some book about the gold rush."

Bending my head and leaning toward them, I quickly related what Maria and I had learned from Charles Bettelheim's diary. When I was done, they both just stared at me.

"Seriously," Lupe said finally.

I nodded. "Test that gold. I bet you find blood on it. But that's not the important thing. At least not right now. Because right now, Odell Radcliffe is using Eureka's research to write the book she was going to before he killed her. That's why he's in Poppyville. Every time I've seen him, he's brought up Eureka's book."

"But why use someone else's idea?" Lupe asked. "And why Eureka's? Wouldn't he know we'd suspect him of murder if he used her research to write his own book? Especially if it sells."

"Not if she *asked* him to help her in the first place. Which is what he claims. And not if he's now writing it to honor her memory. Plus, he can't use just any old idea. A book about Alma Hammond's murder would be based on a real crime. You know, like *In Cold Blood*. I'd think that you'd have to have the right story to start with for that to work, to spark the interest of the reading public, don't you? And boy, this one's a doozy." I sighed.

Straightening my shoulders, I said, "Which is exactly why I told Odell about Charles Bettelheim's diary. I told him it's locked away in Heritage House, and that the police won't let anyone inside. If he killed Eureka, he's not going to pass up the chance to get the final piece of the puzzle."

"You laid a trap?" Felicity hooted, then quickly checked to make sure no one was nearby to overhear.

"In the museum," Lupe said wryly.

"Exactly. Have you released the crime scene yet?"

She shook her head.

"But you could, right?"

"Oh, Ellie. You've got to be kidding."

"You'll know once and for all that you have the right guy if he shows up," I said, all sweet persuasion. "And no harm, no foul if he doesn't. Max doesn't have to know anything about it. Neither does the chief."

She shook her head. "I don't feel good about that."

I shrugged. "Then tell him."

After a few seconds of hesitation, she capitulated. "Tell me what you have in mind."

"Maria said the chief asked her to remove the valuable items from Heritage House, but Odell wouldn't know that, right? So, I told him the diary tells the whole story behind Alma Hammond's disappearance, a crazy story that's darn near unbelievable and utterly gripping." I grinned. "If he killed her and stole her laptop, he's going to fall for it hook, line, and sinker. Not to mention, it's true!"

Felicity leaned forward. "Detective Garcia, it can't hurt. If we say it's at the museum and no one shows up, then we're just out some time and effort." She gave me a look. "But if Ellie's plan does work, we've netted ourselves a killer."

"I don't like all this 'we' talk," Lupe grumbled.

"Well, I have to work until the wee hours, covering for a sick employee," Felicity said. "So you can take me out of the 'we.'"

Lupe said, "I think I can get the crime scene released. When do you think he'll show up?"

"After dark. I'll talk Astrid into waiting with me in Heritage House."

"I'll be there, too," Lupe said. "But let's leave Thea and Gessie out of it."

"Why?"

"Too many of us, and he might catch wind of what's going on. Keep it simple."

"I get it. And thank you." I meant it.

"You're going to be the death of me," she said.

"Don't even joke about something like that."


O N the way back to the shop, I made a detour down Gilpin toward Dr. Ericcson's office. On Saturdays, Astrid attended the front desk until one o'clock, when the vet's office closed for the rest of the weekend. It was just after that now, but I knew she rarely left on time. I hoped to catch her, so I could tell her about tonight's plan to trap Odell in person.

I turned the corner, and sure enough, there was her rickety old car parked right in front. And in front of that, a shiny Corvette that I hadn't seen around town before was snugged up to the curb. As I approached, a woman with wild blond curls exited the vehicle and stood looking at the front of the building.

Walking up beside her on the sidewalk, I saw Astrid through the window. She sat at the desk, phone in one hand while she jotted something in the giant appointment book with the other. Dr. Ericcson was a Luddite if ever there was one, and my friend was always trying to get him to digitize his office operations. She apparently hadn't had much success.

There was movement behind her, and I recognized Dylan. He must have gotten back from that morning's estate sale and was waiting for her to get off work.

*Great. The last thing I need is that guy trying to horn in on our plan to catch Odell.*

The woman on the sidewalk turned and looked me up and down. She was sporty looking, like she played tennis and ran marathons and golfed the rest of the time. In fact, something about her reminded me of Astrid, but I couldn't put my finger on it.

"The sign says they're closed until Monday," she said.

"I know," I said. "Are you looking for the vet?"

She sniffed and turned back to the window, where neither Astrid nor Dylan had noticed us looking in at them. "I'm looking for my husband."

*Ohhhhh.* And *uh-oh.* And then: *I knew there was something off about that guy!*

"Dylan Wong?" I asked casually.

"Oh, God. Not you, too."

"Um, no. But that's my friend in there. It's not her fault."

Her jaw set. "It never is." She marched to the front door.

Sighing, I followed. At least there wouldn't be a big audience for this confrontation.

She tried the door, but it was locked, so she commenced to bang on the glass with her fist. A few seconds later, Astrid came around the corner, a concerned expression on her face. Of course, she'd think anyone pounding on the door of a veterinarian's office would have an animal emergency.

Then she saw me and stopped, tipping her head to one side in puzzlement.

Dylan came up behind her to see what was going on. Then he saw it was his wife making the ruckus. I'd never seen anyone go so pale so quickly in all my life.

He said something in Astrid's ear and tried to pull her away from the door.

Big mistake.

Her eyes flared with anger, and she shook him off. The door was unlocked and open in a flash.

"Please," she said. "Come in. I understand you're probably here for this guy." She grated out the last two words.

"And I understand from your friend here that you're an innocent bystander."

"Not as innocent as I'd like," Astrid said, glaring at Dylan, who was cowering in the corner like a frightened puppy. "Ellie was right. There's something wrong with you. And I was too stupid to listen to her. At least I followed my own instincts and never let things get too physical."

I saw Dylan's wife relax a bit at that. Would she forgive him? I had the feeling she had before. And probably would again, though shame was rolling off her in waves. I ached to give her a dose of betony, lavender, and geranium oils to make her feel better—and give her the strength to leave the jerk once and for all.

However, she wouldn't thank me for butting in right then.

"Come on," she said flatly. "You're coming home."

Dylan hesitated, then scurried past Astrid without looking at her.

"Sorry," his wife said quietly as she followed him out to her car.

"No, hon. I'm sorry," Astrid said.

We watched them drive away from the doorway. "You're the one I should tell I'm sorry," she said.

I waved that away. "Nah. Besides, it could be worse. He's just a cheat. I was afraid he was a killer."

She made a funny sound that I thought was a sob. When I looked at her, though, I saw she was laughing. At first it was silent, and then it bubbled out like seltzer. Soon we were both whooping and snorting, stumbling inside and shutting the door so the whole town wouldn't see us making a spectacle of ourselves.

Finally, we ran down and sat grinning at each other in the tiny waiting room.

"That felt good," Astrid said.

I nodded. "It feels like forever since I laughed."

"I think Eureka would have liked it."

"I think so, too. And speaking of Eureka, I stopped by to talk to you for a reason."

Her eyebrows went up.

I told Charles Bettelheim's story one more time, and then filled her in on Odell's fake alibi and his desire to write Eureka's book now that she was gone.

"He's at the library doing research," I said, and then told her about the trap I'd set. "Lupe's in."

My friend gave a firm nod, all trace of humor gone. "I'm in, too."

# CHAPTER 25

MAGGIE left soon after I got back to the shop. A few customers came in and browsed. I greeted them but otherwise left them alone. I was thinking about that evening. About facing a killer. At least I wouldn't be alone.

I called the clinic to check on Ritter. Dr. Scott said he was doing well, but I detected a note of concern in her voice.

"There's something you're not telling me," I said.

"It's not anything to worry too much about."

My heart beat a little faster.

"He doesn't seem to be regaining the memory of what happened as quickly as I thought he would. I'm sure he will, though. It's just that it doesn't usually take this long."

"When can he come home?" I asked.

"This evening. His sister is going to come get him in a few hours."

"Okay, good. Can I talk to him?"

"Sure. Let me transfer you."

When he picked up, Ritter sounded like his old, strong self, and I nearly wept with relief. What was a little memory problem, after all?

"I hear Thea's going to take you home in a while."

"Thank God. I want a shower and some sweat pants like you wouldn't believe. You want to come over and watch a movie or something? I know it's not much of a date, but . . ."

"Oh, Ritter, I can't. Not tonight. I'm so sorry."

"You have plans," he said, sounding defeated.

"Well, sort of." I debated not telling him what my *plans* were, but that wasn't the kind of relationship I wanted for us. "We're setting a trap to catch Eureka's killer tonight."

"Excuse me, but you're doing what?"

"At the museum," I said. "And I don't know how long it will take for Odell to show up."

"The professor?" he asked.

"We think he killed Eureka to steal her book research. Maggie broke his alibi."

Another long silence. Then a strange sound.

"Are you okay?" I asked, alarmed.

The sound morphed into laughter. Not as hysterical as Astrid's and mine had been earlier, but still genuine mirth.

"You are something else, Elliana Allbright. I'm so glad you're in my life."

"So you're not mad at me?"

"Well, I'm coming with you, of course."

"Oh, no. You're going to stay at home with your sister. And I'll let her know to keep an eagle eye on you."

"Elliana—" he began.

"I'm no wilting violet," I said. "I can take care of myself. But if you're really worried, Lupe will be there, all official with her police training and weapons and all."

*"Hrm."*

"I promise to text when it's all over."

He gave a little snort. "It does make me feel better that Detective Garcia will be there."

"Good."

"But, Elliana?"

"Yes?"

"If you get hurt, I'm going to be really mad."

"Then I won't get hurt," I said.

A STRID and I stopped by the Juke Diner for dinner. I couldn't remember eating a better hamburger. Then we headed to the library, where Maria was waiting for us. Lupe showed up soon after.

"Thanks for helping us," I said to her as we gathered by the side door of the library.

She pressed her lips together. "If this works out, I'm golden. If something goes wrong, I could lose my job."

Astrid and I exchanged looks that said we both regretted dragging Lupe into this.

She noticed and held up her hand. "I know you two. You'd do it anyway. At least I'll be on the inside with you."

"Odell just left," Maria said. "He asked me if I knew anything about a diary, and I acted like I had no idea what he was talking about. He looked relieved. Then I mentioned that the police were talking about confiscating the entire contents of Heritage House and closing it down until they solved Eureka's murder. He didn't seem to like that idea."

"I bet not," I said. "He needs to see what's in the diary for himself. Nice job, Maria."

She grinned. "Thanks."

"Finish closing the library, then go home and lock your doors," Lupe told her.

"I have every intention of doing just that," the librarian said with a nod.

Lupe looked at Astrid and me. "Okay, angels. Let's do this."

T HE museum was a lot colder than I'd expected. There was only the one chair, too, and the floor was hard as, well, as a floorboard. We sat for what seemed like hours, quiet as mice, phones on silent. Finally, I flicked the screen on long enough to check the time and saw we'd been there less than forty minutes.

I sighed and shifted into a more comfortable position.

A loud snapping sound startled me awake. Across the room, I heard a rustle as Lupe moved. Rolling to my feet, I backed against the wall where she'd told me to stand earlier.

The padlock rattled as it was pulled through the hasp. There was silence for several seconds. I tried not to breathe too loudly, but it was hard since my heart was going a million miles a second.

The door slowly creaked open, and a tall figure stepped into the room. The door closed again, and heavy footsteps crossed the floor. The narrow beam of a penlight split the darkness. From where I stood, I watched it play over the desk and empty display cases.

There was a click, and suddenly the entire room was bathed in the light from the overhead fixture. Odell Radcliffe stood blinking like a bat, his face the picture of confusion.

"Gotcha!" I said.

Lupe sighed. "Ellie."

But I was grinning too hard to care. My plan had worked!

Astrid strode out from the alcove by the restroom where she'd been stationed and came to stand by me.

"What is the meaning of this?" Odell boomed.

"Odell Radcliffe, you are under arrest for the murder of Eureka Sanford," Lupe intoned.

"Murder?" He sounded stunned. "That's ridiculous. I . . . I adored Eureka."

I asked, "You're here for the diary, right?"

"Of course I am."

That stopped me, but only for a couple of seconds. "And you killed Eureka for her research? So you could write her book."

He sidestepped Lupe's handcuffs and peered at me with a baffled expression. "Young lady, I haven't the slightest clue why you say such a thing. Eureka was my friend." He hesitated. "Earlier today you implied you didn't want anyone to know she broke into that time capsule. I thought it was so no one would think less of her. Well, I'm sorry, but if you truly knew Eureka Sanford, you'd never think less of her for being a brilliant, curious woman in search of the truth—even if she did cut a few corners in the process. She did break the seal on that old butter churn, and when she discovered what was inside, she called me in Berkeley. That was eight days ago."

His eyes bored into mine, and I found myself unable to look away.

"She was so excited! She asked me to come to Poppyville to see what was in the butter churn—it wasn't a time capsule at all, she said. It was evidence of a long-ago murder. She wouldn't give me details, however. Wanted me to see for myself." He licked his lips. "She wanted to collaborate with me on this writing project, she said, and thought I'd like Poppyville as much as she did." He sighed wistfully. "I'm retiring at the end of this semester. She suggested I might want to move here, so we could work together. I liked the idea immediately. Perhaps I even dared to hope for more than a working relationship."

Lupe snagged my gaze as she said to him, "We can figure all this out at the police annex, Dr. Radcliffe. At the very least, you entered this building illegally."

"Ellie, I don't know about this," Astrid murmured in my ear.

I nodded my agreement. My mind was racing as I reevaluated everything I'd learned. The more he spoke, the more I believed Odell Radcliffe hadn't killed Eureka Sanford—or tried to kill me.

Then who had? Warren and Trixie, as Lupe thought?

No.

Odell's alibi had come from his daughter. Shy Haley with the big glasses and sad wardrobe, but smart enough to be pursuing a PhD at Berkeley.

I'd assumed she'd lied about where her father had been the night Eureka was killed to protect him. But what if she'd lied to protect herself?

But why on earth would she kill Eureka?

And then I realized Odell had just given me the answer. "Hold on a moment, Detective Garcia," I said. "Odell, you were at the Roux Grill on Wednesday night, right?"

He nodded.

"So, when your daughter said you were with her—"

"Daddy, there you are!"

I turned to see Haley had silently pushed the door open and stepped into the museum.

"I was afraid you might decide to come here." She smiled at Odell, then transferred it to Lupe. "This was just a little mistake, Detective. Don't worry. We'll just be on our way. In fact, we're leaving town this evening."

Odell blinked, as if that was news to him.

"I'm afraid that's not possible, Ms. Radcliffe," Lupe said, though she put her handcuffs away. "Your dad broke and entered. I can't just let him drive out of town."

Haley stepped farther into the room. "Oh, *pshaw*. Of course you can. This isn't the big city, after all. He hasn't harmed anything. And wouldn't you rather avoid all that paperwork?"

Beside me, I heard Astrid draw in a breath. She was starting to suspect what I had already figured out.

Maybe Lupe was, too. But neither of them had seen how Haley and Odell interacted like an old married couple, finishing each other's sentences without thinking. It had been just the two of them since Haley was a little girl. For all I knew the only interruption in their twosome was when Odell and Eureka had been an item years ago.

Astrid and I had thought Haley needed to claim her independence from her father. Perhaps we'd had it the other way around.

"What did you think about your daddy moving to Poppyville after he retired, Haley?" I asked.

Startled, she transferred her attention to me. "Now, Ellie. Why did you trick him into breaking the law like that? That wasn't nice at all. He only wants to continue the work dear Eureka started."

"Which I imagine you're fine with," I said. "As long as he stays with you while he does it."

Odell frowned at his daughter. "What is she talking about?"

"Nothing, Daddy!" She gestured toward the door. "Well, if we have to go to the police station before we go, let's get it over with, shall we?"

"Did you break into Eureka's house before you killed her, or afterward?" I asked her.

She blinked. "What a silly question."

"Why did you lie about where your father was the night of the murder?"

The blood drained from her face, but she rallied. "I didn't lie. I was in my room in our suite that evening. I had a headache."

I looked at Odell. "You agreed to her giving you an alibi. Why?"

He made a face. "Well, after she said that to the police, I didn't want to contradict her. After all, it didn't really matter. I knew I had nothing to do with Eureka's murder."

"So you didn't go along with it because you knew your daughter had killed her?"

He stared at me. "What?" The word came out thickly, but his eyes shifted to the side as he, too, started to put things together. Suddenly, he gave a Haley an incredulous glare. "What did you do?"

"Daddy . . ." She faltered. "I didn't . . . no. How could you think such a thing. Don't let this *woman*"—she glared at me—"cloud your thinking."

"You left fingerprints at my house when you poisoned the wine," I said.

She looked smug.

"Not on the bottle. On the back door."

Fear flickered across her face. "I don't know what you're talking about." But she didn't sound so sure of herself now.

"Oh, Haley," Odell said, the sorrow on his face making him look a decade older than he had only moments before. "Why would you kill Eureka?"

"I didn't . . ." She trailed off, drawing her ratty old cardigan closer around her.

Their eyes were locked. She knew he knew.

"Daddy, you were going to move here for that woman! That horrible woman. God, she hated me. Laughed at me when I tried to tell her what a terrible writing partner you'd make."

He gaped at her. "Why would you tell her that?"

"So she'd let you stay with me in Berkeley! Daddy, I can't move here with you right now. I'd have to leave my teaching position, give up everything."

"I'd never ask you to move here," he said. "I thought it would be good for you to be on your own."

"Good for me! I gave up everything to keep you company. My whole life!"

"But I encouraged you to leave the state for college," he said, utterly bewildered. "I didn't need you to stay with me forever."

"Ha! Of course you did. And I gladly made that sacrifice, Daddy."

I wondered if rationalizing a fear of striking out on her own qualified as hindsight bias. I felt bad for her, though. She really was a frightened little girl at heart. Maybe she could get therapy in prison.

"But killing Eureka!" Odell said, astounded. "How could you?"

"I didn't mean to! I went to talk to her, but she was leaving. She laughed at me. Said to 'cut the apron strings' and let you go. So I followed her here, and after she'd been here a while—I wanted to let her calm down a little—I tried again. But she wouldn't listen! We struggled." She pulled the cardigan closer, and I wondered if she hadn't been wearing it for three days straight to cover bruises from grappling with Eureka. Her arms had been bare at the ceremony on Wednesday afternoon.

"We struggled, and, well, things got out of hand, Daddy."

"You hit her over the head with a mining shovel," Astrid grated out. She wasn't feeling sorry for Haley at all now.

"Well, yes," Haley admitted.

"You . . . you . . . ," Odell spluttered.

"And then you stole all the items from the time capsule," I said.

"Well, yes," she said again. "I was kind of upset, you know, but I kept thinking to myself that if Daddy could write Eureka's book, then maybe he wouldn't be disappointed about not moving to Poppyville."

We all stared at her.

Haley continued. "She was in a hurry when she left her house—wanted to get away from me, I guess—and didn't arm her alarm system. When I got a really good look at the stuff that had been in that stupid butter churn, I realized there had to be something else. Something she'd taken. Something no one else knew about, and so it wouldn't be connected with her death. It had to be at her house. But when I went inside, I couldn't find anything. Not a dang thing that looked promising."

"So you grabbed her laptop and ran."

She nodded, but she wasn't really telling anyone this story except her father. Her eyes were locked on his face, which was a study of horrified realization of what his daughter had done. "I was back at the hotel before you returned, Daddy."

"Oh, honey," he said sadly.

"I did it for you," she said in a small voice.

"Did you try to poison me for him, too?" I asked.

She whirled to face me. "You're a snoop, you know that? Digging into everything. And that woman, the bartender at the place where Daddy was when I was, well, you know."

"Murdering Eureka," Astrid supplied.

Haley ignored her. "I found out she works for you."

"And you were afraid she would mess up your alibi. Well," I said. "You were right. And you made my boyfriend really ill." I glanced at Lupe. "Add a charge of attempted murder to the mix."

She nodded and reached for her cuffs again. "Come along, Ms. Radcliffe."

Haley looked around wildly. "You can't let them take me to jail!"

"Honey, I can't stop them," Odell said.

She glared at him. Suddenly she pulled a small black boxy-looking thing from the pocket of her skirt. From the corner of my eyes, I saw Lupe reach for her gun, but Haley had already stepped to Astrid's side and held the box against her neck.

"Daddy got me this thing for protection. If I ever needed protection, it's now."

I felt the blood drain from my face.

Astrid, on the other hand, appeared unfazed. "It won't kill me, Lupe. Go ahead and shoot her."

Haley asked, "Are you sure about that? Ever been tased in the neck before?" Her voice was dreamy.

Astrid didn't say anything.

"Go back to the hotel, Daddy. Pack your bags. We have to leave."

He shook his head. "No, Haley."

"There are police out there," Lupe said. "You can't get away."

Haley frowned. "We'll see." Her hand moved down to Astrid's back, and I heard a quick buzzing sound.

My best friend's eyes grew round, then her face squeezed in pain and she collapsed to the floor.

"Astrid!"

Lupe pulled her gun, but Haley was already running. But she was too close to me, and Lupe hesitated instead of shooting. In that split second, Haley was out the door. The detective followed on her heels.

I heard another buzz and saw Lupe drop to the ground.

Haley took off running again. She was faster than I would have ever expected. Odell ran out the door after her.

Astrid moaned, and I dropped to my knees beside her. Her pulse was fast, but she was conscious. I went outside to check on Lupe when I heard the shot.

Lights came on all over the library park. Where had they come from? Then I saw Chief Gibbon striding toward us.

"Lupe's hurt," I called.

A paramedic came over. "Not as hurt as the girl who was shot. I'll be back."

Gibbon stopped in front of me. "Well, Allbright. It looks like you weaseled your way into another official investigation."

Lupe rolled to her knees, and he helped her to her feet. She was breathing hard.

"You okay, Garcia?"

She nodded. "Sure, boss. Thanks for the save."

"My pleasure. And, Allbright? Nice job."

My jaw went slack with surprise.

Astrid staggered out of the museum. "What happened?"

I put my arm around her. "Apparently, Lupe decided she didn't want to lose her job if things went wrong."

The detective winced, then grinned. "And boy, did they go wrong."

"Yeah," I said. "Is Haley dead?"

Gibbon shook his head. "Max winged Ms. Radcliffe. She's unhappy, but not too damaged. Her father is with her."

# CHAPTER 26

"Lupe called me this morning," I said. "They tested the stuff that was on the gold nugget, and sure enough, it was blood."

"You sound almost happy about that," Ritter said, leaning back on my love seat and lacing his fingers over his abdomen.

"Well, not happy, exactly. But it's nice to be right."

"Mm."

The air was redolent with the scents of bacon and onions, chicken and red wine. I'd finally managed to make it to the grocery store, and we'd finally had our dinner date, albeit at home. I'd put my coq au vin up against any restaurant meal.

Ritter seemed to agree.

He'd made a full recovery, except for being unable to remember what he'd said in the truck on the ride to the clinic. All he knew was that he'd confessed to sacrificing his work for our relationship, and I was having none of it. He'd made the call, and thankfully, the research team hadn't filled the position he'd turned down.

I had three months with him before he had to go. However, this time, he'd only be gone for two months, and I'd already bought a plane ticket to go visit him in the middle. Between Maggie and Larken, Scents & Nonsense wouldn't lose a beat during the summer season, and Dash would stay with Astrid.

Even though I was as much of a homebody as they came, the thought of a real vacation in the wilds of Montana was appealing.

"Spence took off, huh," Ritter said.

I frowned. "I thought you were going to stop worrying about him."

"I'm not worried. I just want to know if he's gone."

"For a while. He's embedded with a team in Somalia. I don't know for how long. I don't think he does, either."

"Somalia. That's probably dangerous."

"Yeah."

"Your men keep leaving you."

"I'm not going to dignify that with a response."

"Good."

In fact, Spence had stopped by Scents & Nonsense to see me before he left. He'd brought me the gift he'd mentioned after he returned from his photo shoot at El Capitán—a smooth agate pendant with what looked like a tiny fern preserved inside the clear stone. It looked like something from a gift shop, but I still liked it. We'd managed to patch things up, but I didn't know if we'd ever be the kind of close friends we were before. I didn't know if he'd really come back to Poppyville, either.

I sat up with a groan. "I'm exhausted."

He straightened. "So am I. Maybe we should go to bed."

"That is a very good idea," I said with a smile.

Dash woofed and ran up the stairs.

As I passed by Gamma's journal, I trailed my fingers over the cover. It was cool as the back side of a pillow.

THE next morning, I left Ritter to his slumber and padded downstairs in the predawn light. Coffee brewed, and I bundled into my fleece robe and went out to the back porch. The wine-stained ottoman had gone to the dump, and the floor was scheduled to be replaced in a week.

Haley had admitted to dosing our wine with jimsonweed. She'd thought I knew more than I did after she heard me talking with Astrid and Dylan at the Roux. She was set to go to trial in six months and, in the meantime, was enjoying three square meals a day in jail.

Eureka's computer, the diary page, the claims map, the restaurant menu, and the town photo had been found in Haley's room safe at the Hotel California, where she put them for safekeeping. They were stored as police evidence along with the photo of Alma, Charles Bettelheim's diary, and the Xavier manuscript that Bongo Pete had found.

Haley had admitted that she impulsively ditched the Xavier manuscript after overhearing me talking to Dylan about it in the Roux. However, she couldn't bring herself to get rid of the other items she'd taken from Heritage House, even though they were incriminating, until she was sure her father wouldn't need them to continue Eureka's work on the book.

The police were working with the forest service to use the claims maps to find where Alma was buried. As Alma's kin, I should have been on board with that. There was something about her being out in the wild that I liked, though, and a part of me hoped they'd never find my nature-loving aunt. If she was out there in the foothills, she was where she belonged, regardless of the tragedy that put her there.

I sipped my coffee and watched the sun lighten the sky as I did most mornings now.

Waiting.

While I waited, I often thought about what Bongo Pete had said about Kell. About how it was all of this. All of everything. The trees and the water and the energy that thrummed though every living being. It was a comforting thought. A feeling of belonging.

I'd been waiting for her every morning, half anticipating, half anxious that the cougar might have hunted her down. So I was both thrilled and relieved when the white doe stepped from the shadows of the trees to gaze at me.

Safe and sound. Strong and delicate at the same time.

She didn't eat. Just looked and looked.

And as I lost myself in her glistening brown eyes, I thought of Gamma's journal.

*Violent death times three.*
*Will summon thee.*

And I finally realized who the daughter of Kell was.
It was me.

# RECIPES
# AND
# AROMATHERAPY

# ASTRID'S CHOCOLATE CRINKLE COOKIES

*These fudgy gems are dense, rich, and not overly sweet. There's no need for an electric mixer—using a hand whisk easily does the job. The perfect cookie to have with a glass of cold milk or a cup of strong black tea.*

*Makes 24 cookies*

1 cup all-purpose flour
½ cup unsweetened cocoa powder
1 teaspoon baking powder
½ teaspoon salt
¼ teaspoon baking soda
3 large eggs
1½ cups brown sugar
1 teaspoon vanilla extract
4 ounces unsweetened chocolate, chopped
4 tablespoons unsalted butter
½ cup granulated sugar
½ cup powdered sugar

Preheat the oven to 325 degrees F and line 2 baking sheets with parchment paper.

In a medium bowl, whisk together the flour, cocoa powder, baking powder, salt, and baking soda. In a large bowl, beat the eggs then mix in the brown sugar and vanilla until just blended. In a small glass bowl, combine the unsweetened chocolate and butter, and microwave at 50 percent power for 2 to 3 minutes until melted, stirring occasionally.

Slowly whisk the chocolate mixture into the egg mixture until combined. Fold in the flour mixture until there are no dry streaks. Allow the dough to sit for 10 minutes.

Put the granulated sugar in one bowl and the powdered sugar in a second. Scoop out the dough 2 tablespoons at a time, and roll it into balls. Drop each ball into the granulated sugar and roll to coat, then transfer it to the powdered sugar and roll to coat again. Arrange the cookies 2 to 3 inches apart on the parchment paper–lined baking sheets.

Bake the cookies, one sheet at a time, until puffy and cracked, about 12 minutes. Rotate the baking sheet halfway through cooking. When the crinkles are ready, the edges will look done but the interior of the cracks will appear underdone. Let them cool completely on the baking sheet. They can be stored in an airtight container at room temperature for up to 5 days.

# Oatmeal Milk Bath

*This recipe welcomes substitutions. Colloidal oatmeal—finely ground to the point where it will suspend in water—is approved by the FDA as a beneficial ingredient to treat skin ailments, but you can also grind quick oats or use baby oatmeal if you're willing to rinse out the tub after bathing. Full-fat milk powder is included here, but there are other lovely milk powders available online—switch in coconut milk or goat's milk, for example. Nonfat dry milk from the grocery store will also work in a pinch. Epsom salts contain magnesium, which calms nerves and can help with insomnia, but you can use sea salt or even kosher salt if that's what's handy. Also, feel free to play with scent combinations!*

*Makes enough for 3 baths*

½ cup Epsom salt
¼ teaspoon lavender essential oil
¼ teaspoon basil essential oil
1 cup colloidal oatmeal
1 cup full-fat milk powder

In a large bowl, combine the salt and essential oils. Stir together with a metal whisk until the oils are evenly dispersed in the salt. Add the oatmeal and milk powder and stir again with the whisk until thoroughly combined. Store in a glass jar with a tight lid.

If you love Bailey Cattrell's
Enchanted Garden Mystery series,
read on for a sample of the first book in
Bailey Cates's *New York Times* bestselling
Magical Bakery Mystery series!

# BROWNIES
# AND BROOMSTICKS

is available from Berkley Prime Crime
wherever books are sold.

THIS was a grand adventure, I told myself. The ideal situation at the ideal time. It was also one of the scariest things I'd ever done.

So when I rounded the corner to find my aunt and uncle's baby blue Thunderbird convertible snugged up to the curb in front of my new home, I was both surprised and relieved.

Aunt Lucy knelt beside the porch steps, trowel in hand, patting the soil around a plant. She looked up and waved a gloved hand when I pulled into the driveway of the compact brick house, which had once been the carriage house of a larger home. I opened the door and stepped into the humid April heat.

"Katie's here—right on time!" Lucy called over her shoulder and hurried across the lawn to throw her arms around me. The aroma of patchouli drifted from her hair as I returned her hug.

"How did you know I'd get in today?" I leaned my tush against the hood of my Volkswagen Beetle, then pushed away when the hot metal seared my skin through my denim shorts. "I wasn't planning to leave Akron until tomorrow."

I'd decided to leave early so I'd have a couple of extra days to acclimate. Savannah, Georgia, was about as different from Ohio as you could get. During my brief visits I'd fallen in love with the elaborate beauty of the city, the excesses of her past—and present—and the food. Everything from high-end cuisine to traditional Low Country dishes.

"Oh, honey, of course you'd start early," Lucy said. "We knew you'd want to get here as soon as possible. Let's get you inside the house and pour something cool into you. We brought supper over, too—crab cakes, barbecued beans with rice, and some nice peppery coleslaw."

I sighed in anticipation. Did I mention the food?

Her luxurious mop of gray-streaked blond hair swung over her shoulder as she turned toward the house. "How was the drive?"

"Long." I inhaled the warm air. "But pleasant enough. The Bug was a real trouper, pulling that little trailer all that way. I had plenty of time to think." Especially as I drove through the miles and miles of South Carolina marshland. That was when the enormity of my decisions during the past two months had really begun to weigh on me.

She whirled around to examine my face. "Well, you don't look any the worse for wear, so you must have been thinking happy thoughts."

"Mostly," I said and left it at that.

My mother's sister exuded good cheer, always on the lookout for a silver lining and the best in others. A bit of a hippie, Lucy had slid seamlessly into the New Age movement twenty years before. Only a few lines augmented the corners of her blue eyes. Her brown hemp skirt and light cotton blouse hung gracefully on her short but very slim frame. She was a laid-back natural beauty rather than a Southern belle. Then again, Aunt Lucy had grown up in Dayton.

"Come on in here, you two," Uncle Ben called from the shadows of the front porch.

A magnolia tree shaded that corner of the house, and copper-colored azaleas marched along the iron railing in a riot of blooms. A dozen iridescent dragonflies glided through air that smelled heavy and green. Lucy smiled when one of them zoomed over and landed on my wrist. I lifted my hand, admiring the shiny blue-green wings, and it launched back into the air to join its friends.

I waved to my uncle. "Let me grab a few things."

Reaching into the backseat, I retrieved my sleeping bag and oversize tote. When I stepped back and pushed the door shut with my foot, I saw a little black dog gazing up at me from the pavement.

"Well, hello," I said. "Where did you come from?"

He grinned a doggy grin and wagged his tail.

"You'd better get on home now."

More grinning. More wagging.

"He looks like some kind of terrier. I don't see a collar," I said to Lucy. "But he seems well cared for. Must live close by."

She looked down at the little dog and cocked her head. "I wonder."

And then, as if he had heard a whistle, he ran off. Lucy shrugged and moved toward the house.

By the steps, I paused to examine the rosemary topiary Lucy had been planting when I arrived. The resinous herb had been trained into the shape of a star. "Very pretty. I might move it around to the herb garden I'm planning in back."

"Oh, no, dear. I'm sure you'll want to leave it right where it is. A rosemary plant by the front door is . . . traditional."

I frowned. Maybe it was a Southern thing.

Lucy breezed by me and into the house. On the porch, my uncle's smiling brown eyes lit up behind rimless glasses. He grabbed me for a quick hug. His soft ginger beard, grown since he'd retired from his job as Savannah's fire chief, tickled my neck.

He took the sleeping bag from me and gestured me inside. "Looks like you're planning on a poor night's sleep."

Shrugging, I crossed the threshold. "It'll have to do until I get a bed." Explaining that I typically slept only one hour a night would only make me sound like a freak of nature.

I'd given away everything I owned except for clothes, my favorite cooking gear, and a few things of sentimental value. So now I had a beautiful little house with next to no furniture in it—only the two matching armoires I'd scored at an estate sale. But that was part of this grand undertaking. The future felt clean and hopeful. A life waiting to be built again from the ground up.

We followed Lucy through the living room and into the kitchen on the left. The savory aroma of golden crab cakes and spicy beans and rice that rose from the take-out bag on the counter hit me like a cartoon anvil. My aunt and uncle had timed things just right, especially considering they'd only guessed at my arrival. But Lucy had always been good at guessing that kind of thing. So had I, for that matter. Maybe it was a family trait.

Trying to ignore the sound of my stomach growling, I gestured at the small table and two folding chairs. "What's this?" A wee white vase held delicate spires of French lavender, sprigs of borage with its blue star-shaped blooms, yellow calendula, and orange-streaked nasturtiums.

Ben laughed. "Not much, obviously. Someplace for you to eat, read the paper—whatever. 'Til you find something else."

Lucy handed me a cold sweating glass of sweet tea. "We stocked a few basics in the fridge and cupboard, too."

"That's so thoughtful. It feels like I'm coming home."

My aunt and uncle exchanged a conspiratorial look.

"What?" I asked.

Lucy jerked her head. "Come on." She sailed out of the kitchen, and I had no choice but to follow her through the postage-stamp living room and down the short hallway. Our footsteps on the worn wooden floors echoed off soft peach walls that reached all the way up to the small open loft above. Dark brown shutters that fit with the original design of the carriage house folded back from the two front windows. The built-in bookshelves cried out to be filled.

"The vibrations in here are positively lovely," she said.

"And how fortunate that someone was clever enough to place the bedroom in the appropriate ba-gua."

"Ba-what?"

She put her hand on the doorframe, and her eyes widened. "Ba-gua. I thought you knew. It's feng shui. Oh, honey, I have a book you need to read."

I laughed. Though incorporating feng shui into my furnishing choices certainly couldn't hurt.

Then I looked over Lucy's shoulder and saw the bed. "Oh." My fingers crept to my mouth. "It's beautiful."

A queen-size headboard rested against the west wall, the dark iron filigree swooping and curling in outline against the expanse of Williamsburg blue paint on the walls. A swatch of sunshine cut through the window, spotlighting the patchwork coverlet and matching pillow shams. A reading lamp perched on a small table next to it.

"I've always wanted a headboard like that," I breathed. "How did you know?" Never mind the irony of my sleep disorder.

"We're so glad you came down to help us with the bakery," Ben said in a soft voice. "We just wanted to make you feel at home."

As I tried not to sniffle, he put his arm around my shoulders. Lucy slipped hers around my waist.

"Thank you," I managed to say. "It's perfect."


Lucy and Ben helped me unload the small rented trailer, and after they left I unpacked everything and put it away. Clothes were in one of the armoires, a few favorite books leaned together on the bookshelf in the living room, and pots and pans filled the cupboards. Now it was a little after three in the morning, and I lay in my new bed, watching the moonlight crawl across the ceiling. The silhouette of a magnolia branch bobbed gently in response to a slight breeze. Fireflies danced outside the window.

*Change is inevitable,* they say. *Struggle is optional.*

Your life's path deviates from what you intend. Whether you like it or not. Whether you fight it or not. Whether your heart breaks or not.

After pastry school in Cincinnati, I'd snagged a job as assistant manager at a bakery in Akron. It turned out "assistant manager" meant long hours, hard work, no creative input, and anemic paychecks for three long years.

But I didn't care. I was in love. I'd thought Andrew was, too—especially after he asked me to marry him.

*Change is inevitable . . .*

But in a way I was lucky. A month after Andrew called off the wedding, my uncle Ben turned sixty-two and retired. No way was he going to spend his time puttering around the house, so he and Lucy brainstormed and came up with the idea to open the Honeybee Bakery. Thing was, they needed someone with expertise: me.

The timing of Lucy and Ben's new business venture couldn't have been better. I wanted a job where I could actually use my culinary creativity and business know-how. I needed to get away from my old neighborhood, where I ran into my former fiancé nearly every day. The daily reminders were hard to take.

So when Lucy called, I jumped at the chance. The

money I'd scrimped and saved to contribute to the down payment on the new home where Andrew and I were supposed to start our life together instead went toward my house in Savannah. It was my way of committing wholeheartedly to the move south.

See, some people can carry through a plan of action. I was one of them. My former fiancé was not.

*Jerk.*

Lucy's orange tabby cat had inspired the name of our new venture. Friendly, accessible, and promising sweet goodness, the Honeybee Bakery would open in another week. Ben had found a charming space between a knitting shop and a bookstore in historic downtown Savannah, and I'd flown back and forth from Akron to find and buy my house and work with my aunt to develop recipes while Ben oversaw the renovation of the storefront.

I rolled over and plumped the feather pillow. The mattress was just right: not too soft and not too hard. But unlike Goldilocks, I couldn't seem to get comfortable. I flopped onto my back again. Strange dreams began to flutter along the edges of my consciousness as I drifted in and out. Finally, at five o'clock, I rose and dressed in shorts, a T-shirt, and my trusty trail runners. I needed to blow the mental cobwebs out.

That meant a run.

Despite sleeping only a fraction of what most people did, I wasn't often tired. For a while I'd wondered if I was manic. However, that usually came with its opposite, and despite its recent popularity, depression wasn't my thing. It was just that *not* running made me feel a little crazy. Too much energy, too many sparks going off in my brain.

I'd found the former carriage house in Midtown—not quite downtown but not as far out as Southside suburbia, and still possessing the true flavor of the city. After stretching, I set off to explore the neighborhood. Dogwoods bloomed along the side streets, punctuating the massive live oaks dripping with moss. I spotted two other runners in the dim predawn light. They waved, as did I. The smell of sausage teased from one house, the voices of children from another. Otherwise, all was quiet except for the sounds of birdsong, footfalls, and my own breathing.

Back home, I showered and donned a floral skort, tank top, and sandals. After returning the rented trailer, I drove downtown on Abercorn Street, wending my way around the one-way parklike squares in the historic district as I neared my destination. Walkers strode purposefully, some pushing strollers, some arm in arm. A ponytailed man lugged an easel toward the riverfront. Camera-wielding tourists intermixed with suited professionals, everyone getting an early start. The air winging in through my car window already held heat as I turned left onto Broughton just after Oglethorpe Square and looked for a parking spot.

Ready to find
your next great read?

Let us help.

**Visit prh.com/nextread**